The Pencil Man

DON MCALLISTER

authorHOUSE®

AuthorHouse™
1663 Liberty Drive
Bloomington, IN 47403
www.authorhouse.com
Phone: 1-800-839-8640

First published by AuthorHouse–07/20/2011

ISBN: 978-1-4634-2985-0 (sc)
ISBN: 978-1-4634-2987-4 (hc)
ISBN: 978-1-4634-2986-7 (ebk)

Library of Congress Control Number: 2011911562

Printed in the United States of America

Contents

This book is dedicated to the memory of
the real Pencil Man
and my dear friend
Rob Williams.
Eternal peace be with you both.

ACKNOWLEDGEMENTS

I'll begin by thanking the readers who loved *Angel and the Ivory Tower*, and who told me so with such passion that it inspired me to try my hand at a second novel.

Once again I thank my brother Dave McAllister for his editing expertise and suggestions for the first drafts. I love you more with every passing year, and I'm proud to be your brother.

My thanks to Director Jim Rementer of the Delaware Tribe and www.talk-lenape.org for the help with the Lenape names.

I also appreciate the reviews and most helpful input from Frances Allis, and Roger and Nancy Tatum.

Karen Kovich continues to inspire me with her caricature art and her friendship (see www.karenkovich.com)

Artie and Lee Granger, as well as Ed and Camille Spencer were paramount in helping me with the cover art. Camille looked great in that original 1950's coat and she posed so well. Wouldn't it be great if *The Pencil Man* became a classic and seventy years from now she could look back and say with an elderly twinkle, "I was that little girl!" I hope the picture conveys to you the idea that the Pencil Man was simultaneously a downtown fixture and invisible to many. I also thank my wife Sue for helping me find the coat used for the Pencil Man in the cover photo.

I appreciate the work of Paula Werne, Director of Public Relations for Holiday World & Splashin' Safari, and for their permission to use a reference to their founder Louis Koch. I went to Santa Claus Land when I was a child. I remember a giant statue of Santa Claus, a train, and a boat ride that I wished I could bring home. Since then the Koch family has grown the park into one of the cleanest and most enjoyable family fun parks in America.

A short drive to the west of Holiday World one can find the Lincoln Boyhood home. The restored settlement is a fine tribute to Tom Lincoln's labor, and the grave of Nancy Hanks Lincoln is a national sacred place indeed.

East and North of Santa Clause, Indiana one can find the monastery of the Sisters of St. Benedict. Twenty years ago we traveled there and found peace, majesty, and our dear friend Sister Sylvia Gehlhausen. Thanks so much Sister Sylvia for your help with some of the characters from that part of the book. I hope I did them justice.

My thanks to the citizens of Anderson, Indiana who have done their part to make this a great hometown. I especially thank Kikthawenund for choosing this place. He was the first to see its potential, and I agree with his vision.

Rob Williams was my friend in real life and the only saint I knew personally. Much he failed, much he overcame, and then many he blessed. When I see a dove I think of you, Rob.

Most of all I thank the Pencil Man. We may never know your name, but you are not forgotten. I pray that you have found that warm paradise that so eluded you in life.

God bless the humble poor.

FOREWORD STEPS

Drawn by Karen Kovich (www.karenkovich.com)

In my first novel, *Angel and the Ivory Tower*, I titled this section "Forward" instead of the proper "Foreword." It was an intentional play on words that indicated that I was ready to do something with my life that I had never tried.

The result of my taking this unnatural step was a pleasant novel that garnered remarkable and passionate praise from my readers. Because I was a new author, it took a while for it to get off the ground from a sales perspective. For the longest time I called it

"America's #1 unknown best seller." The friendships I kindled and rekindled (no pun intended Amazon) with that book are worth millions to me.

We now have another play on words with "Foreword Steps."

Life is a series of steps. Some steps take us in a better direction, while some stumble us into a worse situation. The ultimate mistake is to stop walking and trying altogether.

Walking itself is a miracle that we too often take for granted. Ask someone who is elderly, or who has otherwise lost the full use of their legs.

Before you in this book is a highly fictionalized account of a very real man. When I was a child I saw this man quite often on the streets of my hometown. I was close enough to him on many occasions to shake his hand. One of my great regrets in life was that I did not do so.

Many people in Anderson remember the man with no legs who propelled himself around town on a wheeled board and who sold pencils. I haven't found anybody who really knew him. Therefore this cannot be an actual history of the man. It is a true-to-life reflection of our own journey through life and of what we might experience if we were thrust into the Pencil Man's situation.

This is a strange story—I'll admit that up front. Some people will get hung up on the mysticism. Some Anderson historians may debate the details of what I remember from my childhood. These are only vehicles for the book, and in many cases a tip of the hat to some of the people I have admired in my life. Some of these people I knew; others are a part of my cultural heritage. There are people like my mentor Gene Brown, the well loved and respected Herman B Wells whom I met in 1967, and the great Miami Chief Kikthawenund, who first saw the potential of my birthplace.

Much of what you read here is personal. These are places that I've studied and touched myself. They are a part of what I use to define the word "home."

The main focus for my readers should be on the characters. Some people say I use too many characters to keep track of them all, but one doesn't "keep track" of the characters in real life. Some of them are "regular customers" who weave themselves into our lives. They are the strong fibers of our "life's material." Others we meet only once. They may entertain, teach, or reinforce a life lesson and then they are gone. These are ones we recall when our memories need a little color.

Some of the main characters are observers of life. They study the life that swirls around them before they react. Others are the instigators of life. Like us, they are imperfect and are thrust into situations that are beyond their control. They make important decisions that lead to results that may be blessings or failings. In either case each decision leaves a mark. Sometimes it's an inscription, other times it's a scar. As you read, ask yourself if you would have made the same decisions.

Perhaps you have met someone like the Pencil Man in your own life. They may be mentally ill. They may be dangerous. They may also be the most remarkable person you will ever meet. I do not pretend to know if or how you should deal with such a person. I cannot advise you nor will I.

I can only tell you this. This book is just a work of fiction.

The Pencil Man was real.

CHAPTER 1

The Pencil Man

It's a miracle that happens every day, but only once in a lifetime. A baby decides that crawling isn't enough. He pulls himself up along the sofa with the greatest effort and balances for a moment—perhaps two. Then—like a bird on the edge of a nest—he steps—maybe once—maybe twice—and his legs collapse into the soft thud of a diapered bottom. For an instant he begins to cry, but his determination to walk takes over and he pulls himself up again. This time one step—two—three—four, and into the excited outstretched arms of his mother or father. There is a wild celebration, for this is one of the true miracles of human life.

Walking—a common everyday action. From the time we first totter and tumble to the time we step into the grave, we walk, and walk, and walk. We get up in the morning and walk to the bathroom, and to the kitchen, and out the door. We walk to our transportation, and from our transportation. We walk into our jobs or schools, where we must always "walk the line." We walk home, and through the stores, and into the arenas. We walk up the church aisle as two separate people and walk back down that same aisle as one forever—at least until one or the other walks out—or until six men walk for us, with somber expressions and heavy steps. Billions of people walk billions of miles everyday, with billions of steps that seem meaningless at the final destination.

When I was a child there was the common ritual of getting dressed up and walking the two blocks up the hill to take the Meadowbrook bus to downtown Anderson. That was where the shopping was. That was where the action was.

There were a few mom and pop stores outside of the mile square of center city Anderson. One could shop at the businesses that fed the thousands of factory families along Columbus Avenue or the Meadowbrook Shopping Center, but it was still downtown, the heart of Anderson, where one found the shopping, the food, the entertainment, the government, and the business of the city.

Downtown was a mighty throbbing engine of commerce and society that pulled us together like gravity.

One could eat at the YMCA or Ferris cafeterias, or at the Good Earth. There was the Toast, or that hole-in-the-wall hamburger joint—Hill's Snappy Service. The high rollers ate at the Anderson Hotel—we almost always ate at home. The one dining treat I remember was the lunch counter at Woolworths, where I could spin round and round on the counter stools and drive my mother nuts while I waited for my hamburger.

We bought my shoes in the basement of the Hoyt Wright department store, where we passed a colorful picture of Custer's Last Stand on the stairs. For church, school, and going downtown Mom bought me "breathin' brushed Hush Puppies." For play she fixed me up with Keds sneakers, which would always make me run faster when they were new.

The rest of the trip was mostly mom stuff. There was the remainder of Hoyt Wright and the other department stores, the Fair store, the Banner store, and J.C. Penney, where the elevator always stopped on the mezzanine, whether there was anybody waiting to ride or not.

These stores held no interest for me except to watch the pneumatic tubes where the clerks sent the money in a brass cylinder to the accounting office and the change was returned with a whoosh.

The big Sears store on Main Street had enough guy stuff to keep a boy interested. I mostly went there with my dad. It took up most of a city block and had its own parking lot with a small white guardshack at the entrance to keep the cars of non-customers out. Downtown parking was at a premium in those days.

The toy aisles at the dime stores, Kresge and McCrorys, drew my interest, but Neumode hosiery was the most embarrassing store in town.

There were three great movie theaters, the Riviera, which was smaller but more ornate than today's theaters; The State, which was a cavernous, domed venue; and the Paramount, a grand palace built in 1928, with a Page organ, and stars in the ceiling. It has since been restored to its glory days and remains one of the few great theaters left in America. Sometimes we would come to a movie as a family, but mostly I came on Saturdays and froze in the alley, with a long line of kids waiting for the ticket office to open for some must-see kid classic like the "Three Stooges in Orbit." In which Moe, Larry, and Curly saved us from Martian invaders.

The city was so full of people that we had scramble bells at the intersections on Meridian Street—the main drag in town. When the scramble bells rang we could cross in any direction, even diagonally, as the cars waited from all four sides.

The town was built around a square that featured an old ornate red brick courthouse with a clock in the tower that was probably never in time. From there the city flowed south onto Meridian Street, flanked by Main and Jackson, filled with shoppers, lawyers, doctors, and the ebb and flow of the retail trade.

Many landmarks remain in my memory, but the one I remember the most was not built of brick or glass. It didn't have impressive window displays or neon signage. That landmark was built of flesh and bone. It was a living, breathing, human being—though I'm not sure he always felt that way himself. He was the Pencil Man.

The Pencil Man was a beggar. He was dressed in shabby clothes and had no legs from just above his knees. His was a condition that compels children to stare and adults to glance away.

My fascination was directed at his mode of transportation. He had fashioned himself a square board with four casters, which he used along with his hands and arms to pull himself about town. He didn't accost anyone. He just sat on his board against some storefront, holding a can of pencils. People would put some change in and pull out a pencil. Others just tossed in the change and walked on. A few cruel ones would take a pencil and give him nothing. After all, what was he going to do, chase them down?

The cruelest of all may have been the ones who passed him with a sharp turn of their heads to avoid his condition. While many were generous with their donations, very few wanted to really know the man.

I remember one time I paused and looked at him, he being one of the few adults at my eye level. He offered me a pencil. I think he just wanted to give a kid a present at Christmas.

We all wondered how he had lost his legs. Some said it was a railroad accident. Others thought he had lost them in the war. What did he do with the money he collected? Where did he go at night, or in the storms, or in the cold? Most thought he was a drunk who spent his daily take on booze.

It would have been simple to answer those questions if we had just introduced ourselves and asked him. Hundreds saw him every day, we all wondered about him, but very few knew him at all.

As my childhood passed into my inevitable (and sometimes questionable) maturity, I became a bit obsessed with this local legend. I scoured the archives of Anderson for some detail of his story and found nothing. Several long-time residents remembered him, but no one could tell me any more than I already knew.

In the opening of the 21st century—I don't recall the exact year—the son of a dear friend of mine died. I hadn't seen my boyhood friend in decades. He had mysteriously disappeared from the scene, and yet somehow I got involved with the disposition of his son's personal effects. The son had died under horrible circumstances and the family could not bring themselves to reenter the house. They trusted me to catalog and box things up to bring to their home. As much as possible I tried to load the boxes with like items. Food went into one set of boxes, clothes into another set, and knick-knacks into another, etc.

I was especially particular about any unopened mail that I found. I opened each one to determine if there were bills to be paid and when they were due. I felt strange getting into someone else's mail, but the family had endured enough grief and I wanted to make their immediate decisions as light as possible.

I brought the cataloged boxes to their home in several loads. From there they would go through the containers and discard the trash or distribute items as appropriate among the survivors. I was asked if there was anything that had any personal value to me and I told them, "Yes, there is one."

Near the chair where the body was found there was a large opened envelope addressed to the son. It had no return address. In that stack of scattered papers I found a note addressed to his mother and siblings, and a loose-leaf journal. It was a story of the Pencil Man.

The rest of what you will read in this book is from that journal. It began with:

I was one of the few who knew the Pencil Man well. I knew him very well. I knew where he came from. I knew of his family. I knew how he lost his legs. I knew the things he loved, and the things he had lost. I knew what he hated, and what he feared. I knew the demons he fought, and the few angels who gave him comfort, and on rare occasions, the thing we value most—respect.

I was his best friend—perhaps his only friend when the time came that he finally "walked" out of our lives. I knew his name.

His name was Mike.

There—that makes him a human being. We have to deal with him now. He can no longer be ignored like a dirty building, or litter on the street. The walking world must take time to see the streets from his level. We can no longer just walk away and ever hope to find redemption.

This is the story of the Pencil Man.

CHAPTER 2

Running

The Pencil Man sat on bustling Meridian Street, at the corner of the building where Penneys met Walgreens. The building stuck out about a shoulder's width, which afforded a slight windbreak, though not much at all.

Anyone who believes that a man who lives outdoors can tolerate the cold better hasn't been in the Pencil Man's situation. There he sat, with his back to a cold masonry wall and less than two inches from a colder sidewalk. He hated the wind—especially when it was damp with impending snow. His coat was too thin and his ungloved hands could barely hold the pencil can. Nobody really gets used to suffering—they just suffer through it.

It was the Monday before Christmas, which was usually a good business day for the Pencil Man, though not as good as the week before when people had more time to shop and would pass at a more leisurely pace.

This was the last-minute warning of Christmas, and everyone was zipping past. The men and boys rushed to every store counter-clockwise and the women and girls mirrored the process in the opposite direction. The small children suffered the most, being carried along by the hand like a kite—their feet barely touching the ground at all. The extended lower lip, the whining and crying, and the dragging of little feet that would have had some force the week before, was now completely powerless before this onslaught.

Very few pencils were taken that day, but the giving was in line with the Christmas spirit. People didn't stop—they just threw the donations at the Pencil Man, forcing him to catch some of the coins like an outfielder who steals the homerun ball from going over the fence.

Running, running, everybody was running. The Pencil Man looked across the street and through the window of the travel agency to see Mr. Collins seated at this desk. He was arranging a trip for a young couple, perhaps planning their honeymoon. Mr. Collins caught a glimpse of the Pencil Man and waved. Everyone else was oblivious to the souls about them. They were like street litter in a swirling wind—running, running.

The Pencil Man returned Mr. Collin's wave, but he too was drifting into a mental swirl trying to find a place in his mind where he could abandon the moist winter cold. As he sat there and shivered he dreamed of his running days.

His dreams took him to the playground at Theodore Roosevelt elementary school. Roosevelt was a fairly new building at that time. It was almost summer, nearing the end of the school year. That day was a good day for recess and a hard day to concentrate on lessons—even for the teachers.

The "Pencil Boy" was ten years old and this would be one of his few remaining chances to impress Debbie, the fair-haired girl, whose house he passed as he walked to and from school on Brown Street Road.

Due to the length of the recess, the boys were able to play only three or four innings of baseball before the bell rang.

It was the bottom of the fourth, and Mike was up to bat. Debbie and her entourage were watching from behind the backstop. It was now or never, he had to deliver. The first pitch was a strike. The second was a clean grounder past the pitcher to Rusty Elliot, the fastest shortstop in the history of playground ball. Rusty vacuumed the ball and fired it to first—a sure out—but Mike would have none of it. He ran for his life and beat it by the skin of his teeth. Both sides weighed in—"Out! Safe! Out! Safe!" Mr. Powers heard the commotion and called it safe. He was standing playground duty a mile away on the steps of the school, and probably didn't see it at all, but nobody argued with Mr. Powers.

With the winning run now on first, one out, and the bell about to ring, Mike made his move. With lightning speed he stole second base on the first pitch. The batter struck out, leaving Mike on second and only one more out in the arsenal. His heart sank when Leroy took his place at bat. Leroy was the worst player in the history of playground baseball. He couldn't hit a basketball with a two by four.

The pitcher threw a ball head high, and Leroy swung and missed it by almost two feet. The second pitch was even worse, as the nervous spider-limbed wonder swung before the ball even got to the batter's box.

On the last pitch, Steve Davis, the most popular boy in school, decided to humiliate Leroy by throwing one right down the middle. Leroy closed his eyes and prayed that he would drill himself into the ground so deep that no one could find him after he lost the game.

To everyone's astonishment the ball hit the bat and bounced deep between the left and center outfielders. Leroy just stood there watching it go as his teammates screamed at him to run. To add even more peril to the mix, it was widely known that even Mrs. Nordair, who the kids thought was the oldest teacher in the world, could have outrun Leroy.

It was up to Mike to make a move and win this thing. With blazing speed he rounded third for home. Steve Hoyer, the hottest arm in the Roosevelt outfield fired the ball like a rocket to Matt Batts, who would later go on to catch in the majors.

Mike laid down a long stretch slide and felt the tag as he touched the plate. By now Mr. Powers was standing over the plate with a clear call. He hesitated for a moment as the return to class bell rang and drowned out all human sounds. When the ringing stopped he called, "SAFE!"

Mike jumped up in triumph. He was covered in dust, his shirt was torn, and his arms and part of his face were covered in a blood rash. Leroy, who had just made it to first, was jumping up and down. At last he was the hero! But nobody paid any attention to him.

Mike looked to Debbie for approval. Instead she looked at the mess he had made of himself and led the girls in a turned up nose chorus of "eeewww!" The only girl who was smiling was Veronica, and no boy wanted Veronica to smile at him.

Long after everyone else had gone back inside, Leroy was jumping up and down on first base with his arms waving in the air. Mr. Powers had to go back outside to call him in.

"Leroy! Leroy! Recess is over!"

"Oh."

Mike had won the game, but he struck out with Debbie. Still his running days were far from over. He was never bulky enough for football, nor could he dribble a basketball worth a hoot, but he continued to play baseball and was a state contender in both cross-country and track.

In his senior year, Mike ran the mile in the state championship meet. The big rival for everyone that season was John Staton. John held the national high school record for the mile, until they measured the Richmond track and found it a yard short. Still John was by far the boy to beat.

The race began with all of the fellows closely bunched. No one wanted to be far from Staton's pace. The runner from Liberty Center was in the lead, with the Richmond great Mike Bennett on his heels. Eugene Brown from Crispus Attucks was in third and another powerhouse runner to watch. Everybody liked and respected Gene. He was a great guy on the sidelines and everybody wanted to be his friend, but on the track none of the runners gave any quarter.

Gene was followed by the runners from Terre Haute and Markleville, respectively. John and Mike traded back and forth for sixth and seventh place with the Gary, Ft. Wayne, and Jasper runners just behind but fading some.

In the fourth turn of the second lap, Gene Brown broke free and took the lead. John and Mike took it up a notch to the third and fourth positions with the Liberty Center runner holding on to second. Gene began to stretch his lead in the third lap, and John shot past Liberty Center to catch up. He was fifteen feet behind as they started the final lap, and Gene wasn't showing any signs of fading. Mike was another ten feet and closing but really feeling the pain in his lungs and legs.

Pain would have to wait. This was the state championship and he had a quarter mile of pain to endure for the last time in his high school career. By the midpoint of the final lap John was five feet from Gene, with Mike another three feet behind John. Coming out of the fourth turn the three runners were welded together. They raced through a final gauntlet of wild cheers and crossed the line in the tightest finish in state history. The three collapsed together on the infield grass, unable to do anything but painfully strain for air.

It was almost an hour before the photo was processed to confirm the finish. Gene had held on to win by a chin, with John and Mike almost imperceptibly separated for second and third, respectively. None of that mattered as all three had shattered the state record, and Mike Bennett took fourth just one tenth off the old mark.

John would go on to other racing glory in college and beyond, but for the rest of his life he would point to that race as the greatest he had ever run.

Gene never went to college. He served his time in the Army and returned to live a quiet life as an ordinary worker in a publishing house bindery. There was nothing "ordinary" about Gene's personal life. He remained a champion who had a profound effect on all who knew him. He was devoted to his faith and made it his mission to inspire and encourage young men over the rocks of early life.

When Mike was sufficiently recovered from his run, he wandered back to the rest area on the northwest end of the track to watch the other events. There he hooked up with the most amazing "event" of the entire meet. A cinder walkway circled the outside of the track, and sashaying toward him was the most vivacious, drop-dead beautiful girl Mike had ever seen. Every eye of every male in southern Indiana was on her every move, and boy could she move! Even more astounding, she was firmly attached to the arm of—you won't believe this—Leroy!

She must have sent Leroy on a mission to get her a soda at the concession stand on the far end of the field. He had this look of, "You dumb broad, we walked past there ten minutes ago." Of course he was powerless to resist, as this knockout owned any man who could find a way to attach himself to her arm.

As soon as Leroy was out of sight she made a bee line for Mike, jumped on him, kissed him, and declared, "Mikey, you were amazing!" Mike couldn't believe his luck, but who was this girl? When she saw the dumbfounded look on his face she volunteered, "You don't recognize me. It's me, Veronica. Remember the old Roosevelt Rough Riders?" As she said this she made a flirty cheerleader move. "Daddy moved us to Lapel. I've been going to school there."

The guy from Liberty Center ran over to catch Mike, as he could see Mike's knees buckle. Leroy came back in time to see enough to realize that he had struck out again. Leroy handed Veronica the drink and walked dejectedly back to the fan bus.

Mike asked the coach to let him ride home in the fan bus. Coach Powell would not normally grant the request, but Mike had just participated in his last high school sports event. Technically he was no longer a part of the team.

Veronica sat with Mike in the front, while Leroy sulked in the back seat alone. Mike walked Veronica home that night, and the next night, and the next night.

Poor Leroy would get over it, or maybe not.

The state championship would be the last race that Mike would run in peacetime. His next running would be for his life.

The Pencil Man's dream faded, and the cold set in. It was 5 p.m. A few men were racing about after work to begin their Christmas shopping at the few stores that stayed open till 6:00 for the late Christmas crowd. The rest had gone home. Mr. Collins closed his shop and walked across the street to buy a pencil. It was his habit to do so each night after closing up his shop. Most of the time he gave the Pencil Man the enormous sum of fifty cents. On very good business days he might buy his one pencil for a dollar. This night he purchased a bright red pencil and gave the Pencil Man five dollars.

"Thank you, Mr. Collins! Merry Christmas!"

"Merry Christmas to you sir. Good night."

Mr. Collins had never asked the Pencil Man his name. He never learned what he ate, or where he slept at night. Mr. Collins wasn't a bad man. Buying the pencils and giving an occasional smile was all he could do. He was far better than most, but the Pencil Man would have given all he had collected that day to anyone would have said "Merry Christmas, Mike."

The Pencil Man closed up shop, put the money in his shabby pocket, stuck his pencil can between his stumps, and pushed himself down the sidewalk to find some warmth in the winter night.

CHAPTER 3

Christmas Eve

When one is a pencil man, one gets a whole new view of human nature. December 24th was a perfect day for people watching. The kids were out of school and wound up tight in anticipation of the big day.

Mothers would relieve the tension by taking their children on a fun outing downtown. By then most of the Christmas preparations were finished. The only major task remaining was to help Santa arrange the gifts late that night. There would be the work of firing up the Christmas meal in the morning, but on Christmas Eve day the mothers would take their children to marvel at the window displays, or to purchase some small toy to tide the tykes over. Some mothers even went to a movie with their children, popcorn and all, while their husbands worked.

The Pencil Man found that 4:30 p.m. on Christmas Eve was the prime time for human nature watching. The harried businessmen, doctors, and lawyers poured out of their offices in a mad dash to begin their long delayed Christmas shopping before the stores closed at five to let the store employees get home for church and other family activities. One frantic fellow was so desperate, after the stores closed, that he offered the Pencil Man thirty dollars for all of his pencils, can and all.

That hour between five and six was the loneliest hour of the year. He would watch the last buses pull away from McCrorys. As the smoke and noise of the diesels faded, it was replaced with an unnatural calm. It was only then that the silent night would be replaced by the ghosts of better days.

Mike could see in his mind the old Salvation Army woman at her kiosk, shouting "Merry Christmas" to all who passed, whether they gave or not. She must have died when Mike was still a boy, but her kindly smile and her Christmas cheer was something one could never forget.

He looked to where the haberdashery had operated and could see Mr. Tuttle, with his camel cloth coat, red plaid scarf, derby hat, and earmuffs. Always a dapper dresser, Mr. Tuttle had given the Pencil Man his first job as a kid and was the most patient of employers. The aging shopkeeper would lock his business at 5:20 on the dot and shuffle home to his apartment on Central Avenue. He always managed to cross paths with Mrs. Mader, the old widow who cleaned the Anderson Bank at nights. Mr. Tuttle would pull himself straight, smile, and tip his hat. He seemed to have had a thing for the old woman, perhaps going back several years.

Somewhere between Main Street and Central, Mr. Tuttle would run across Oscar, the orphan kid who lived somewhere downtown. Oscar walked close to Mr. Tuttle, as the old man was looking a little unstable in those days. Oscar tried his best to make it appear that he wasn't there to help his friend, but he was always prepared to catch Mr. Tuttle, as he had fallen several times lately. Sometimes Oscar would stop to tie his shoe when he suspected that Mr. Tuttle needed a rest. He always seemed to need his shoe tied near a street bench or the Sears parking lot wall, where Mr. Tuttle would also sit down and politely "wait for his young friend."

As they walked together Mr. Tuttle would share the events of the day. He would speak of some customer or a new store item. Oscar would ask for more detail to keep the conversation going, but he rarely volunteered what he had been doing that day. At the apartment steps, Mr. Tuttle would give Oscar a quarter and encourage him to use it to buy a good supper. Then he would pat the boy on the head and say, "Good night, son."

Oscar was too dirty to attend Mr. Tuttle's funeral at Central Christian Church when the old man died. He would have been welcome, of course, but Oscar was a dirty ragamuffin prone to self exile. Oscar listened to the funeral from the alley. It was a hot summer day so the church windows were open. While the mourners, including Mrs. Mader, filed past the casket for the last time, Oscar walked across the 10th Street bridge to the East Maplewood cemetery gravesite. There he stood in the background until the family, a few cousins and a nephew, left the cemetery. Only then did Oscar approach the grave. The dirt on his face turned to streams of mud as he cried his heart out. He had lost the only "father" he had ever known.

The ghost of Mr. Tuttle faded from Mike's mind, and the Pencil Man saw a new vision. It was his own wife and son, gleefully taking in the animated Christmas display in the window of Standt's Jewelry Store. They turned and looked right at him. Then they spun in the other direction and ran away, as if playing some eternal game of tag. He knew that they were just playing. He knew that he could readily overtake them with his strong fast legs. In his mind he ran and ran. The Pencil Man's "steps" grew heavy as if he were running in tar. Then the memory of his beautiful wife and son vanished into the snow flurries. As the Pencil Man's dream crumbled in the winter cold, he found himself, half a man, lying next to a wheeled board, with coins and pencils scattered on the sidewalk.

The annual fantasy was over. It was time to go to church. The Pencil Man collected his things and rolled himself to St. Marys. He drug his board up the front steps and hid it behind the stairs. From there he pulled himself up into the balcony to hide in the shadows for the early Christmas Eve Mass.

When he found his usual secret place he was surprised by a large package, which was labeled "To: Mike, From: Fr. Metzger". It was a small Army backpack that he could use to carry the things he could not otherwise easily handle when he had to use his hands to move about. Inside was a wool blanket, a few packs of matches, two cans of beef stew, a P-38 can opener, a pair of warm leather gloves, and a sterling silver spoon with etched Marion roses.

Father Metzger was one of the few people in town who knew the Pencil Man by his real name. Just before the people began to filter in, he went up to the balcony to visit with Mike, who he knew would be there.

"Won't you come down and sit with us tonight?"

"Thank you, Father. I want to enjoy the kids, not scare them."

"But you know you would be welcome."

"I know, Father, but I'll stay here. Merry Christmas."

"Merry Christmas, Mike."

The Pencil Man clung to the dark, but he pulled himself up enough to see the children as they marched in, ringing their bells. He loved the children and their Christmas spirit. He loved the memories of his own parade down that same aisle, with his mom and dad smiling, and his older brother thinking he was too old for the procession. The Christmas music was sweet comfort for his ragged soul.

The homily of course was about the Christmas story. When Father Metzger got to the part where there was no room in the inn, his voice broke. Tears began to seep from the corners of his eyes and he looked toward the balcony for just a moment. The parishioners thought Father was just getting into the story. He alone knew of the half-man hiding in the shadows of his church, and his heart went out to the Pencil Man. Mike mouthed a silent "thank you" to his friend.

During the Eucharist, the Pencil Man slipped out unseen and made his way to the First Methodist Church. He hid in the shrubbery along the 12th Street side near a stained glass window to hear the midnight service. They always had a fine orchestra for the midnight observance.

Sheltered from the wind, and armed with his new blanket, he would slip into Christmas Day with beautiful music, and visions of beef stew dancing in his head. Inside, the warm Methodist congregants raised their candles to an a cappella "Silent Night."

CHAPTER 4

The Pencil Man's Father

As I mentioned in the last chapter, the Pencil Man had a mother, a father, and an older brother. They sound like a perfect family in what you know of them so far, but that wasn't always the case.

This may seem like a radical and extended departure from the Pencil Man's story, but bear with me, for without the story of his parents one cannot fully understand Mike's story.

His father had been christened Thaddeus Joseph, but he always went by Joe to anyone but his mother—and Joe hated his mother. Both of his parents were stern beyond reason. They used the normal tools of discipline as weapons. The razor strap was a weapon, chores were a weapon, and even the Bible itself was a weapon—it was sometimes used as a physical weapon to the boy's head and body.

In those times one could expect a stern father, but not one this cruel. Joe's mother was a woman of absolutely no maternal comfort, who always finished any punishment given with a warning on how Joe needed to be more respectful.

Joe was not allowed to go to school. They would say "Learnin' makes boys think they're better than their parents." At night, Joe would sneak away to Miss Lackey's home. She lived with her father, a watch maker. Miss Lackey would secretly teach Joe to read, write, and do his ciphers. Mr. Lackey taught Joe the watch making trade, so that he might someday have a chance to make his way, should he ever escape his situation.

Often Joe was discovered when sneaking back home and was severely beaten for his "transgressions." After several of those occasions Joe's father would walk to town and stand in the street outside of the Lackey home. He would loudly proclaim the vilest threats against Miss Lackey. She in turn was protected by her father, who was older but still a good-sized man. He was seething for Joe's father to cross the line. One day he did, and the old man began to punch and pound on Joe's father without mercy. The townsfolk came out to watch, as old man Lackey gave Joe's dad every blow they would have given him if they had had the courage.

Joe's father staggered home and gave the boy what little he had left. It was followed by a lecture from his mom on how it was Joe's fault that his father had been humiliated by that old man.

That night Joe bound his wounds and left for good. He never saw his birthplace, his home county, or his parents again.

The boy was fifteen and had nowhere to go. He worked where he could, ate where he could, and slept where he could. He rode the rods under the train cars and lived in hobo camps, where he was frequently robbed of his possessions and food.

Joe found his way to New York City, where he ate out of garbage cans and slept behind them. One night he was rescued by a Captain Giarusso of the Salvation Army. Captain Giarusso took Joe to a shelter, where he could get a decent set of clothes, a good meal, and a warm bed. Joe was allowed to stay for as long as he wished, no strings attached. He was always invited to the worship services, but was never forced to go.

Joe was confused but very grateful. It was the first time in his life that he had seen Jesus used for love and not for a beating.

He began work in the collecting and sorting of donated items to help pay back his benefactors. When he asked them why they were devoting so much to down-and-outers who couldn't begin to pay them back, he was amazed at their responses.

Joe wasn't ready to make any commitments about this new-found use of the Bible, but he began to have a crude understanding of the motivation for these people and folks like the Lackeys. He also started to see that God was not the enemy. The people who abused God's word were the real enemy.

For no special reason, Joe joined the Army in 1916. He found Army life hard but with a purpose, unlike his father who was hard on Joe just for the pleasure of it.

The drill sergeants at Camp Upton were just plain mean, and Joe's was the worst. Sgt. Del Gustanski had served in the Spanish-American War. Those were his glory days, and these days were far from glorious. The Army was stripped down to nothing. They had to drill with broom sticks for guns. They rationed all ammunition. Each soldier had ten rounds a week for range practice. The guards walked their posts with unloaded weapons.

That left the sergeants with two affordable options in training—either march the men to a lather, or to have them dig holes. The drill sergeants used these training tools to excess.

After a cold sleepless night in a tattered Army tent, the men were kicked out of bed and quick-step marched to the outdoor sinks for a cold water sponge bath, and a cold water shave. The recruits had fifteen minutes to complete these tasks.

They were then quick-step marched to the mess tent for a fast breakfast of porridge and coffee, or beans and coffee, with a slice of bread or cornbread on Sundays only.

After breakfast they would march in formation around the parade field for an hour, with Sgt Gustanski screaming in some poor soldier's ear the whole time, whether they were in step or not. He was equal in his punishment, and everyone had a chance to be the target of the day. Sgt. Gustanski was mad at the world, and his world consisted of twenty sorry recruits.

After drilling, they were given a ten-minute latrine break and marched to the exercise field for calisthenics. The man who didn't get his chest dirty or muddy was sure to feel Sgt. Gustanski's boot on his back.

After calisthenics, they had thirty minutes to clean up their tents for inspection. As they stood at attention, Sgt. Gustanski would rail at them for every wrinkle and every speck of dirt on the uniforms he had just pressed into the mud. As they continued to stand in the cold winter air, he would pick out a tent and enter it to kick everything inside to kingdom come. Those men would then be put on report for not passing inspection and were made to stay up after curfew doing KP for the next day's breakfast.

The final duty was to march, with full pack, twenty miles at a brisk pace, ten miles double-time, or five miles at a dead run. When they got to their destination they were forced to dig a trench tall enough and long enough to bury the entire squad chest high. Joe always dug harder and faster than any other soldier. The anger of his childhood was exercised with every blow of the shovel. After digging the trench they were given a ration of water and marched back in the same fashion for a lunch of bean soup, or cold sandwiches.

In the afternoon they would march away their lunch for an hour, and then do some type of combat training—hand-to-hand, bayonet, or rifle range. Sometimes they would crawl under barbed wire through mud to simulate real combat. Dynamite was used to get the feel of artillery shelling.

The next day they would repeat the process: only this time they would fill in the trench they had dug the previous day.

By the end of boot camp, these men were in the best shape of their lives, but no one forgot or forgave Sgt. Gustanski.

Things did improve for Joe after basic training. He was placed into the 77th Division, where he made the first real friends of his life. There were two Indiana boys, Burley Burke and Leon Taylor. They became a part of the four musketeers, along with Joe and a fellow from Maryland named Rowe Montillo.

Both Rowe and Burley were natural-born lady killers. Rowe gave the girls that shy quiet baloney. Burley, with his slim strong build and his stylish brown hair with the trademark curl descending on his forehead, looked like the uniform was designed for him.

Leon was neither shy nor outgoing and was a good listener and a good conversationalist. He was a man full of big ideas and had the ambition of opening up a tailor shop in Indianapolis. He even had the signage figured out. He was going to put his name in a bow at the top of the sign with a straight "Tailor" below the name—it would read, "Leon Taylor Tailor."

Joe was slow to make friends, but when he did one could trust him with his life. Girls were another matter altogether. Joe had a real conflict between the models of the loving and supportive Miss Lackey, and his horrible mother. He was attracted to women, but when it came to trusting women, Joe was like a dog that had been beaten too much by its owner.

Every soldier lives for his liberty and a chance to go to town. Liberty for the four musketeers usually consisted of a dash for the nearest dance hall or church social. It didn't matter as long as there was a gathering of girls. The boys had a system. Burley would walk in, looking good in his uniform, and draw all of the female attention to their group. Rowe, with his shy good looks, and Leon, with his smooth, yet unthreatening style, would thin the herd and match up the couples. The woman with the most maternal instinct would take Joe. When they broke up for the night, it was every man for himself.

When they reassembled in the morning, they would ask each other how they had made out. Burley would more often than not say that he had done all right, which usually meant that the girl was interested in his good looks and nothing more. Rowe was a gentleman and wouldn't say either way. Leon, who was the talker of the group, just kept his mouth shut and smiled a lot. Joe, in his shy tone, would say, "She was a nice girl," and leave it at that.

Of the four, Joe was the most likely to have been kissed. Every girl who went out with Joe could see his hurt and wanted with all her heart to heal him.

In advanced training, Joe became a Browning automatic rifle, or B.A.R. man. The B.A.R. ate up a lot of ammunition, so it required an assistant, to keep it supplied. Leon became Joe's B.A.R. assistant and back-up gunner.

Burley had an eagle eye and could hit six out of six every time. They put him on the line with a specialty as a sniper.

Rowe was regular infantry, but he had good leadership skills and soon made corporal.

In time, Woodrow Wilson changed his mind about the fighting "over there," and the Army began seriously preparing for war. The 77th Division was a part of that effort, and the boys were sent to France in June of 1918.

Much to everyone's chagrin, Sgt. Gustanski shipped over with them. He was still the biggest jerk in the Army, but he was back in his element. He carried a smile from ear to ear, and he was hankering to lead the boys through some good sticky French mud.

The 77th was first deployed to the relatively safe Baccarat sector for training. There was still some trench action taking place, but nothing very strong on either side.

That being said, one could still manage to get killed by sticking one's head up at the wrong time, and the planes from both sides would dogfight above and strafe each other's trenches.

It was here that Rowe gained his appreciation for the pilots, as he watched them duke it out in the blue skies over the tortured mud below.

On two occasions Rowe was able to slip away to the nearby airfield and meet some of his heroes. There was a fellow from Texas by the name of Slim; Bill Brown from Decatur, Indiana; and a guy by the name of Harley from Detroit. They were real friendly fellows. The pilots showed Rowe their planes and gave him a quick ground school. Harley seemed to be the airfield expert on the French girls.

The leaders of the group were a quiet fellow named Roscoe and a strange man they called Felix. They looked up to Roscoe because he pushed the kind of preparations that would get the job done and everybody home. Roscoe was the guy who would come out of nowhere to pick off that German you couldn't shake off your tail.

Rowe saw Felix on two occasions. The first time Felix was practically doing cartwheels and was bubbly as all get out. On the second visit, Felix was sullen to the point of doom. The story goes that Felix had been there longer than the others and was the only one left of his original squadron. When Felix was in the air, he lived for two things—flying and blood. He had become a man who loved to hunt and kill Germans. For that matter he really didn't care if he killed the German, or the German killed him. He just wanted someone to die.

Felix and Roscoe were the best of friends. Once on the ground, Roscoe could calm Felix like no other human being. He had a patient way of transforming Felix back into a regular guy, who loved flowers, little children, God, and good times.

By observing the diverse personalities of these pilots and the men who counted on each other in the trenches, Rowe learned to listen long to the soul of a man. It made him very successful later in life.

Burley had a very different experience in France. As the 77th moved up through Vesle, the fighting changed. They were more on the march, and sometimes susceptible to sniper ambushes. As the platoon sniper, Burley would have the job of spotting and picking off his German counterpart. He did this three times, with each job becoming more difficult to stomach.

The night after his second kill, Burley went off into the woods. Joe was worried and went to look for Burley. He found him at the edge of a stream, shaking and crying. Joe sat down next to Burley like a priest while Burley made his confession.

"It's different, Joe. When you see movement on a ridge, or over a trench, you just shoot at it. You never know if or what you hit. When I use that scope . . ." Burley couldn't finish the thought; at least not out loud. "Joe, please, I just want to go home."

Joe put his arm around Burley's shoulders and let him cry. "Tell me about your dad Burley. He's a great guy, isn't he? Tell me about your mom and dad. Did you grow up on a farm?" Joe kept up the small talk to get Burley's mind on better days. He also kept Burley's secret to himself.

Two days later Burley had to kill again. When they approached the tree, they found that the German sniper was a boy no more than fourteen who had been chained to the tree by the Germans so he couldn't desert. Burley lost his mind on that one. Rowe, Leon, and Joe whisked him away so Sgt. Gustanski wouldn't see him in that condition.

Two days later Burley's war was over. They were caught in the open by a German shelling. An explosion behind Burley sent a fragment through his left lung. They had to leave him there. When the shelling stopped, Rowe got to Burley first. He did what he could to stop the bleeding, but it was clear that Burley was near death. Sgt. Gustanski ordered Leon, Rocky Angelo, and the medic Ben Porter to carry Burley to the nearest aid station.

Burley survived his wounds but lost his lung. He was on borrowed time from that day on.

Joe's battalion commander was Major Charles Whittlesey. Major Whittlesey had been a lawyer in civilian life. He looked more like a college professor than a soldier, but the men thought of him as the best officer in the field.

On October 3, 1918, Major Whittlesey's 550 men made the mistake of advancing too fast into the tangled mass known as the Argonne Forest. Visibility was limited to a few feet, and they found themselves surrounded by an invisible enemy, who made their presence known with nearly continuous mortar and machine gun fire.

During the next five days, 249 of these men would be wounded so badly that they had to be carried from the field, and the "Lost Battalion" would see 107 of their soldiers and officers killed.

One of these was Sgt. Gustanski, who was killed in a German assault on the first day. Despite his bravado in boot camp, he completely fell apart in his first real combat. He ran from the line, leaving Rocky Angelo exposed to Germans on both sides. Rowe came to Rocky's rescue by killing a German at his left. Sgt. Gustanski was shot in the back as he ran into the woods. No one mourned the old coward.

During that week there was little food or water for Major Whittlesey's men. There were tempting streams in the woods, but they were guarded by the Germans, and any man who dared approach one to sooth his parched throat was an easy kill. This is where Joe found his personal hero in Father Francis Courtney, who was assigned to the battalion as a chaplain.

Father Courtney didn't carry a weapon, but he fought the battle with greater daring than any soldier. He helped the medics tend to the wounded. He pulled men to safety, even under murderous fire. At night he would crawl on his belly for several yards with a canteen in each hand to recover water for the troops. He couldn't carry more than two, as they would rattle and give him away.

It would take him all night to retrieve anywhere from four to eight canteens full, before the light of day stole his opportunity. Here again Joe was a confused witness to Jesus being used in sacrificial service to mankind, and not as the weapon his mother and father had perfected.

On the fourth night, Father Courtney's luck ran out. The Germans heard him and dropped a mortar round right on him. Joe could hear Leon respond in a whispered shout, "No, God, no, not Father Courtney!" There was a curious pause, and Leon appeared to be talking to someone. Then he clearly said "Yes, now!"

A second mortar round landed right in front of Leon and Joe's foxhole. Joe's B.A.R. was torn from his hands and shattered like a china cup. Joe was covered in painful fragment cuts, but not seriously injured. When he was able to crawl back to Leon, he discovered that his buddy had lost both hands—and his dream of his tailor shop.

Joe used his belt and Leon's to make tourniquets to stop the bleeding. Though dazed and wounded himself, Joe tried to heave Leon on his back to carry him to the pile of wounded soldiers in the center of the battalion formation.

As he struggled with his load, Joe heard the voice of Father Courtney, who had crawled unscathed back to safety. It was a true miracle. Joe had seen the mortar hit Father Courtney square, and yet here he was without a scratch.

The next afternoon General Alexander's men broke through to relieve the Lost Battalion. Those men would never see combat, or for that matter be the same again. Joe's quick action saved Leon's life, and he was cited for doing so. Rowe made sergeant for his leadership in the fight.

Thirty-three days later the "Great War for Civilization" ended. Many in the Lost Battalion were bitter that they had endured so much with the end so near. Some of them would never get over the feeling that their friends had somehow died in vain.

While they were waiting for transportation home, Rowe paid one last visit to the airfield, where his friend Harley took him up for his first plane ride. That experience made aviation an integral part of the rest of his life. Nine days before the war ended, Bill Brown was killed in a dogfight.

Father Courtney was changed by his experience. He was like a man who had come physically face to face with God. On the ship home he took Joe aside and made a confession. Father Courtney knew Joe well enough to know that he could trust Joe with his secrets.

It was a strange and sobering story. "On the night that Leon lost his hands, I was dead, Joe. I could see my body. It was torn to pieces. I went to Heaven, Joe, not in a dream but physically I went to Heaven. I saw God, and Moses, and my sister, and then I was sent back into a whole unscathed body. When I climbed the hill, I wasn't in the slightest discomfort. I could feel machine gun bullets strike my body, but I wasn't hurt at all."

Joe didn't say anything. He nodded his head. Joe believed Father Courtney, but like so many other things in his sad, mad world, he couldn't fully comprehend. Neither could he comprehend Leon's thinking. Here he had lost both hands—an aspiring tailor suddenly without hands. Somehow Leon didn't seem to mind. "It was my choice, Joe. I got what I prayed for, and I'm grateful."

Leon's statement never fully registered with Joe, but Joe didn't pursue it further. He had a natural aversion to any questions that contained the word "why."

CHAPTER 5

The War Comes Home

When they arrived in New York, Rowe, Leon, and Joe were discharged from the military. They had each been in the Army a few years before the 77th was formed and had more than served their time.

Rowe remained in New York and began a career in theatrical work. The four musketeers kept in touch, but not as well as they should have.

Burley had already gone home to Indiana, where he would battle for his life over the course of the next three years. Every cold, and every allergy, turned into a morbid struggle. With only one healthy lung, any labor that he could have easily performed before the wound now left him breathless and weak. Sleep was beyond him. At night Burley would see the faces of those he had killed.

Burley's death was an act of mercy. Rowe was unable to attend, but Joe and Leon were there. Leon wore gloves over his prostheses to appear less hideous. Burley had full military rights, and when the guns fired their salute it tore through Leon and Joe like they were being shot themselves. At the playing of Taps, Leon fell to his knees beside the grave and wept. Joe knelt down and put his arm around Leon. Leon did the same to Joe. Leon's hook felt odd on his shoulder, but Joe valued the touch of his friend. Joe did not cry. As always, he kept it inside. Tears had been beaten out of him when he was a boy.

After their discharge, Joe followed Leon back to Indiana. He had nowhere else to go, and he felt an obligation to help Leon get settled in life. Joe also felt a personal need to stay close to someone who understood the traumas of combat.

Joe and Leon lived a hair trigger existence for quite some time. A night without nightmares was rare. Fireworks were out of the question. An unexpected tap on shoulder, or the snap of a twig, could cause a violent and swift reaction. When a reporter or some well-meaning person would find out that they had been a part of the now famous "Lost Battalion," they would shy away from comment. They had just left Hades, and Valhalla was still too distant.

Joe stayed with the Taylors for the first two years. Mother Taylor was grateful that Joe was there to help Leon regain his physical and mental place in society. She really struggled at first with the changes in her little boy. She had all of the skills of a good mother and taught Joe a great deal of what he had missed in his own childhood. Still, she had no cure to mend her broken son. On the surface, Leon appeared to be mostly normal and happy, but there are things that mothers see and others never will.

She tried to hide her concern, but Joe could see the strain. One day he took her aside and let her talk. She told of how Leon had changed, and how she felt so helpless. Then she asked the tough question. "Joe, what did Leon see over there?"

Joe hesitated. His natural inclination was to never think about it again, but he knew there would be no peace in Ma Taylor's soul until he bared his. He told her things that only a soldier would understand.

When Joe was finished, she buried her head in his chest and cried and shook for her boy. It felt strange to Joe. His own mother had never cried, nor did she ever hug Joe or seek tenderness with him.

After their frank talk Mother Taylor knew what to do. She would just be Leon's mother. She would love him like a mother and she would wait for him like a mother, until the day when Leon decided he needed his mother.

Mr. Taylor was not like any man Joe had known. He was neither kind, like Mr. Lackey, nor was he cruel like his old man. Mr. Taylor was a realist. He didn't believe that Leon would ever be able to take care of himself. "A man with no hands—I just don't see it," he told Joe one night as they walked around the block. "I hope he proves me wrong, Joe. I hope he doesn't give up."

That was Joe's hope as well. He worked with Leon everyday, and pushed him to master and do more and more with his prostheses. Leon had already learned the basics in the hospital—like how to attach his hooks, dress himself, and eat a meal. Joe pushed Leon to the finer details of learning to live everyday life again.

One day Joe said, "It's time to go to work, you bum!" Joe put a needle on the floor and said, "Pick it up!" Leon tried over and over to pick up the needle. He did this for hours. Exhausted and frustrated, they gave up for the day.

The next morning, after Leon had dressed and eaten breakfast, Joe took the needle and dropped it to the floor. Leon tried again and again. He cursed, he kicked, he stormed out of the house—and then he walked back in and tried over and over. This went on for days until Joe had the idea of drilling a small hole in the metal of Leon's hook. It was just big enough to allow the needle to lodge firmly in position. Again Leon struggled for days to master the task. Finally Leon stood back up with the needle in his hook.

Leon started to yell and carry on so much that his father put his newspaper down and came running. Then Leon dropped the needle, and everyone gasped. As it turned out the needle hadn't slipped from Leon's hook—he had dropped it on purpose. Leon reached down and picked it up again, and dropped it again, and picked it up again, over and over. Leon started dancing around the room with his mother, who was bawling a bucket. His dad was patting him on the back saying, "Son, I'm so proud of you—that's wonderful, boy!"

Joe broke the mood by slamming a spool of thread loudly on the table. He looked at Leon and said, "Thread the needle!" For weeks Leon struggled with a problem that most people with two good hands have trouble doing. In time that task too became natural.

Leon went on to sew two scrap pieces of cloth together—ragged at first, evolving into a finely tuned professional stitch. Mastering this, Leon set out to become lord of the sewing machine. Eventually Leon decided to make Joe a tailored suit. He measured, he marked, and he perfected his own method of cutting the material. The result was a fine, first-rate, professionally tailored suit. It was finally time to open his shop—"Leon Taylor Tailor."

Leon and Joe found a good location for their store. Joe would have a section of the store for his jewelry and watch repair business, and Leon would tailor in the other part of the store. The combined businesses would draw customers for each other. They went through the various exercises of building a business plan. Finally it was time to approach a bank for financing.

Bank after bank turned them down with a variety of excuses.

"You boys have no business experience."

"I don't see the need for a tailor shop in that part of town."

"Sorry boys, you don't have enough collateral."

The honest ones came right out and said, "How are you going to sew if you don't have any hands?"

After hearing that last excuse one time too many, Leon asked the loan officer if he had a penny. The banker pulled one out of his pocket, and Leon instructed him to lay it on the desk, which he did. Then Leon picked the penny up and stood it up on edge on the desktop. After that Leon pointed to Joe's suit as evidence that he could produce a fine product. The banker was shamed, but he stuck to his guns.

"I don't think so, son."

The last banker was downright blunt. "If you had hands sir, it might be different, but no normal human being would want to be measured and gone over by a man with hooks for hands. You'll scare away your customers. Face it, son—you have to realize your limitations."

Leon rose to his feet. "I apologize for not being able to produce my original hands, sir! I gave them away to a German mortar round, while trying to preserve your comfortable American way of life! I'm sorry that my sacrifice offends you!"

That night, his spirit broken, Leon simply walked away and was never seen again.

Once again Joe's own hope in life was beaten down. All that he had gained was gone, and he had little heart to start again.

Chapter 6

Midnightmares

Joe stayed with Ma and Pa Taylor for a while. But there was so little he could do to ease their loss. There came a point when they all realized it was time for Joe to move on.

Joe left Indianapolis and found work at the Delco Remy plants in nearby Anderson. The factory wage was better than most, but the work was hard, dirty, and noisy in those pre-union days. It was a psychological drain on the soul.

Joe had learned from his experiences with Leon that men with money have power, and he was tired of being under the thumb of the world. It was with this in mind that Joe lived a Spartan existence, saving as much money as he could. There was no thought of socializing or love. He had seen enough friendships turn to dust, and his cruel mother had left him with no desire to place his trust in a woman's advances.

Joe's daily routine consisted of working a 10-hour shift, walking home to his shabby apartment on Pitt Street, scrounging something for supper, and going to bed. It wouldn't be long before the nightmares would start, and by midnight sleep was useless. Sometimes Joe would walk the streets to work off his restlessness. Most people were asleep, and the town was his. Solitude meant a lot to Joe, even if it was oppressive at times. On occasion some drunk would stagger home to an angry wife, and once he watched as a burglar climbed into a back window. Joe didn't try to stop him. Life and possessions had no value to Joe.

One day Joe found out about Mr. Tompkins, a jeweler who was retiring, and wanted to sell his business. It was the first thing in which he had taken an interest for a long time. It would be a way out of the factory, and Joe's only real joy in life was watchmaking. Looking through the magnifying lenses and bringing those small parts together to make a beautiful and useful piece gave Joe the same sense of satisfaction and accomplishment that God must have felt when he created the tiny Earth and all of the intricate parts of its living creatures.

Joe took off work that Wednesday and had lunch with the owner to talk the deal over. Mr. Tompkins took a liking to Joe and negotiated a purchase price that met both men's needs.

Living alone and working as much overtime as he could, Joe had set back enough for a sizable down payment. He went to see Mr. Duncan at the bank, and the loan was easily obtained. Joe appreciated Mr. Duncan's faith in him, but the good feeling was tempered with the memories of the cruel loan rejections Leon had endured.

On Thursday morning Joe told his foreman, Mr. Vinson, what he had done and that he was giving his notice. Mr. Vinson wished Joe well and told him that he could finish that week and work another two if he wanted, or that he could leave after the Saturday shift if Joe would prefer that option. It didn't really matter to Delco Remy, as there were plenty of other men whose souls were available to grease the cogs of factory production.

Joe chose to take the shorter leave, and spent the next three weeks working with Mr. Tompkins to make the transition. Joe kept the name Gransengetters for good name recognition and to honor old Horst Gransengetter, the original owner.

Many of Mr. Tompkins's loyal clientele were disappointed, but he played up Joe and his better watch repair skills. The male customers liked the fact that Joe was a regular guy who wasn't a pushy salesman. He didn't make a fellow feel small for being indecisive on a gift for his sweetheart, or for not knowing a karat from a carrot. He worked with the fellows who wanted to impress their girls but who couldn't afford the outlay all at once.

The women who frequented the store admired his taste in jewelry. They also liked Joe because he was cute, needed their maternal care, and would make a great match for their daughter, granddaughter—or to heck with them—herself.

One of Joe's best customers was his old boss, Mr. Vinson, who would come around every month or two to buy something for his wife, or one of his daughters, or his mom. His first purchase came about a week after Joe went solo with the business. He ordered a diamond encrusted Masonic ring. Mr. Vinson's word of mouth was good for Joe. He knew a lot of the big shots in town, and he would often suggest Gransengetters to any of his workers who were mulling what to get for their wives or their girlfriends.

Despite his pleasant demeanor with his customers, Joe remained a solitary man. He left his apartment on Pitt Street and moved into the back room at the store to save money and to keep his place secure at night. After closing he would do his bookwork and place his orders. Then Joe walked the day's haul to the Anderson Banking Company's night deposit box.

Having no social obligations, Joe would usually grab a bite to eat at the YMCA and walk the meal off, enjoying the town at his leisure. After that exercise, Joe would go back to his bed in the back room and try to sleep. Three or four hours after he hit the pillow, he would begin hear gunfire and the screams of dying men calling for their mothers. Other times he would be pushing away his father's blows, with his mother's voice scolding him to show more respect. When those nightmares came around, Joe would usually walk the darkened city streets. Every third shift cop and hooker in town knew Joe and respected his privacy.

It was the summer after Joe had opened his store, on one of those midnight haunts, that Joe first met a beggar everyone called Kelly. Nobody ever knew if that was his name for sure, but that's the name everyone used. Joe first saw Kelly urinating on the City Hall steps, around three in the morning. It turns out that Kelly hated the mayor, and that's why he chose that spot. The mayor grew angrier and angrier at the affront and had the police conduct extra patrols in the area to catch the offender. As it turned out, the cops hated the mayor even more and always claimed that they had just missed the guy.

During the daylight hours both Joe and Kelly were, in a sense, established downtown businessmen. Kelly did most of his begging on Meridian Street, while Joe's jewelry store was on Main.

At night Kelly lived in the narrow passage between two buildings off the alley between Meridian and Main streets and bounded by 12th and 13th streets. He had lost most of one foot, three fingers, and the eye on his left side. He had the look of a land-locked pirate. All he needed was a parrot on his shoulder. Kelly never offered to tell much of the story, but Joe was pretty sure that he had lost them to a shelling or a mine in the war.

At the close of business each day Joe would walk to the bank to make his deposits and would pass Kelly as his own "business" was closing. The two young war Veterans usually hooked up and swapped bits of Army stories as they walked "home." That was the way Joe talked, in bits, but Kelly could easily fill in the blanks, for these were two fellows of common experiences who understood each other without the need for excessive talk.

As their friendship grew, Joe made sure that Kelly had at least a sandwich every day, and he allowed Kelly to sleep in his shop on bad nights. Kelly didn't sleep much inside, as he had been hunkered down for the night in a small building in a French village when he sustained his injuries. He much preferred the lesser known "shadow" spaces of outdoor Anderson.

By day Kelly was a helpless crippled beggar, humbled by the stares and aversions of the crowd. By night he had the power to rule the town, slipping in and out like a superhero/villain, taking what he chose and creating mischief on his own terms. It was strange that Joe's own son would someday be a crippled beggar—and that a man named Kelly would be his helper and friend.

CHAPTER 7

The Delaware Girl

For every lost soul there is a savior, and one day she walked into Joe's store. Her name was Keku, which was a nickname derived from her Lenape (Delaware) name, "Kèku hàch kuwatu," which roughly translates to the English "What do you know?"

Keku was a devout Catholic who attended Mass at St. Mary's every Sunday and once or twice during the week. She was also a direct descendent of the city's founding father, Delaware Chief Kikthawenund. While Keku was a modern girl of the twentieth century, she maintained close ties to the traditions of her Lenape heritage. In church she saw no separation between the God we call Jehovah and the God she called Grandfather. They were one and the same, and responsible for all life and creation. This doesn't mean that she worshiped the Earth, but she did see in nature her brothers and sisters created by God. As she left the Mass, Keku would genuflect and, in doing so, thank Jesus for his sacrifice, God for his universal creation and love, and her brother and sister trees for giving her a comfortable place to sit and kneel.

It was this modern girl, with this deep spiritual awareness, who entered Joe's shop on her lunch break from the phone company. She had a broken necklace, an ancient piece given to her by her grandmother. The bell on the door rang as she entered the store. She was alone for only a moment before Joe appeared, but in that short time she sensed that powerful "demons" were present. These were spirits that would either have to be exorcised with gentle patience—like a mother using cold washcloths to relieve a child's fever—or removed with violence. There was no in-between.

34

It was only after this moment that she first saw Joe. She thought he was certainly an attractive man, and—as with the other women who frequented his store—his maternal needs drew her heart. Still it was the demon spirits haunting Joe that drew her compassion and set her sights on helping the troubled jeweler. She quickly discerned that she would have to approach Joe with gentle steps.

Joe marveled over the beautiful and delicate necklace. It was so unique in its design. He asked her its history and she told him, using only the words necessary and nothing more. She sensed that Joe would respond only to a quiet woman who listened more than she spoke. As he studied the piece, she studied his eyes, and gave only a hint of the caring smile that was building in her heart.

Joe felt very strange in her presence. It was that unconditional love and goodness thing that he had encountered with Miss Lackey, the Salvation Army Captain Giarusso, and Father Courtney. It had never made sense to Joe, but here it was again, and stronger than ever. Who was this woman? He had to learn more.

Joe wanted to see her again, so he made up an excuse that he would need more time to do his best work and asked if she would be willing to return the next day. He apologized for the inconvenience and asked her if she wanted him to clean the piece as well. She said yes to the cleaning, and that it was no inconvenience to come back as she worked two blocks away at the phone company.

Keku turned to walk out of the shop, and Joe suddenly realized that he hadn't captured her name and phone number.

"Oh, wait! I need . . ." She cut him off and told him her name and phone, as if she were a clairvoyant.

"That's an unusual name."

"I'll tell you all about it sometime," she said with a faint smile. Then the bell rang as she exited the store.

Joe's heart jumped. She had given him signals that she wanted to spend time with him and for them to get to know each other better.

All afternoon he was anxious to work on the necklace, but his promised workload and an unusual number of customers that day kept him from his desire. He was outwardly polite, but inwardly seething about all the interruptions.

Joe finished Mr. Hunt's watch around 4:30, but he had Mrs. Furnace's to repair before the next morning and it was a disaster. The paperwork that evening was a tangled mess, and it was almost 7 p.m. before he could run—and I do mean run—the receipts to the night deposit box. On the way back he grabbed Kelly and pulled him along to the diner, as he apologized for being late. Joe rushed in and ordered a hamburger and a vanilla cola, thumping his fingers the whole time it was cooking. He threw a five at the waitress and said, "Keep the change." Exiting the diner, he shoved the burger and cola at Kelly and said, "Nice talking with you," as he ran back to the shop. A stunned Kelly, who hadn't had a chance to say a word in Joe's vacuum, watched Joe speed around the corner, and replied to the air, "Thanks Joe, enjoyed the conversation, have a good night." Kelly rolled his eyes, shook his head, and ate his sandwich.

It would be 10:00 before Joe would be finished with Mrs. Furnace's watch. Mrs. Furnace was a sweetheart of a woman, a bit on the small side, and full of zest in her demeanor. Every day seemed to be the greatest day of her life, and no one could be near her for very long without smiling. A high school French teacher, she loved everything French, especially French cooking.

This was not the first time Joe had fixed her watch. She had a bad habit of dropping it into bowls of French stuff. The next morning when Mrs. Furnace saw Joe's restoration of her poor marinated watch, she shouted, "Voilà! merci, merci, Monsieur Joe!"

It was after midnight when Joe finished the necklace. With a little dedication and jeweler's magic, the broken piece was fully restored to its original glory. Joe had no idea what time it was when he called Keku to let her know she could come in any time to pick it up. It was only after she picked up the receiver that Joe realized the late hour.

"Oh, I'm sorry. Were you in bed?"

"Well, actually yes, I was. I have to be at work at 6, but thank you for working on it so late. I'll be by at lunchtime. Goodnight."

Joe hung up the phone, pounded his fist on the table, and shouted "You idiot!!!!" Then he left the shop and kicked a can all over town. The police kept an eye on Joe to make sure he didn't hurt himself. Kelly could hear Joe's tirade all the way from City

Hall. He had endured enough of Joe's moodiness that evening and decided it was best to avoid his friend like the plague that night.

On the other end of the receiver, after Keku had hung up the phone, she smiled and whispered to the air above her bed, "Goodnight, Joe."

CHAPTER 8

The Redemption of Joe

Like a Hollywood movie, Keku's visit to Gransengetters led to a courtship and a wedding. They had dated for over a year before Joe worked up the courage to propose. When the evening came, Keku knew what Joe was about to do. She could read his spirit like a book.

Joe started to propose in the Shamrock diner, but Keku cut him off. "I ate too much, Joe,—let's go for a walk." Having a strong sense of history, she maneuvered Joe to the hill above White River where Chief Kikthawenund's village had once stood. With the spirit of Kikthawenund bearing witness, Joe got down on both knees and asked Keku to marry him. His past being what it was Joe was still terribly unsure that she would say yes. Keku knelt down and held Joe. "I was yours from the moment I walked through your shop door, Joe. Of course, I will marry you." Kelly and Officer Dodd watched it all from the steps of City Hall and welled up like two parents who were losing their son.

The marriage was a healing balm for Joe, and Keku had a man who would be devoted to her for the rest of their days. However Joe's problems were far from over. The nightmares and the scars remained with Joe for several years after their marriage. As was her way Keku would sponge off what demons she could and remain patient for what she could not do. Joe was eternally faithful and grateful to Keku. He never raised a hand to her, always turning his anger inward, not knowing that this hurt her just as much as if he would strike her with a physical blow.

Keku worked for the phone company for another year. They lived on Joe's income and saved hers, and during that time they were able to purchase the rest of the building that housed Gransengetters and Mrs. Dempsey's flower shop. Joe and Keku transformed the top floor to a very nice apartment.

They loved living in the city. Each evening, just before Joe closed his store, Keku would come down to do the paperwork so they could enjoy more of the evening together. By 5:30 they would walk together to the night deposit box, rain or shine. It was her best time to teach Joe about the goodness of life. While others might curse the rain, Keku would thank the rain for its life-giving refreshment. She would never despair over the hot summer sun. She raised her face to feel its power. Joe did not understand the way she thought. Neither did he understand the way he felt when she spoke of these things. On the surface these were just pleasant times with his wife, but in another dimension Keku was fighting a spiritual war. Keku's purity was pushing back the evil that had dominated Joe's life.

On their way from the night deposit, they would catch up with Kelly and treat him to a sandwich, or take him home to share their evening meal. It meant a lot to Kelly and he enjoyed his visits, but he couldn't stand to stay indoors for very long.

At night Joe would have his nightmares, and Keku would follow him out the door. Sometimes she would walk beside Joe. Sometimes she would walk a few steps ahead. Because of his war experiences Joe would have turned and killed her if she had approached him from behind. There were times when she would walk on the other side of the street to give Joe the extra room he needed that night.

This is not meant to imply that all combat Veterans are half crazy. A majority just tend to shy away from talking about their experiences and live perfectly normal lives. Joe's case was special. The war had served to magnify the anger and the hurt of his childhood abuse.

These evening walks would often end the same. The two would return to the apartment in silence where Keku would cradle Joe's weary mind in her healing flesh.

In the second year of their marriage, Keku became not only pregnant, but pregnant with twins. Joe was both excited and scared to death. He treated Keku like a china doll. He worried himself sick about being a father. He had no role model to follow except his wicked old man.

Kelly got into the act as well, feeling the babies kick, and asking all sorts of naive and sometimes embarrassing questions. He was always bringing toys for the babies, most of which were clearly worn, and had plenty of teeth marks. Keku's intuition told her that Kelly may have pulled some of them right out of some poor baby's mouth.

For all of his doting and excitement, Kelly didn't live to see the babies born. One Friday night a small gang of teenage punks found him walking around downtown. They started to shove him from one kid to the other, like a medicine ball. They made fun of Kelly and laughed at their power over the crippled street bum. Finally they shoved him, and he fell head first into the sharp corner of the Citizens Bank building. Kelly was dead before he hit the ground.

The word of what happened got around quickly, but there were no witnesses except the boys and therefore no evidence to convict. The mayor was embarrassed that the crippled bum had made his living in his city, so the investigation was only a half-hearted one. Officer Dodd tried to pursue it further, but he was told to drop it. Both he and Joe knew who the culprits were, but the evidence was too scant and it would be some time before there would be any justice for Kelly.

During those nine months, and well into the babies' early lives, the nightmares either went away or Joe was just too focused on his responsibilities to notice them. Joe went crazy during the long labor, and when he saw his children for the first time he was petrified with fear. Hand-to-hand combat paled next to the doubt he had at that moment. Joe's business was doing well enough that he knew he could provide for them, but with his limited education how could he help them with their schoolwork? How could he give them a happy childhood when he had never had one himself? How could he discipline them without becoming his own father? But there they were—ready or not—a little boy named Tony and a little girl named Toni (which they pronounced "tone knee" with the emphasis on the "knee" to distinguish between the two).

Joe worked his regular hours in the store. Keku would come downstairs with the babies around 1 p.m. and bring him some lunch. Then she would usually take the twins for a stroll around town to meet their adoring public. Sometimes she would take them to the bluff along the river to mingle their spirits with the spirit of the great Anderson chief, who was their great-great-great-grandfather, Chief Kikthawenund.

In the evenings and nights, Joe took over most of the care of the twins. He bathed them, he played with them, and he changed their diapers. Joe would pull them up by one leg to slip the clean diaper under them. He had a crazy idea that over time this would cause one leg to stretch out longer than the other, so he was very diligent about alternating the leg each time.

Keku cooked the evening meal and, of course, she fed the babies. During the night it was Joe who got up to bring one or the other to their mother. It was during one of these wake-up calls that Joe watched his son turn over in the crib for the first time. Had he been the average father of the day, he would have missed this once-in-a-lifetime moment. Joe loved to watch his wife feed their children. It was more beautiful to him than anything in the universe.

After the twins were baptized by Father Williams, Joe began to go to church with the family. Joe liked Father Williams. He had a great mind, and he observed people much as Joe had done in his own life. He felt a kinship with the priest, who was about Joe's age. Father Williams had one thing over Joe—he had a relationship with God, while Joe was still afraid to let go and trust anyone or anything to that extent.

The truth be known, Joe favored Toni. Even at the age of two she was daddy's little girl and would sit for hours on his lap, while her brother toddled about the apartment in search of adventure. When he came up after work, Toni would be the first to leave her toys and crawl or toddle to her daddy's leg. He loved her big, wet, whole-mouth kisses on his cheek as she tried to imitate her mom.

Three months and two days after their second birthday, Keku contracted the flu. Joe closed the shop early to help out. He had gone to the drugstore to get some medicine for Keku when she became violently ill as she was boiling some water for tea. While she was in the bathroom, Tony started to play with a dishtowel, flipping it around. He hit the stove and it caught on fire. He started screaming, and when he pulled it down it fell on Toni and set her clothes ablaze. Despite her vomiting, Keku ran into the room to find that Toni had broken through the gate and was falling down the stairs out of her grasp. By the time Keku was able to reach her daughter, Toni was too badly burned. She died on the way to the hospital, and Keku was also seriously burned.

Joe turned the corner to see the ambulance pulling away from his home. Mrs. Dempsey had heard the screams and had called the ambulance and the fire department. The firemen turned off the stove and quickly extinguished the small fires, as Mrs. Dempsey checked over Tony to make sure he was all right. He was, but he was scared to death and crying uncontrollably. She gave Joe a quick overview of what had happened and promised to care for Tony so Joe could go to the hospital.

They had no car, so Joe started running the ten blocks to the hospital. A block or two into it Officer Dodd caught up to Joe and drove him the rest of the way, with the siren blaring.

After Toni's funeral, Keku went through several months of painful healing from her burns, and a crushing load of grief and guilt over the loss of their baby girl. Joe fell further into the abyss and grew cold to the world in general and also, unfortunately, to his son.

Little Tony may have had it the worst. He was now terrified of the stove that had come alive and had made his sister scream. Tony was too young to understand why his mother couldn't hold and comfort him. His daddy would have nothing to do with him. The hardest part was trying to understand where his sister was. "Where Toni? Where Toni?" he would say over and over. He thought that Toni didn't like him anymore and was hiding from him. Joe couldn't stand it and walked away from his son. It tore at Keku's heart every time he said it, and Tony said it a lot.

Joe could have repaired the damage in the apartment, but not the horrifying memories, so they moved to a small house just north of 38th Street. Joe took the bus to work each morning and sometimes walked home after working past the last bus run. He knew that Tony and Keku needed him, but his fear of loving and losing was so great that he was emotionally paralyzed. All of the demons Keku had sponged from Joe's brow were back and more.

It would now take an act of violence to drive them out. That would come in the form of a high school hot-shot.

J.T. Batten was the most popular boy at Anderson High School. He was an all-state quarterback and an all-star forward on the basketball team. All of the guys wanted to be on his "team." J.T. could have any girl he wanted. More than one girl "got into trouble" because of J.T. He was the only child of a rich father and a trophy mother. The smug teenager drank, smoked, and did anything that pleased his mood. He was the only boy who had his own car when he was a junior. It was a brand new car and plenty fast. He didn't have to work. His weekly allowance was greater than half of the adult men's weekly wages in Anderson. Worst of all, J.T. was the leader of the gang who had killed Kelly. He had even bragged about the killing, but no one dared to witness against him. He was too powerful in school, and his father was too powerful in Anderson.

J.T. came into Joe's shop one afternoon to buy a diamond bracelet to impress a girl. When he found one he liked, he told Joe, "I'll take that one. Wrap it, old man." Joe told him that that particular one had been purchased and the man was going to pick it up after work. Joe swallowed his loathing for the boy and asked if he wanted to look at anything else in the case. J.T. had a fit. No one had ever told him that he couldn't have what he wanted, and he demanded that Joe sell it to him. Joe had had enough. "Get out of my store boy!"

No one had dared to speak to him in that manner—not even his father. An hour later J.T. came back in an uncontrollable rage and this time with a gun. He pointed it at Joe and screamed at the "old man" to give him the bracelet.

Something popped inside of Joe. It boiled up and exploded through the top of his head like an erupting volcano. HE WASN'T GOING TO TAKE IT ANYMORE!

He grabbed the boy by the wrist just behind the pistol and pulled him across the glass case like a rag doll. The gun exploded in a report and fired a round into Joe's stomach. The pain was intense, but Joe's rage was greater. He slammed the boy to the floor and put his knee in J.T.'s chest. He punched the boy in the face over, and over, and over, and over as he cut loose on his father and his mother, and on Sgt. Gustanski, and the people who had destroyed Leon, and the punks who had killed Kelly, and the fire that had destroyed his little girl and his family. He kept punching, and punching, and punching, long after the boy fell limp.

Mrs. Dempsey heard the shot and called the police. Before they could arrive she rushed into the store to grab Joe and try to pull him off the boy. It was no use. She was too small and Joe was too strong and enraged, so she just climbed on his back and held on. "It's over, it's over, Joe. Stop! Please, Joe, stop! It's okay, Joe. It's over. It's over."

Finally Joe began to hear her voice, and he stopped hitting the punk. Weak from his own blood loss, he now easily fell back onto Mrs. Dempsey's stomach, where she held him like a child. Mr. Huggins rushed in from the nearby office supply store followed by Officer Dodd. The ambulance arrived seconds later to rush the boy and Joe to surgery.

Joe would survive with several weeks of pain, but no permanent damage. J.T. also survived, but every bone in his face was broken. He was no longer the prettiest boy in school. For that matter he never went to school again.

Officer Dodd called in the detectives and they found enough evidence to convict J.T. of armed robbery. At the trial his father was outraged that his son was being accused of a serious crime. "He was just getting some harmless kicks. He was just being a normal boy. Meanwhile you do nothing to the man who nearly killed my son. He should be arrested!"

There were several students present at the trial, including a few girls who had had to leave school because of J.T.'s love-em-and-leave-em style. Coach Gast took the entire football team to the trial. He wasn't there to support J.T.—he was there to show the other boys what happens to kids who act like J.T.

J.T. himself was angry and unrepentant. He couldn't believe that he was being punished over a stupid bracelet. Daddy had covered for him before. He knew that his old man's lawyer would get him off the hook. He couldn't wait until the judge would be forced to apologize to his face.

The jury saw it differently. They convicted J.T. on all counts. At the sentencing Judge Smith looked down at Mr. Batten and told him that if there was a law against being a jerk of a father, "I would sentence you to Death Row." J.T. was sentenced to 20 years, and with his attitude he served every day of it. The Battens never bothered to visit J.T. in prison. They were always too busy.

Joe didn't stay for the outcome. He gave his story to the court, and after he testified the court went into recess. Joe left the court and didn't return. He had seen enough lives destroyed. If that boy wanted to ruin his life, that was his business, but Joe didn't have to stay to watch it.

With guarded steps from his still tender wound, he left the courtroom, and he asked Keku to walk with him to St. Mary's. As they walked, they did so hand-in-hand. Joe hadn't held Keku's hand in a long time. When they arrived at the entrance to the sanctuary, he let go of her hand and walked up the aisle alone. Keku followed a few steps behind. When Joe reached the altar, he fell before it on his hands and knees, with his head dropped. Keku lurched for him, thinking that his wound had opened up again. She stopped short of Joe as he let out a long, loud, mournful cry and said, "I can't do this anymore! I need your help! I've hurt my wife. I've hurt my son. I've hurt you. I'm so sorry. I'm so sorry. Please help me."

Father Williams was in the sacristy when he heard Joe's lament. He came out and knelt by the contrite man, with his hand on Joe's shoulder. Keku knelt by her husband's other side and placed her hand in the middle of his back.

With that one violent shout, a door had opened in Joe's soul and the demons fled. Over the next several months Father Williams' good council and Keku's love would heal Joe's soul and give him new life.

CHAPTER 9

A Child is Born

Joe was indeed a new man, but he had a lot of fences to mend. For the first time in his life Joe was happy. He wasn't magically spared from life's heartaches, but now he began to understand that the goodness of life could be separated from the bad. He took the extra effort to return the love that Keku had shown him. Joe learned to appreciate and apply the principles of Christian charity that he had seen in Captain Giarusso and Father Courtney.

The nightmares were gone, but so was his chance to be a complete father to Tony. Things between them did improve dramatically, but there would always be a wedge between Tony and his father. From that point forward Joe was devoted to mending the rift with his son. He took Tony fishing. He played catch with his son. He even taught Tony the watchmaking trade, which fascinated the boy and gave him a sense of accomplishment. Tony loved this change in his dad, but there was always the lingering fear that it would end at any moment.

Tony was troubled but not deeply scarred by his father's lapse. On the surface he was a normal boy. Even under the surface he knew he was loved and valued by his parents, especially by his mother. Keku had shown Tony nothing but love, even though at times she was masking some natural human anger at him for starting the fire that killed her daughter and caused her own physical pain.

Keku's ability to love her son and control her anger was borne of several visits in the hospital by the spirit of her great-great-grandfather. When Kikthawenund sensed Keku's trauma, he came to her. He would sit quietly as the nurses tended to Keku's burns. When they were alone, Keku and Kikthawenund would talk about what had happened.

"I should never have left my children alone."

"You were violently ill. You had no control over this, Keku."

"I should have turned off the stove. I should have done something."

"If you could do this, Keku, then you would have the power to go back in time and cure all things. You must teach me this power."

"I do not have this power, Grandfather."

"Do you merely say you do not have this power, or do you know you do not have this power?"

"I know I do not have this power, Grandfather. I have no power at all."

"This is not true, Keku. You have the power to love and forgive your son. You need only one thing more, Keku."

"What is that, Grandfather?"

"The power to forgive yourself."

Kikthawenund held out his hand to Keku, and in his palm was a great light. "I can only carry this gift so far, Keku. You must take it from the Great Spirit."

Keku's physical hands were immobile, so she reached out with a set of spiritual hands and accepted the gift. As she did, Kikthawenund pulled aside his robe to reveal her little Toni, affectionately clinging to her great-great-great-grandfather's leg.

"We call her Mamalis (sounds like mah-MAH-leese) which means in your English, Fawn. She is a great joy to me, Keku. I thank you for your labor, and your nurturing care."

With that Toni's spirit kissed her mother, as did Kikthawenund. He brushed the tears from Keku's cheeks, and the two spirits vanished. They took with their exit, a great deal of the pain from Keku's burns. So too, her anger and guilt no longer consumed her. Keku would never completely forget the bitterness and the sorrow. Sometimes her human side would take the upper hand, but she now had the power to overcome her shame and anger. She made it her goal to love Tony even more than before.

That being said, Tony always struggled with himself. As he grew older he began to understand Toni's death and his part in it. The love and support of his parents helped him channel his guilt into positive pursuits. He drove himself to be a better student, a better athlete, and a better citizen. That drive only intensified when his little brother Mike came along.

Baby Mike was a chance for a new life for Joe and Keku. He was also a do-over for Tony, who was almost like a third parent to Mike. Tony, keeping in mind his sister, was often overprotective. This caused some friction from time to time, whenever Mike tried to emerge from his brother's protection. Still, Mike was so proud of his big brother Tony the valedictorian, Tony the star hitter, Tony the star quarterback, and Tony the varsity basketball starter and leading scorer. Mike was never as good as his brother in any of these pursuits, but he became a better person as he tried his best to emulate Tony.

Keku knew before anyone else in the family that Mike would be a great athlete. Her labor with Mike was made easier when Kikthawenund and Mamalis entered the delivery room to watch the birth of his new grandson, and her baby brother. Mamalis was growing into a very pretty girl, and it pleased Keku to see her daughter, and to speak to her in Lenape. This of course confused the heck out of the delivery room nurses, but they had heard it all and wrote it off as the ramblings of a woman in the throes of labor.

Right after Mike was born, Keku asked to be alone with her son. When the nurses and the doctor left, Kikthawenund and Mamalis approached the bed. Mamalis kissed her brother and left a small birthmark on his forehead. Kikthawenund said to Keku, "His name is kshamehële," (which sounds like Sham-hay-lay and means "He runs fast").

I've already told you about Mike's prowess at running the bases to impress the fair Debbie at the Roosevelt baseball game, and his strong finish at the state track meet. As a boy he ran all of the time, mostly trying to keep up with Tony. It seems that the only time Mike didn't do much running was when Veronica was chasing him.

As it turned out, Leroy was the last fellow to date Veronica, before she turned to Mike for good. If he had been any competition, it didn't matter. Leroy decided to drown his sorrows by joining the Marine Corps that fall and pretty much disappeared into the military. On December 7th of that year the world changed for all of the "Teddy Roosevelt" boys.

In the summer of 1941, Mike spent every moment he could with Veronica, and she distracted his mind every minute they were apart. Mike had taken a job at The Toast restaurant to earn money for college. Keku and Joe laid down the law when the time he spent with Veronica began to affect his work. They firmly reminded Mike of his obligations and his goals. Mike had earned a track scholarship to Taylor University. It would take quite a bit of sacrifice by Mike and his parents to see it through, but it meant the world to Joe. Mike would be the first "man of the family" to graduate college. Joe kept thinking of the words of his parents, "Learnin' makes boys think they're better than their parents." He couldn't wait for Mike's commencement day when he could pop out his "proud papa's" chest and shove that phrase in his miserable old man's face.

It was a foregone conclusion that Mike and Veronica would get married as soon as he graduated college, but all of that changed dramatically when Tony fell into mortal danger. It didn't matter how much he loved Veronica, there was a new goal now that surpassed all others. Tony was in trouble and Mike had to save his brother.

When Tony graduated high school in 1938, the job market was still pretty bleak, so he joined the Army. At the same time that Pearl Harbor was being bombed, Tony was in Manila serving in a coastal artillery unit. When the Japanese 14th Army swept through the Philippines, Tony's company was decimated and scattered like so many others. He and his friend Ernie joined up with the remnants of the U.S. forces on Bataan that had formed a final buffer between the Japanese onslaught and Corregidor, where the Army was pushed back to make its last stand. Our guys fought a gallant defense for almost five months before they were forced to surrender. If these brave soldiers had known what lay ahead, they would have fought until the last man was dead.

They might as well have been dead. The Japanese marched the survivors up the Bataan peninsula in an exhausting forced march. They perished from disease and malnutrition. They died of heatstroke, lack of water, and exhaustion. Many of them were beaten to death or shot for sport and left along the shoulders of the road.

Over the next three years, the star athlete from Anderson High School would become a barely living bag of bones. He would suffer from malaria and dysentery. He would lie in filth that one cannot imagine. He was so malnourished that at times he would lose his sight, and even become literally paralyzed by the lack of sufficient vitamin B in the meager diet. Then there was the ever-present cruelty of the guards.

Tony would not have survived without the help of his buddy Ernie Griner. They patched each other's wounds and sacrificed their starvation rations to the one who needed it most at the time. They gave each other hope when there was no hope at all.

One particular night in the fall of 1943, Tony was nearly blind from malnutrition and unable to stand. He was delirious with fever and almost certainly on the verge of death. Ernie was also very ill and barely able to help Tony. Ernie did his best to cool Tony's fever, to hold him when he went into convulsions, and to encourage him to hang on. Too weak to go on himself, Ernie slipped into a semi-conscious state and began to feel his own life slip away.

As Ernie became increasingly unresponsive, Tony gave up and fell into a deep restless sleep. It was during this time, when Tony was utterly isolated from the world around him and near death that he began to dream, and as he did so a spirit kissed his forehead. It was Mamalis, whom Tony began to recognize as his now-grown sister.

In his delirium, Tony begged her forgiveness for the fire he had started. Toni told her brother to look at her, and asked him if he saw any scars. Indeed there were none. All Tony saw was a beautiful young woman his age. She had a healthy smile and showed her brother only love.

Mamalis told Tony how proud she was of the man he had become, and how he had been such a good example to their little brother Mike. Then Mamalis said, "We are here to give you back your spirit. It is not your time to join us, but I will always be in your heart. I love you, Brother."

With that Mamalis vanished, and a large fire appeared in the center of the camp. This was impossible, as the camp was kept dark at night for the wartime blackout. Around this fire danced a very old man. The old man sang a song in a language that Tony did not understand. When he had finished his song, the old man looked at his great-great-great grandson for a moment. Then the old man, the fire, and Tony's fever vanished. Tony stood up and found some water to help Ernie.

It would be several days before Tony would see his own reflection. When he did, there was a mark on his forehead where his sister Toni had kissed him. It was just like the birthmark he had seen on Mike.

At the moment the old man vanished into the night, on the other side of the world Keku jerked up in bed and shouted "kikeha," which means "He healed him." Joe shot awake at her outburst. He didn't understand what she had said, but he knew it was important and that the spirit was not to be broken.

Mike was a thousand miles away. He too jumped up from his sleep, not knowing why, but that something very important had happened. The next letter from his mother would be very mysterious and disturbing.

CHAPTER 10

The Pencil Man Goes to War

As soon as the news broke of the invasion of the Philippines, Mike was chomping at the bit to get there as fast as he could to fight beside his brother. The word of Tony's MIA status would come later and would intensify Mike's drive to reach his brother. For a week Mike studied the situation and made his decision.

"Enlist? Enlist! Are you crazy? Don't you love me?" Veronica was not taking the news well.

"Of course I love you. I think of you all the time, but I have to do this, Veronica. I have to reach my brother.

"But why the Marines? Tony is in the Army."

The Army would have made sense if Mike had known that the Army would be sent to liberate the Philippines, but he didn't know that at the time. He did know that President Roosevelt's publicly announced general plan was to send most of the Army to Europe to fight Hitler. The Marines would be deployed in the Pacific to take on Tojo—so Mike went with the odds.

Keku was worried sick that her last remaining child was running into mortal danger. They could have kept Mike home as the sole surviving son—especially since Tony's situation was uncertain at best, and very likely he was already missing or dead. Keku strongly sensed that Tony was in peril, but she also knew that she could not keep Mike's spirit in a bottle—especially considering the kinship between the two boys.

Joe was in the unhappy position of having his boys in a situation he knew too well. Mike may be able to send home cheerful letters to his mother, but Joe would know the truth.

Mike enlisted on a Wednesday, ten days after Pearl Harbor, and by Saturday he had passed his physical. He was given a week to settle his affairs, and the following Saturday he was on his way to New River, North Carolina.

The scene at the bus station was pretty sad. It was the first time he had ever seen his father cry, and neither one of them knew how to handle it. Keku was broken hearted and would go to Mass every day thereafter and say the rosary three times a day. Veronica was dressed to kill, in hopes it would change Mike's mind. She made quite a scene, and Mike almost had to drag her into the bus to get things rolling. I don't think any of the guys on the bus would have minded, but Mike pried her loose and left her pouting.

As they rolled down Highway 67 to Indianapolis and Union Station, Mike saw his world falling behind the bus. There was Pendleton, where he had watched Tony hit a game-winning grand slam against the Irish. In Fortville, Mike had broken the school record in the mile. The bus stopped in McCordsville to pick up Bob Frazier, who was also heading to New River. Mike didn't know Bob, but they became friends on the way down. Oaklandon and Lawrence were next, and then the big town, Indianapolis.

Back then Indianapolis was a large busy city. It has since become much larger and busier, but it is also much cleaner. The coal furnaces in the homes, the factory smoke, and the locomotives in the Beech Grove yards made it a dirty gray town back then, but even in 1941 Indianapolis was a place of excitement for an 18-year-old boy from Anderson.

As the bus traveled down Pendleton Pike, it turned west onto 38th St., toward the home of the Indiana State Fair. At the impressive limestone tower of North Methodist Church, the bus turned south on Meridian—the main artery into the heart of Indy. Where Meridian crosses Market Street, the ornate Soldiers and Sailors Monument rises in the midst of a circle that represents the center and the spiritual heart of Indiana. The monument is to Indianapolis what the Eiffel tower is to Paris or the Golden Gate to San Francisco. To Hoosiers going to war, the Soldiers and Sailors Monument was their Statue of Liberty, and a symbol of coming home.

As the bus went around the west half of the Circle, Mike realized for the first time that he was really leaving home. Mike wondered when he would see it again. He was too young to think the words "IF he would come home."

One block south of the Circle the bus turned west onto Washington, and then, two blocks later, south onto Capital, where they pulled into Union Station. Bob and Mike took one more look around before entering the station. Bob told Mike that after the war they would walk to St. Elmo's and he would treat Mike to a big steak dinner. Neither boy had been to St. Elmo's, but it had a great reputation then, and still today, of being the best place in the world to get a steak. It was a "man" plan for two boys just taking their first step into the wide world.

The boys were overwhelmed by the marble majesty of the vast Union Station lobby. The nearest comparison Mike had seen was the ornate lobby and dome of the Carnegie Library in Anderson. The nearest Bob could come up with was the large cemetery marker for Mr. McCord on the south edge of McCordsville.

With nervous anticipation of first-time travelers, they looked for their train. They sat in the train car for the longest time before the locomotive lurched forward out of the station and headed south for New Albany. There they said goodbye to Indiana and wound their way south and east through Kentucky, Tennessee, Virginia, and North Carolina, and what would be for them the end of the world—a brand new base called Marine Barracks New River, N.C. A few months later it would be named Camp Lejeune.

From the station they took a Marine truck to the base. Mike told Bob that a base that bordered the Atlantic sounded a little exotic for a couple of Hoosier boys who had never seen any water wider than the White River.

It was exotic all right, but not in a way that Mike could have fathomed. The camp was so new that there were no buildings yet—just tents mounted on wooden decks with wide gaps that seemed to suck in the cold coastal night air. It was exotic—if you love swamps, snakes, chiggers, sand, and mosquitoes.

Then there were those gentlemen of the 1st Marine Division in the big round hats who greeted the boys on arrival. The language employed by these gentlemen was unlike any they had heard back home.

In what was left of the day, the boys were stripped, shot, shaved, and scathed. The gentlemen also let the boys know just how far they were from their mothers and that the following day they would be meeting their new mothers.

That next morning started awfully early, and when Mike met his new "mother" his jaw dropped. Remember the tall gangly nerd Leroy? Well since the last time Mike saw him, Leroy had a new name—Drill Sergeant!

The day Leroy was dumped by Veronica, he vowed to make some changes. He was still tall, but there wasn't an ounce of "gangly" on him. The line of his massive shoulders made a nearly perfect triangle to his narrow waist. His arms were as big as his legs had been, and his legs were large enough to do some serious kicking.

The only thing that hadn't changed from the day Mike won Veronica from Leroy's arm was his memory. Drill Instructor Leroy made Mike's introduction to the Marine Corps a living hell.

Mike never managed to pass inspection, despite his best efforts. His bunk was never made right—especially after Drill Instructor Leroy kicked it over. His rifle was never clean—after Drill Instructor Leroy dropped it in the mud. Mike's uniform was torn—after Drill Instructor Leroy yanked on a button or two

Mike "earned" extra K.P. He learned to holystone the tent decks, polish his boots till they gleamed, and do endless push-ups. He was forced to crawl for miles and often had to run around his squad with his rifle over his head singing loud praises to Drill Sergeant Leroy as the squad marched.

One day Drill Instructor Leroy asked Mike if he would like to know "how Drill Instructor Leroy had become so strong." Mike's only response could be "SIR, YES SIR!"

"I got to be this strong by digging a hole six feet square by six feet deep with this tablespoon. Would you like to be as strong as me?"

"SIR, YES SIR!" Mike shouted. It was good that Drill Instructor Leroy couldn't hear Mike's thoughts, for it would have only given Leroy more satisfaction.

Despite his natural anger, Mike was actually thankful for Leroy's harsh treatment. It made Mike a much tougher Marine than he would have been under another drill instructor, and it propelled him closer to his goal of saving Tony.

Mike's boot camp graduation held an even greater surprise as Veronica came down to attend. When Veronica saw her man she was overpowered by his new powerful physique. Always a good looking athlete, Mike was now a knock-out!

Leroy was staring with lock-jawed jealousy at the couple, and Mike finally had a chance to invoke his revenge. He took Veronica in his arms and gave her a kiss that raised the temperature of the place another hundred degrees. Veronica's arms fell limp and Leroy's veins nearly exploded.

Now before you begin to feel too sorry for Leroy, there was another bizarre twist. Veronica had brought along her friend Debbie. Remember the fair-haired Debbie from the Roosevelt baseball game?

Debbie caught a glimpse of Leroy and nearly drowned in her own smile. She had no idea that this was the geek from Roosevelt, and Leroy wasn't about to remind her.

The next 72 hours of liberty took Leroy's mind off of his feud with Mike. When the boys put the girls back on the bus for home it was clear that Leroy and Mike's personal war was over. As they watched the bus go over the horizon they simultaneously and slowly let out a good old Marine "HoooooRah." With a broad grin stuck on both of their faces they shook hands and settled their war with an Old Breed "Semper Fi!"

CHAPTER 11

The 1st Marine Goes to War

When Mike enlisted it was a case of Mike against the world. In boot camp he learned to be part of a unit greater than himself. He had been a boy—now he was a Marine. He understood things, like watching out for his fellow Marines and obeying a superior's order without question. From boot camp forward he would kill for the corps or die for the corps, even if Leroy gave the command or needed help.

In advanced training Mike learned to operate a B.A.R. (Browning Automatic Rifle), just like his father. The B.A.R. was a fairly heavy weapon and used a lot of ammunition, so B.A.R. men worked in teams. Eddie Spencer, a kid from Missouri, was assigned to be Mike's B.A.R. assistant. Eddie was a good guy. He was a quick study and would do anything for you. He was always good for an interesting conversation. Eddie would ask all kinds of deep questions, like you were God and had all of the answers. Everybody liked Eddie. He may have been the only guy in the Corps who didn't make any enemies.

Bob Frazier, Mike's McCordsville, Indiana friend, was assigned to the intelligence unit as a scout. It suited him well and he was pretty happy with the M.O.S. (Military Occupational Specialty). Later Mike would think a lot about that conversation and how happy Bob was then.

Advanced infantry training wasn't as hard as basic, but it was still very intense, and at the end of the day the rack felt pretty good. The worst part of their training was that it was based on a general knowledge of war and tropical terrain. The real detail of how to fight the Japanese was unknown to any American fighting man except the men who were captured when the Philippines fell and the poor fellows who were overrun in the valiant stand at Wake Island. The 1st Marine would be the first advancing division to experience the tactics of the enemy, and those lessons would come at a high cost.

In the late spring of 1942 things began to stir. The upper brass knew that the Japs were threatening Australia again and that they may be building air bases in the Solomon Islands. The average private couldn't have told you where the Solomons were if you paid him, but they knew something was up. The instructors had a stronger sense of urgency in every exercise they led. The inspections were more stringent, and the men were pressed to keep things battle ready and mobile.

One day the word came—they were moving out! The scuttlebutt was that they were going to Australia, but when they boarded the train the troops were in their winter greens, so some of them thought they were going to be sent to Europe. Mike's stomach tightened at this news, as it was his personal mission to fight in the Pacific and find his brother.

When the train headed north, that only reinforced the European rumor, but the guys were really confused when they woke up the next morning and found themselves somewhere in Florida. A guy everybody called "Bomber" was dead-sure they were headed to Cuba. Bomber's real name was something Brown and his dad had fought in the last World War. Bomber had been a professional boxer before the war, and he wasn't too bright. Most fellows said he had been hit in the head too many times and they wondered how he had made it into the Corps, but he was one tough Marine and a likeable guy one could depend on in a fight.

From Florida they headed to New Orleans and points west. After the train had passed through most of the major cities, the security restrictions were eased and the boys were allowed a little more freedom to raise the window shades. Mike saw a world he never dreamed he would see and picked up some good memories that would last a lifetime.

Somewhere in Texas the boys were met by a cheering "crowd" of a dozen or so townsfolk. The train had to make a fairly long scheduled stop, and the boys were let off to stretch their legs. It was a small, dry town in the middle of nowhere, so it was a safe bet that none of the Marines would be tempted to go over the hill. Within an hour the people of the town descended on the boys with sandwiches, fresh milk, and pecan pie.

In Nevada the troop train passed a very old man in a Spanish-American War uniform standing next to the tracks as far from any town as anyone could get. The ancient soldier stood at rigid attention and saluted the train till it passed. A flood of tears streamed down the man's spotted and wrinkled face. Some of the fellows made fun of the old codger. Others reacted like Mike, wondering why the man was crying. In a few weeks even the scoffers would find out.

While most Marine units in the war might have spent a few extra weeks of training in California, these guys went straight to San Francisco to board a ship and headed west as fast as they could sail. The grunts didn't know where they were heading or the reason for the hurry. As implied before, this was new territory for even the officers, as no American infantry force had gone on the offensive in the Pacific. We had been on the injured side of the Japanese onslaught plenty since Pearl Harbor. This time was different—we were now the invaders—this was our time!

Still there was an uneasiness in the stomachs of even the toughest punks when the boys were alone with their thoughts. There was also the queasiness felt by some 8,000 landlubbers squeezed together in a bobbing troop ship. Mike's quarters were five decks down, where the Marines slept in bunks six high. Pity the poor sucker who was stuck with the bottom bunk when the seasickness began.

Mike was no exception—he was sicker than a dog the first three days. He finally found a sympathetic old salt who advised him to stay on deck and to keep his stomach full. From that time on he stayed topside as long as he could and followed the old mariner's advice.

About the fifth day out Mike was surprised to find an officer on deck that he knew well. Lt. Paul Loftus was just two years older than Mike and was also a member of St. Mary's in Anderson. Paul was a guy with Hollywood good looks, but you couldn't find a fellow who was nicer to be around or who would do more for you. He was also a quick study and could recognize a dangerous situation quicker than many officers. Paul would later keep his guys out of unnecessary trouble and give it to the enemy, which gained him a lot of respect in the ranks. Mike was sorry that he wasn't in Paul's company, even though he would be well served by his own Lt. Army. Lt. Army was a great Marine, but he sure took a lot of kidding about his name until he made colonel.

Officer's country was off limits to the regular enlisted men like Mike, but Paul made a special effort to meet every day with his hometown friend. Neither one had been to sea. They both enjoyed the many unusual sights that greet the men who sail her. There were dolphins and sharks. There were those odd flying fish and an occasional ship of war or commerce. One day they watched a giant old sea turtle swimming slowly in the opposite direction. He seemed to be tired of the war and was lumbering as far from the fighting as possible. In the months to come, Mike would sometimes think of that turtle and envy its ability to just swim away.

Social life aboard a troopship was a mixed bag. Some fellows read books, from classics to comics, or wrote letters home. Others played cards or gambled on anything and everything. Some would lie on the deck at night and study the stars. Some participated in Bible studies. Everyone cleaned his weapons, but nobody shined his shoes.

Benny Dauber from B Co. was one of the more interesting characters on board. He spent most of his time asleep. Benny could sleep in any position or in any place day or night. Noise didn't bother him. Salt spray didn't bother him. He could have slept on the floor of the engine room. The big joke was that B Co. always had its dauber down. The northern boys didn't understand the joke, but the southern boys howled when it was told.

The conversations contained lots of swearing, and bragging about things they probably never did. Almost every guy talked about a girl. Some of the girls were wives, some were prostitutes, and some were the All-American sweethearts next door. Mike talked about Veronica. Paul talked about a good-looking, tough-minded Navy nurse he had met in the officer's club. Leroy shared a little too much about his Debbie and all the guys thought he was bragging, but Mike knew it was true. Bob Frazier went on and on about a girl he had met at a dance in Fortville. Well, he hadn't actually "met" her, but he sure was in love. He was determined that she was "the one," and if he had worked up the courage to actually say hello she would have found out that Bob was a great guy.

Of course, there was the endless scuttlebutt. There was always some guy who "absolutely knew" where they were going. Phil Peacock was dead certain that they were headed to New Zealand. Greg Ellis had them going to Hawaii. Wendell Amos said that they were heading "Straight to Tokyo, straight to Tokyo!" He always said it just like that. Frank Czninski said that we were headed to the Philippines to "get them bastards!" Mike was hoping that Frank was right. His whole purpose in life at that time was to find and free his brother. Mike had just found out about Tony's MIA status. He couldn't bring himself to think that Tony might be dead, so he told himself that Tony was captured and that "little brother was on his way!"

As it turned out, Phil was the winner. There before them was the most beautiful island in the world. It was paradise to every guy on the ship, but for different reasons. New Zealand really was an appealing jewel before them, but the only scenery some of the guys wanted to see was the broads and the booze. Whatever their tastes, everyone wanted off that miserable ship.

Their ship had arrived late in the convoy. They lay at anchor for a day, savoring the island and waiting to debark for some much-needed shore leave. Then their hopes were dashed as the engines came to life and the ship began to turn out to sea. The men on board cursed their luck and watched beautiful New Zealand shrink into the ocean—some with tears in their eyes.

A day later it was all over the ship that the Japs were nearing completion on an airstrip that threatened Australia, and that they were going to some sort of canal. The officers brought their men together and up to speed. They were back on accelerated PT. Their weapons were checked and cleaned and rechecked. The lieutenants were shown maps and drilled on their objectives. The sergeants reviewed combat moves and signals. In the last days of July the transports made a stop at Koro in the Fijis to do some Higgins boat practice before moving on to the real show.

On August 7, 1942 they stood off Guadalcanal and Savo islands. Most of the guys were nervous, but few of them were afraid. That would come in later invasions after they had tasted the realities of war.

At first the invasion seemed to be too good to be true. There was only one casualty the first day, and that was some bonehead private who cut himself while trying to slice open a coconut. The airfield was taken in two days and renamed Henderson Field after Marine pilot Lofton Henderson, who had lost his life at Midway.

The first major "battle" on Guadalcanal itself was the battle to get supplies ashore in a hurry. The Japanese navy was lurking within range, and Admiral Fletcher was more concerned about losing his ships than landing supplies. He withdrew early, leaving the Marines with severely reduced rations that they had to supplement with captured Japanese supplies.

On August 12th word came that a group of Japs was asking to surrender. When the Intelligence Officer Lieutenant Colonel Frank Goettge led a patrol to bring them in, the Marines were ambushed. They spent most of the night under fire, pinned down and dying on the beach. By morning only three Marines were alive. Two had been ordered to swim back earlier for reinforcements, and the third, Sergeant Frank Few, was the last man alive. He managed to make it to the sea where he too swam back to safety. Looking back to shore he could see the Japanese swords glinting in the sun over the bodies of his friends.

Mike's company was one of three sent in to take on the Japs who had slaughtered Col. Goettge's patrol. None of the bodies of the Goettge patrol were ever found. One of the missing bodies was that of Bob Frazier. Three months later Mike came across a Guadalcanal native who had found a small cross on the beach partially buried in the sand. Mike recognized the cross as being a lot like the cross Bob's mother had given him, but there was no real proof of the fate of his buddy except the fact that he was gone.

The first night that the Marines were engaged in battle with what might be called "Japanese lines" was bizarre to say the least. First of all, the word "lines" is loosely defined. The enemy and the Marines were more intermingled than fixed across from each other in trench lines.

In the pitch dark of Guadalcanal the enemy seemed to be everywhere. All during the night the Japanese would call for help to make us think that there was a Marine in trouble. Others would shout things like "You die, Marine!" There was even a Jap dog that wouldn't shut up all night. Over near B Co. there was one Jap soldier who was particularly obnoxious. He howled like a werewolf, and he called out things like "All Marines die!" and "I will have your woman!"

Finally, at about 0100 Benny Dauber went totally unglued. He threw every grenade he had. When his foxhole buddy calmed him down, the night became quiet again and they didn't hear another sound from then on. In the morning the Marines found six dead Japs where Benny had attacked. When his buddies asked Benny what had gotten into him, he said "I couldn't sleep with all that @#!* Jap noise!"

The battle for Guadalcanal raged for another six months. It was a back-and-forth struggle to the death, with the Japanese shipping in more reinforcements and the still ill-supplied Americans pushing back the Japanese attacks over and over.

The Battle of the Tenaru was one of the major victories for our boys. Under the cover of darkness and in a coordinated attack from the sea, the Japanese commander drove his troops toward the mouth of the Tenaru. The American commanders started the process of calling up reinforcements for Company G, which by now was fully engaged. Marines came from everywhere in the dense jungle and began improvising on the spot.

The overconfident Japanese quickly found themselves enveloped in what became a disastrous turkey shoot. In the early light the Marines finished off the remaining Japanese troops, completely crushing the entire invasion attempt.

Mike gained a new level of respect for Leroy at the Tenaru. Leroy was one of the sergeants who distinguished himself by quickly recognizing the situation and organizing his men while bringing his lieutenant rapidly into play. It was Marines like Leroy who put the training on the line and made one feel proud to be a part of the Corps.

While the Japanese Army was to be respected, it was the Japanese Navy that Mike feared the worst, especially on the "Night of the Battleships." This was the night that two Japanese battleships opened fire on Henderson Field for nearly twelve hours, lobbing thousands of shells, each the size of a small car. Mike was on duty near the field that day, and he quickly dove for one of the bunkers that had been constructed for the frequent air bombardments and naval shelling. The ground shook all night. The bunkers were full of rats who feared the Japanese Navy, but who had no fear of the Marines. The air was thick with cigarette smoke, tropical sweat, and the dust of the dirt seeping through the coconut logs with every heavy THUD.

This particular shelling was in advance of the heaviest Japanese effort to retake the island. They failed, of course, but Mike lost another friend, Jake Eisenstein.

Jake was a Jewish kid, originally from Germany. He narrowly escaped the Nazis when a Christian family took him in. They were the parents of his friend Otto Marks, whom he was visiting when a gang of Hitler's followers smashed Jake's father's store. They killed his mother and father in the attack. Things were spinning out of control, and Otto's parents could see the fate of Jews in general. A week after the riot that had killed Jake's parents, the Marks made arrangements for Jake and Otto to travel to France with their cousin Karl. Even in France there were anti-Jewish elements, and—realizing the risk—Karl made arrangements to get Jake and Otto jobs aboard a tramp steamer heading to America.

Otto's parents were later arrested for hiding Jews and were taken to a concentration camp, where they eventually died. Otto actually died before his parents. When America entered the war Otto joined the 10th Mountain Division and was killed in the Apennine Mountains in northern Italy.

Jake made his way in life as best as one could do in America in those days. As the Depression wore on it became increasingly harder to get by. He joined the Marines in 1937 where he knew he would get three squares, clothes, and a place to live. When the war broke out Jake wished he had joined the Army so he could get a better chance to go after the Nazis who had killed his family and his dear friends. Still he was proud to be a Marine and was well liked by his fellows.

Mike enjoyed many long conversations with Jake, mainly because he was Jewish. It was a faith that was so different, and yet was the root of his own religion. Jake in turn was fascinated with Mike's mixture of traditional Catholicism and Lenape ways. On several occasions Jake wrote to Mike's mom to ask questions about these things, and Keku was more than happy to give Jake his answers and a little motherly affection.

Jake was on guard duty the night of the battleships and was caught in the open when the shelling began. There was nothing left of Jake except his mutilated dog tags and his Star of David that Jake had often fingered like a rosary.

October was Hell Month for the Marines. It was also the month when for the first time one could see both our victory and our defeat within reach. The Japs gave us all they had on opposite ends of the island. Mike was sent to the western front on the Matanikau River. There were several all-out battles where the issue was in doubt more than once, but the Marines beat them back each time.

By February it was over. More Marine and Army Divisions were brought in to finish the fight and to finally give the 1st Marine much-needed relief. Many of the 1st Marine was so wasted by months of battle and malaria that they had to be lifted into the waiting ships. Mike was one of these. He had lost thirty-five pounds.

In the end Mike felt almost sorry for the Japs. On his final patrols Mike would see scores of Jap soldiers literally starved to death. They could have surrendered and would have had food and medical treatment, but they were driven to die. This sight, even more than the battles he had experienced, made Mike realize that the effort to save his brother Tony was an almost insurmountable task.

Mike had fought what most men would consider a whole war over the last six months, and Tony was still several thousand miles from Mike's reach with more "Guadalcanals" between them.

CHAPTER 12

Peleliu

The Old Breed was a ragged lot when they reached Australia for some much-needed rest and regrouping. Their equipment was shot and their clothes were a hodgepodge of whatever they could find to replace what they had worn out. Most of the guys were dressed in what could be considered regulation, but there were some strange variations. Most of the socks had crumbled in the first few weeks, and underwear was pretty tattered. One fellow had a shirt taken from a dead Jap and a pair of pants "borrowed" from one of our Army guys while he was bathing in the Teneru. Another guy had on a pair of real fancy cowboy boots. There was all kind of speculation about how he came up with those. Everyone seemed to have a button from a Japanese uniform to replace the ones they had lost.

Several Marines collapsed on the dock when they tried to walk. Many of the men were weak from contracting malaria, and they had all lost several pounds of weight from the wear of battle, various illnesses, and the starvation rations they had been forced to endure for so long. They had lost so much weight that Mike thought the transport rode higher in the water than it did when they were being shipped to Guadalcanal.

The worst part of going to Australia was that they were now under the command of Douglas MacArthur. MacArthur's staff didn't give a rat's meow about the Marines. They were billeted in a swamp near Brisbane, where the cases of malaria climbed at alarming rates. When General Vandegrift demanded better housing, he was told that there wasn't any other place to send the men.

General Vandergrift's determined staff finally found that the city of Melbourne was willing to take in the ragged Marines. With a lot of resistance from MacArthur's boys and a great deal of help from Bull Halsey they were finally relocated. To dig the Army staff a little deeper, Halsey used as his primary transport a ship named West Point.

The 1st Marine stay in Melbourne was wonderful. They were treated like the heroes that they were. The Old Breed had saved Australia from the advance of the Japanese, and the Aussies knew it. They opened their city and their homes to these tattered boys and made them feel like men again.

All good times must end, and end they did for the 1st Division when they were called up for the invasion of Cape Gloucester, New Britton. It was one of the lower profile battles of the war, but very intense and miserable in terrain. There was too much jungle, too much rain, too much mud, and too many Japs.

Anyone who missed that one had no reason to sulk, and yet there was Mike feeling left behind. One day before the Old Breed's departure, Mike was clobbered with what the doctors first thought was a relapse of his malaria, but it was odd in its symptoms and lasted far too long. The doctors finally took some additional tests and found that Mike was seeping blood from his large intestine. It could have come from the concussion when a Japanese shell exploded near Mike on Guadalcanal, or maybe it was a lingering problem from that bar fight with an Army corporal in a Brisbane pub. Mike didn't exactly write home about that incident.

He must have been seeping blood for some time before the malaria outbreak intensified the situation. He had been feeling a little weak, but Mike had written it off to the miserable conditions in Brisbane and the soft living of Melbourne. A simple operation fixed the problem, but it kept Mike out of the New Britton campaign.

Mike's next big battle would be at Peleliu. He was released from the hospital midway through the Cape Gloucester campaign and assigned to duty back in Guadalcanal, where he helped with the training of some of the new replacements coming in from the States. In early August of 1944 Mike and his replacements were sent to Pavuvu to receive invasion training for Peleliu.

In Pavuvu Mike caught up with some of his old buddies and was given some hazing for his soft living while they had suffered at both Cape Gloucester and this so called "rest camp."

Pavuvu turned out to be one of those islands that looked like a paradise from the air, but it was a real quagmire once one got used to it. It had been a coconut plantation. With the interruption of the war thousands of unharvested coconuts had layered the island with rotting ooze. The monsoon season forgot to end, and the mud was almost unbearable. There were thousands of large rats that owned the night, and they didn't mind sleeping with the Marines. If you killed one, it seemed like four more sprang from its carcass. By the time Mike arrived, the coconuts had been cleaned up and the bivouac area was covered in crushed coral. Some of these paths had been paved by Marines who had hand carried the coral in their helmets.

Mike's "hazing" was soon put behind as he and his replacements were mixed into the intense training for the Peleliu invasion. This battle would be a new chapter for the Japanese. They would not have the hope for reinforcements as they had on Guadalcanal. Their strategy was singular and gruesome. This time the Japs would dig in, drag out the battle, kill as many Americans as possible, and then die for the Emperor.

There they were, staring up at the rugged spine of Peleliu, which was filled with caves and well-disguised pre-sighted defensive positions. Any Marine who approached the entrances to these fortifications was exposing himself to almost certain death. There would be no foolish Banzai charges as Mike had seen on Guadalcanal. This time it would be his Marines advancing in full view and range of the Japanese.

Unlike the uncontested initial landing at Guadalcanal, the Japs opened fire with their big guns while the Marines were approaching the beaches. On Mike's LVT the coxswain was killed, and there was a mad scramble to get the craft under control. A few seconds later a shell came screaming right at the center of their landing craft. The sun flashed in Mike's eyes and everything STOPPED. The sounds of the battle ceased, the waves were frozen, and the shell halted its flight in mid-air. Then Mike saw the spirit of Kikthawenund who held out his hand and pushed the shell harmlessly to the side. In that instant everything returned to reality. The other Marines made comments about the near miss, for they had not seen the vision that Mike had seen. On the other side of the world Keku jumped up in bed and shouted "wtikamao," which means "he defended him."

Once on the beach Mike's unit was pinned down for several hours by the murderous fire from Umurborgol Mountain and mortars that seemed to come from everywhere. There was sniper and machine gunfire from a maze of jungle, bunker, and spider-hole positions. The beaches were heavily mined, and the terrain ranged from coral to thick jungle to mangrove swamps.

At 1600 they dug in for the night near the edge of the airfield. One hour later the Japs tried to drive them back with tanks, but it was poorly executed. Mike was nearly crushed when a tank missed him by less than a yard. Along with this peril our Marines gained the proximity and opportunity to shove grenades in the treads, stopping the tanks and making them helpless before our boys, who were now just plain mad.

It took almost three days of brutal fighting to take the airfield, and then the real fight led into the moon crater maze of the island's center spine. The Umurborgol mountain range was a sharp, jagged, twisted mass of tangled rocks and roots. Everything that could be bruised or cut was punished by the sharp coral. The heat was over a hundred degrees, and water was always in short supply. Several men simply fell to their deaths from the unsure footing.

By the sixth day the 1st Marine was down to two-thirds strength and was losing its ability to fight effectively. With his own platoon decimated, Mike was assigned to Sgt. Tarvin for a small patrol up into the west central part of the mountain.

Sgt. Tarvin had a reputation for being one of the toughest Marines on the island. He was a large, powerful man who kept his feelings in check and his mind on the task at hand. If he feared anything, nobody could have guessed what it would be.

Mike was one of four Marines who were replacements in the platoon. Nobody knew their names or anything about them, and that's the way the regulars wanted it. Mike understood, for he had lost too many friends as well.

The rest of the squad had been through the war together. Besides Sgt. Tarvin there was Doug Wilson, whom everybody called Digger, partly because his name was Doug, and partly because he could dig a foxhole faster than anyone in the Corps. Joe Longusser was the corpsman, so they all called him Doc. Warren Peese had a soft-sounding moniker, but he was a professional middleweight boxer in civilian life. The fellows were afraid to give him a nickname. Jimmy Lane was such a good looking kid that they called him Killer. No guy wanted to have Jimmy come along when they took liberty because Jimmy would attract all of the girls. The funny thing was that he was so shy that he could hardly look them in the eye. The last regular was Donald Wayne. As a kid, Wayne was a rabid fan of John Wayne and wanted everybody to call him Duke. Unfortunately boys will be boys and they started to call him Duck. Much to his chagrin, he was stuck with Duck.

Duck was the B.A.R. man, and Warren was his assistant. Digger was the flamethrower. It was a lousy job that made a Marine an easy target and could get him incinerated along with any Marine close by, so Tarvin gave him an M-1 for this patrol. Joe, of course, was the corpsman. Killer was the sniper, if one were needed. Killer had magnificent eyesight, and had saved the patrol on several occasions when he had spotted trouble before the others. They preferred to keep Killer on point, and he liked it that way.

Mike and one of the other no-names were assigned to carry extra satchel charges. The other two were told to "follow along and try not to screw up."

An hour into the patrol the Japs began to pop up from the rocks and holes and from all sides—sacrificing themselves for the possibility of killing at least one American. Killer was able to spot most of them in time for the patrol to pick off each ambush, but about two hours into the mission his luck ran out. Jimmy spotted a spider hole at the ten o'clock. The men dispatched that one pretty quickly, but a simultaneous shot from the three o'clock position hit Jimmy in the side of his rib cage. Sgt. Tarvin ordered two of the no-names to carry him back to the battalion aid station. It was close, but Jimmy survived and was evacuated to a hospital ship before the day was through.

It was a bad sign, and the men were uneasy over losing their best set of eyes. By midday the men were pretty beat. It was miserably hot, and the terrain was sharp and twisted. Every man had bumped all of his joints on the sharp rocks. Most had twisted their ankles, and all of them had fallen at least once on the craggy terrain. On the plus side, they hadn't encountered any more snipers.

At 1330 all hell broke loose. Warren stepped on a mine and was killed outright. The explosion sent an alert to a Jap Nambu machine gun nest that was positioned ahead and slightly to the left. They quickly spotted the Marine patrol and opened up. Duck was hit in the carotid artery and almost instantly bled to death. Doc was hit in the stomach and went down calling for his mom. He twitched like a man being electrocuted, and then he froze in a fetal position and died. Digger, true to his reputation, buried himself behind a man-sized rock, with the other no-name hunkered behind him and slightly exposed. Mike was across the ravine from Digger, and Sgt. Tarvin was lying next to Duck and appeared to be dead.

Mike was more in line with the machine gun, but he had found good cover. In a low voice Mike asked Digger if he was all right, and he heard the response that he and the new guy were good. Sgt. Tarvin didn't respond.

Suddenly a 47mm located just to the forward right spotted the partially exposed no-name and fired on the position. The big gun split the rock, causing it to shatter and spread through the bodies of Digger and the no-name. A thick cloud of dust enveloped the scene and Sgt. Tarvin yelled "Let's Go!" Mike jumped up and followed Tarvin into a fissure that had been carved by the 47mm. Sgt Tarvin had gathered up Duck's B.A.R. and a satchel charge that had scattered when they were attacked. He ordered Mike to go back and get as many satchel charges as he could carry before the dust settled and their cover was lost.

As the air cleared, the Jap Nambu chased Mike through the ravine while he scrambled to find the charges. The bullets nipped and tore at his clothes without any serious effect, except to make Mike run faster than he had ever run.

Mike managed to grab three more charges and made it back to Sgt. Tarvin. The two survivors crawled up to the left side of the cave entrance. They were out of sight of the 47mm and the Nambu. The two Marines coordinated their plan. Sgt. Tarvin would jump into the cave entrance for a brief burst of suppressive fire, and Mike would throw the charges into the opening. They would both drop just below the entrance and wait for the results.

Sgt. Tarvin signaled "on three." One-Two-Tarvin jumped up and laid down a heavy burst. Mike tossed in two satchel charges and dropped to avoid the blast.

When Sgt. Tarvin rose to fire, three bullets were returned from the Japanese rifles in the cave. They formed in a circle smaller than a human fist and stopped in the vacuum of time two inches from Sgt. Tarvin's heart. Everything froze as he witnessed the Jap bullets dissolving like sugar in water before his chest. Then time resumed and, in the next instant, Sgt. Tarvin found himself hunkered next to Mike. BOOM! BOOM! The dust rose and the cave entrance fell shut on its defenders.

As the dust cloud drifted into the blue equatorial sky the noise of war turned to a peaceful calm. Normally a stoic man, Tarvin's eyes were of a boy who had seen a ghost. He asked Mike, "Did you see that?"

"See what?" Mike replied.

Sgt. Tarvin proceeded to tell Mike about the bullets in detail. Mike shared with him the mysteries of his family experiences, and speculated that he had just seen such a spiritual miracle.

"Let's not tell anyone about this," Sgt. Tarvin responded.

Sgt. Tarvin resumed a normal civilian life after the war. He was a complex man who listened long and spoke little as a rule. He was not an evangelical per se, but whenever someone would mock God or say they didn't want to worship anything they couldn't understand, Tarvin would lean menacingly into the guy and respond that "One doesn't need to understand the Almighty, but you'd better respect him."

A lieutenant from a nearby platoon was able to observe enough of the attack to spot the position of the 47mm. He called in naval gunfire, and the position was obliterated. Mike and Sgt. Tarvin picked up the body of Duck and carried him back to Battalion HQ. Battalion in turn sent out a unit to recover the remaining bodies.

The next day Mike slipped while climbing a slope and fell just far enough to break his left arm. It wasn't as bad as it could have been, but it was enough to force his evacuation.

While recovering on the hospital transport USS Tryon, Mike met Lt. Colonel Austin Shofner, who was wounded on the first or second day. It was hard to tell. Both days had blended into one long firefight.

Col. Shofner had been captured at Bataan and was a rare escapee from the Japanese prison camps. Mike was eager to learn more detail. When Mike told him about Tony, Col. Shofner lit up a bit and asked if Tony had been with the coastal guns. When Mike said that he had, Col. Shofner said, "I thought so. You boys look alike." He went on to tell Mike that he had seen Tony at one of the prison camps and explained just how bad things were. The Colonel tried to give Mike some hope. "Tony has a strong character. If anyone can survive, it will be him. If you don't find him in the Philippines, don't give up. They will probably move the POWs closer to the home islands when we invade the Philippines." Colonel Shofner kept his real thoughts to himself. He was certain that the Japs would kill the prisoners before we could get to them.

A few days later U.S.S. Tryon transported the wounded Marines back to Pavuvu. As Mike watched Peleliu fade into the ocean, he wondered why Kikthawenund had waited till Peleliu to visit and defend Mike in battle. Why had he appeared to Sgt. Tarvin? Was he helping Tony? Mike had heard his mother tell many times of Kikthawenund, but this was the first time Mike had witnessed one of the old chief's miracles.

Far from Peleliu and in the still of the warm ocean day, Mike's mind began to clear of the trauma of the battle. Once more he refocused on his personal mission. Where was his brother Tony, and would he reach him in time?

CHAPTER 13

Operation Iceberg

As the years wore on, Tony's situation grew worse. In the back of their minds the POWs longed for the return of the American forces, but one was almost afraid to hope.

As it turned out, both emotions were justified. With the American gains in the Pacific and the impending invasion of the Philippines, the Bataan prisoners were indeed transported to the Japanese home islands on what became known as the "Hellships." These were mainly troopships that were overloaded and devoid of the minimums of sanitation. Hundreds died in the miserable conditions, and many were killed by our own submarines. These ships had no markings to indicate they were transporting prisoners and were therefore fair game to our sub commanders.

Those who survived the transfer were often pressed into slave labor for the Japanese war machine. While it was almost impossible to live, let alone work, there was some advantage as the POW laborers were given slightly more rations, and the act of work is always good for the mind if not kind to the body.

The conditions in the camps were stark. There was no "will to live" at that juncture. A mass execution would have been welcome as a means to die like men with some shred of dignity.

Tony survived on the occasional visits of his sister's spirit and the fading support of his friend Ernie. By 1945 it was clear that Ernie was dying.

Mike had recovered as much as one could from the physical beating of Peleliu. The 1st Marine Division was re-equipped and was in the mode of intense training for the next battle. The news was already filtering in from the 3rd, 4th, and 5th Divisions' struggles on an island called Iwo Jima. To Mike it sounded a lot like Peleliu and maybe worse. For the moment the rank and file 1st Division Marine had no inkling of where or when the next battle would be, but there was a general knowledge that we were closing in on Japan itself. The feeling in the stomachs of the Old Breed was that they were headed for the toughest struggle yet.

The only thing for certain was that they were steaming west in an ever-growing armada of ships of every sort. On the way to the battle, the brass gave the fellows a stopover at an island called Mog Mog for a little recreation in route. They were allowed one hour each on the island and two beers. Mog Mog was an island paradise, but a fellow could see the whole place in fifteen minutes.

In route they saw the aircraft carrier USS Franklin pass by on its way to repairs in the States. It had been torn apart by a Japanese air attack off Okinawa and was a gruesome sight. It was so badly damaged that every fellow who saw it had a lump in his throat. Jim Lester, who was still a kid in Goldthwaite, Texas when Mike was on Guadalcanal, had a cousin by the name of Billy Dennard, whom he knew was stationed on Franklin. Jim, of course, was pretty upset and had no way of knowing that Billy had survived by the grace of God and Medal of Honor recipient Donald Gary.

As the convoy cruised toward its target, it grew in size daily. The great Pacific seemed to be giving up every man of war that had ever felt her embrace. The knots in the stomachs of those who had tasted combat also grew in size with each nautical mile, for they knew that the pleasant gift of Mog Mog was a harbinger of doom.

A few days later the officers were called on deck to view a map of their target. The word soon rippled through the division of a place that was pronounced more often than not "Okay in away."

Okinawa had once been a place of beautiful terrain and gentle, carefree people. They were very much a part of Japan and simultaneously quite separate in their culture and ideals. Unfortunately it became a vital part of the Japanese war machine and a vital target of ours.

In August of 1944 the die was cast. General Mitsuru Ushijima was placed in command of the Japanese defense. He knew before they started building their fortifications that his men would not be relieved. They became nothing more than a glorious speed bump in the path to our ultimate victory. They would buy time for the Emperor at a grievous cost.

Opposing General Ushijima was General Simon Bolivar Buckner, Jr., whose American 10th Army consisted of four Army divisions and three Marine divisions.

It was a collision of the titans with hundreds of thousands of Okinawans in the middle. In the end over half a million soldiers, sailors, marines, and airmen would fight for the 10th Army. Of those almost 13,000 would be killed in action, with the largest single group being the sailors who were lost in the overwhelming kamikaze attacks. Of the 100,000 Japanese soldiers, all but 1,000 would die either in battle or by their own hand in defeat. Nearly 150,000 Okinawans were killed by the shelling, by trying to filter through our lines at night, by the hands of the Japanese, or most alarmingly, by their own hands, either in suicide attacks on our troops or by mass suicides. More civilians died on Okinawa than in both of the atomic bombings.

The naval shelling began on March 15, 1945 and didn't end until an hour before the invasion on what was called L-Day, April 1, 1945. It was April Fool's Day. It was also Easter Sunday. A sumptuous breakfast was served, and the call was broadcast to climb down the rope ladders to the waiting boats. The day was sunny and there was no firing from the defenses as there had been on Peleliu.

As they approached the island there was the air of vacation versus invasion. They landed to extremely light resistance. This continued all day, to the point where all of the landing parties captured their fourth-day objectives on the first day. The greener troops were elated at their good luck. The seasoned veterans were more on edge than ever. It was too good to be true. Eventually the combat veterans' dread materialized, but not for a few more days.

The 1st Marine crossed the middle of the island and cut it in two, along with the 7th and 96th Army divisions just to the south. A few days later the 7th and 96th were joined by the Army's 27th Division in a drive to the southern third of the island. The 6th Marine was sent to capture the northern end of the island and the 77th Army division was assigned to capture the nearby island of Ie Shima, where Ernie Pyle was killed on April 18th.

By April 19th the 27th, 96th, and 7th Army divisions were hopelessly mired in the Ushijima's masterfully prepared Shuri line. They became stalled to the point where General Buckner was forced to reconfigure his offense. The 27th was pulled back and the line was realigned from the western shore of Okinawa to the eastern side. From west to east the line consisted of the 6th Marine Division, the 1st Marine, the 77th Army Division, which had captured Ie Shima, the 96th (Deadeye) Division, and finally the 7th Army Division.

The Deadeyes had the awesome task of taking down the Conical Hill complex. The 77th was square on to the massive Shuri Heights defenses. The 7th captured Yonabaru. The 6th Marine had perhaps the toughest assignment in capturing Sugar Loaf Hill, an eight-day battle that decimated the 22nd and 29th regiments.

Mike's 1st Marine took on Wana Ridge and Wana Draw, which was described by one officer as "an ideal place to get your sorry self killed" (not a direct quote). It was here that Mike's war would end.

Mike was now reporting to his old friend and nemesis Leroy, who was the new Fox Company Lieutenant. Mike had made corporal for his actions on Peleliu. He could have been promoted to sergeant, but his focus on saving Tony distracted his thoughts. He was afraid that he lacked the concentration he would need to properly lead his men. Mike expressed these concerns each time he was presented with promotion and his superiors appreciated and respected his candor.

Leroy, having full knowledge of Mike's abilities, made Mike his runner. It is the runner's job to transfer communications from the lieutenant to his command post and vice versa when other forms of communication could not be trusted. It was a vital task and an easy way to get killed.

The battle of Wana Ridge and Wana Draw was not a battle in the sense of two armies lining up and shooting at one another as one sees in the movies. It was an insane theater of the mind. The enemy was everywhere and no where. The Japs would pop up from any direction and fire off a few rounds. In the next instant a Marine was either dead or he heard the sonic crack of the bullet that had just missed. Every step was either a lucky one or it would fall victim to a precisely placed artillery round, or a machine gun, or a mine.

Beyond the normal expectations of battle was the intense psychological warfare that preyed on every man's mind. No one outside of combat could appreciably understand all of the factors that work on a combat soldier's mental and physical exhaustion.

All sequence of time and story dissolved as Mike later recalled the Shuri Line. He remembered only mental snapshots, like the bullet that put a nick in his helmet, his races across open fields of fire, and Jim Lester flying through the air after a mortar hit just a few feet to his right. The most heroic images were reserved for the Corpsmen who made themselves prime targets time after time as they scurried forward to save the wounded.

Leroy was an excellent commander in the field, and his actions saved many a young Marine. Mike and Leroy were also a great team. Mike raced to and fro as he delivered instructions between HQ and Leroy. As he ran he felt the thump and twist of the rough terrain and the snip and snap of the bullets that were always chasing him down.

The gun emplacements of Wana Ridge poured down thick fire upon the Marines as they entered Wana Draw. It was joined by accurate Japanese artillery from Shuri Heights. Mike remembered the overpowering desire to cry like a schoolboy telling the teacher about the schoolyard bully. Swaggering bravery is a farce in such situations. A few months or years ago, these were boys who had never left their mothers. It was only by the strength and faithful execution of their training that these scared boys survived.

The morning they made their final drive on Shuri Castle, a Japanese 105mm shell landed near Mike's position. Leroy was killed by the concussion. His body was essentially unscathed. He looked like he had just lain down in the field and had gone to sleep in his mother's arms.

Mike was thrown several feet and was deafened by the blow. The air had been sucked out of his lungs. He was now in a world of half-awareness and half-dark. He tried to get up and fell over.

He couldn't feel his legs and feared the worst. Trying to examine his wounds, Mike had no sense of where to direct his reach. As he turned his head to look—the world went black.

CHAPTER 14

The Star Spangled Banner

Nothing ignites the American people as much as the sight of the Stars and Stripes. We decorate our politicians with it to make them seem more "American." We wave it in celebration on patriotic occasions. We raise it like a prayer on Memorial Day and during times of national distress.

Nobody sees the American flag like a Veteran. It makes their chest swell and their eyes moist. It causes them to remember moments that no one should ever have to experience in the first place.

We didn't know it at the time, but the last battle flag of World War II would be raised at Ara Saki on the southern tip of Okinawa by the men of George Company of the 22 Regiment 6th Marine Division on June 23, 1945.

Long before the battle was over, Mike found himself on a hospital ship headed for Guam. It was a bizarre world of yin and yang. On one hand there were pretty nurses in sterile white. Here was shelter from the war, and the smell of clean fresh air that had so eluded the warriors on Okinawa. On the other hand, there were indescribable horrific wounds and death on a daily basis. There was hope for all who had made it to the hospital ships, and yet that hope dissolved for so many at the most unexpected moments.

Long rows of hospital beds lined the outer sides of Mike's ward. There was also a double row of beds in the center of the room. These beds faced toward the beds along the hull. Each bed had the minimum of space between them so it was easy for Mike to keep tabs on the half dozen or so men who were closest to his bed.

To Mike's left there was a soldier from the 96th who was left blind by a sniper's round. The bullet was still pressing on his brain, and the doctors seemed uncertain as to how to proceed, except to keep him in a fixed position. It must have been misery for the boy, but he could still talk and seemed to be in little pain except for an ongoing headache. He told Mike that his name was Bill and that he was from Indianapolis. They struck up an instant bond when Mike mentioned that he was from nearby Anderson.

Their conversations were brief, as they kept Bill pretty heavily sedated. When they reached Guam, Bill was flown to Hawaii. Later Mike would often wonder what happened to him.

Ahead of Mike and to the left of his bed was a Marine from the 6th whose left arm was missing at the shoulder. He was angry and didn't speak a word except to let loose with a long, vile tantrum of profanity in the middle of the night he died. Several fellows speculated that he could have survived his wounds, but he was just too angry to live.

The sailor immediately in front of Mike was the victim of a kamikaze strike. He had burns all over his face and upper torso, and he must have been in terrible pain, but he made a lot of jokes about his condition. He'd say things like "got too close to the weenie roast," or "You should have seen the other guy." The sailor grimaced as he spoke, so you knew he was suffering, but he refused to let it beat him. The fellows around him were inspired all to heck.

When they landed in Guam he was flown out with Bill. While Mike never saw him again, he thought of the sailor often and remained in awe of his ability to overcome the worst that life can dish out.

In front and to the right was a soldier from the 27th. He wasn't physically hurt, but he lay there like a statue. His mind had been completely fried by the things he had seen on the Shuri Line. He was just a kid, maybe seventeen at the most. He must have had his parents sign for him. He hadn't had a lick of combat experience before Okinawa.

The reaction from a few was that he was some kind of a coward, but any man who had been there knew that they too had been no more than a fiber away from the same fate.

Early on, when Mike was just beginning to come to his senses, the man on his immediate right died. A few hours later a new patient was placed in that bed. Mike was surprised to see that his new "neighbor" was Jim Lester, from his own platoon, who had been severely wounded. Mike had been convinced that Jim was mortally wounded in the explosion and was quite surprised to see that he was alive, let alone right there next to him.

Jim's skin was as white as the hospital ship. He had lost almost all of his blood supply and had some serious damage to several internal organs. By all rights he should have been dead, but there he was and in fairly stable condition for the wear.

As the two men improved, Mike and Jim played cards and caught up on the lost time between them. They each received a large stash of mail one day and they swapped the ones that weren't too personal. Mike had received a few letters from Veronica that were almost too personal to read to himself, let alone to the other guys. Jim's Aunt May had died, and he was pretty choked up about that one. Mike read a few of his mom's letters to Bill, the Indianapolis boy. Anderson is only forty miles up Highway 67 from "The Circle City" and it made Bill feel closer to home.

The next to last day before they landed in Guam turned out to be a bad one. The Marine from the 6th Division died during the night, and a few minutes past 1000 the next day, Jim Lester died without the slightest warning. The doctors speculated that he had passed a blood clot. It was a terrible shock. Jim was doing so well and improving every day, and then BOOM he was gone.

The next morning there was a burial at sea for those who had died during the previous 24 hours. Mike was allowed to come out on deck to pay his respects to his platoon mate.

A burial at sea is a somber thing beyond words. Jim's parents would have no body to bury. Their last memory of his face would be when he waved from the window of the bus that took him to the train and basic training. His last letter home and the few personal effects that were returned would become a shrine. A dad had lost his only son. A mother had lost her first-born baby. A sister would cry inconsolably for her big brother.

Mike was on the deck level above the scene as each serviceman was placed on a board. That beloved flag was placed over the body of each corpse. A few words were said and then the weighted body slid into its watery grave. This was repeated until all of the men had been committed, then the rifles were fired and the bugler played Taps.

When the service was finished Mike had time to think about all he had seen since he had left home. He had profoundly changed, he had sacrificed too much, and Tony was still a prisoner—or maybe dead. Most of all he wondered why Kikthawenund had not appeared when Leroy was killed and he was wounded.

In the months to follow he would learn from his mother that "Kikthawenund was a great chief, but he isn't God. His spirit could only be in one place at a time, and your brother needed him more."

Forty-four days after George Company raised the flag on Okinawa we dropped the atomic bomb on Hiroshima. Three days later we did the same to Nagasaki. On August 15, 1945 the Japanese surrendered.

Twenty-six days before George Company raised the flag at Ara Saki, Ernie died in the POW camp in Japan. Tony was lost without his survival buddy. They had kept each other alive for over three years, and the war for them had no end in sight. Ernie had endured beyond the farthest extremes of human suffering. He simply had nothing left.

It was an hour or two before Tony could accept that Ernie was dead. So many of the POWs that had appeared to be gone still harbored a thread of life. Tony sat in a blank stare with his back against the wall of the hut, holding Ernie's corpse as if he were only sleeping. For more than three years he had survived because Ernie had survived, and Ernie had survived because Tony had survived. It was like some morbid competition with each man thinking, "If he can endure this so can I."

As the hours wore on, heavy deep thoughts moved slowly through Tony's mind. He thought of his mother and how it would hurt her to lose another child. He thought of his father and how Joe had overcome a horrible childhood and the tragic death of his sweet little girl. Tony wished that he would have had just a little more time to heal the remaining gap between them.

Tony descended into a deep remorse as he thought of how he had killed his sister. No matter what anyone had said, he still held himself to blame for her painful death. He wondered if his little brother had been caught up in this terrible war and where in the world he might be. Tony had no inkling that Mike was only a thousand miles to the south and also facing death at that moment.

The thoughts drifted past each other and through each other as the life faded from Tony. In the midst of this trance Kikthawenund's spirit materialized into view. He sat across from Tony with little expression as he listened to his great-great-great-grandson's thoughts. Kikthawenund spoke first.

"I am proud of your life, Grandson."

"I don't see how Grandfather. I took my sister from my family. I have accomplished nothing."

"Your family did not own Mamalis. Mamalis does not own herself. We all belong to the Great Spirit who gives us life, but does not make us live by his will. We demand freedom but are not willing to pay its costs. You have borne much, Grandson, and have carried it on your shoulders like a man. Why should I not be proud?"

"I have no more strength, Grandfather. Will you be proud of my death?"

"That is up to you, Grandson. How will you die?"

Kikthawenund's spirit vanished, and for the next two days Tony remained in his trance as Ernie's body began to deteriorate. It was time for his friend to be carried to the pile where it would be burned with the others, like so much garbage.

Tony was dying and he knew it. It was time to choose his final act while any life remained.

In the past three plus years Tony had been a victim of the demeaning culture of the Japanese war machine. He had witnessed and experienced dysentery, untreated wounds, starvation, and random beatings by sadistic guards.

Tony would have killed all of the Japs if he had had any strength to lift his hands. There was one act of defiance that he could still muster. It was the same action of the heart that had taken down the mighty British Army in the Revolution. Tony's patriotism and love for his country was the only power he had left to overcome the might of the Japanese Empire.

Before the Japs took Ernie's body away, Tony tore a section of Ernie's shirt in a large rectangle. He pressed the corner of the rag into the mud, for he had nothing else to darken the field. Then he took a sharp rock and tore small holes in the field so it would look like stars when the sunlight passed through the field. With the same rock he cut himself, and carefully used his own blood to paint the red stripes. It was a pathetic dirty rag, but it was also as beautiful and inspiring as the original Star Spangled Banner.

As the world of Tony's spirit began to mingle with the world of Ernie's spirit, he could feel Ernie's hand on his shoulder. Ernie gave Tony a "V for Victory" sign and breathed a prolonged Y E A H!

Captain Richard Brown witnessed Tony's last act and hid the flag from the guards. He showed it to the other prisoners to give their waning spirits strength. When they were finally released, he tied the flag to a stick and held it high as they marched out of the compound. One cannot describe the act of men—beaten, ragged, and barely alive—struggling to their feet and attempting to stick out their humbled chests to march out like men. No human is so strong that they could witness such a sight without tears.

After the war Captain Brown came to Anderson to give the flag to Keku and Joe and to tell them the details that Keku had already sensed.

Captain Brown went on to become one of the most sought-after professors of business in the country. He was loved and profoundly respected by his students. They never fully understood why he would occasionally stop at the campus flagpole, stare for the longest time, and sometimes weep unashamed.

As the life was draining from Tony, and the Japanese artillery was pounding Mike, Keku was deep in her prayers at Mass. As she prayed she began to realize that her boys were in mortal danger. She could not see her sons, but she could feel the shock wave of their situations. The torment rose to a crescendo, and she cried inhuman sounds of grief that could be heard all over the church.

Father Williams did not stop the service. He could not, for he was in the midst of the consecration, which had a power that day beyond any he had ever experienced. He could not see Keku, for in those days the Mass was said with the priest's back to the congregation. He could hear Keku's screams. He could feel his own spirit being pulled into the moment. He somehow knew, as Keku did, that the boys were being swallowed by the evil of death. Some mystery of God told Father Williams that this very act of consecration—this sacrifice of Jesus that makes possible our victory over death—was presently the only power blocking war's all-consuming thirst. In this consecration Father Williams was literally fighting that day for the lives of Mike and Tony.

One of the ushers started to approach Keku. Doctor Lamey, who was sitting near her, saw that Keku was in no physical danger so he waved the usher off.

The Latin, the mother's cries, the crucifixion, the prayers of the parishioners, and the spiritual warfare were frightening and intense. At the end of the consecration Father Williams was drained.

The Mass and Keku's torment ended in concert. Father Williams started to approach Keku but stopped short. Some of the parishioners also moved toward Keku, but he motioned them away and waved them out the door.

Father Williams stood alone in the sanctuary with Keku. They both had tears in their eyes as he watched her slowly rise. The words caught in her throat as Keku genuflected, thanked Jesus for his sacrifice, God for his universal creation and love, and her brother and sister trees for giving her a comfortable place to sit and kneel. Then she walked out of the sanctuary with head bowed and heavy steps.

She knew in her heart that one son was in danger and that one son was dead. Brokenhearted, she walked home. Her only concern now was how she would console her husband when the War Department telegram would eventually arrive.

As Keku walked past the telephone office she heard the flag flutter on the mast. She looked up and saw the Star Spangled Banner as she had never seen it before.

CHAPTER 15

The Magic Carpet

Mike was coming home after several months of convalescence in Hawaii. His injuries had not been life threatening, nor would they have much permanent impact on his physical health, but they took some time to heal. The explosion had cracked several ribs and had broken bones in both legs and his left arm. There were several major organs that were bruised from the concussion and at one point the doctors were concerned about his left eye, as it remained bloodshot for an unusual length of time. It took hours to pick out all of the bits of blasted rock and metal from his torso. Some pieces of the shrapnel worked their way to the skin surface a year later. Mike picked those out himself in his own bathroom back home.

Mike's concern for Tony remained a galling factor to his own healing. He had failed to rescue his brother, and now he had lost the means to continue the attempt. This concern eased a bit when the war ended. The news of Hirohito's surrender came as Mike was in transit between Guam and Hawaii. Then he began to wonder if Tony would beat him home and a little bit of that old brotherly rivalry began to rise in Mike. That was replaced with more fear when the weeks passed in Hawaii and the news from home reflected no knowledge of Tony's fate. He thought that surely the liberated POWs would go home first. Still the weeks rolled on and there was no report.

It would be months before Mike would know the fate of his brother. Mike's immediate agenda was the process of returning home. The front lines of battle now consisted of a line of typists with volumes of orders to cut for thousands of military men and women scattered from China to South America, and Alaska to

Australia. The post-war logistics were an effort almost as great as the war itself. Every soldier, sailor, airman, and marine had earned the right to come home to their mothers, fathers, brothers, sisters, sweethearts, wives, children, and—for many—the babies that they had never seen.

Men had to be located. Points had to be assessed. Material and equipment had to be disposed of and damage repaired. Transportation had to be matched to the people who had to be transported, and provisions had to be matched to the transports for thousands of men traveling for weeks on end. Then there was also that so-and-so who just had to fall in love with a local girl and start the complicated maze of paperwork to return with his war bride.

Mike would always have some recurring pain in his left elbow and some loss of hearing in his left ear, but otherwise he was ready to go home and rejoin civilian life. Arrangements were made for him to make the short hop from Pearl Harbor to San Francisco aboard the carrier USS Independence.

CVL-22 was an odd-looking duck. It had been hastily constructed in the early months of the war when we were desperately short of aircraft carriers. It began life in the shipyard as the light cruiser CL-59 Amsterdam, thus the merging of the CV for carrier and the CL for light cruiser into the designation CVL. From the flight deck down it looked like a cruiser, but from the hull line up it looked like a carrier that had landed on a cruiser with the cruiser bow sticking several feet forward of the end of the flight deck.

Despite its odd appearance USS Independence had been a real workhorse. She had served in the Solomons, the Gilberts, and the Philippines. She had been torpedoed at Tarawa, and had faced swarms of kamikazes at Okinawa.

Now she was a part of the largest and best operation of the war—Magic Carpet—the effort to bring millions of boys home from the war. The sailors of Independence made trip after trip to the States and back out again. It was great to be taking those fellows home in peaceful seas, but they too had served and wanted to go home as well. Each trip back out had to be a bitter pill for the Independence crew.

Mike's "magic carpet" sailed out of Pearl Harbor past the wreck of USS Arizona. Arizona had already become an honored memorial that had come to represent the war itself and the sacrifices of all. As they passed, the sailors lined the deck in a solemn salute. The others on board may not have been so formal, but no one spoke. Part of this was out of respect for the sailors entombed in her wreckage, and part was their own memories of the buddies who had been so young, and who would never see their mothers again.

It's hard to describe the thoughts of a man who is returning from combat. Perhaps the better word is impossible. Two years ago, three years ago, or even six months ago these were boys who would normally be playing baseball, working on cars, going to school, entering the workforce, and chasing girls. They were returning as disciplined wild men who had been aged by chasing women and hard drinking (where available), military order, crude living, and death in every imaginable form.

They wanted to go home so badly, but at the same time they feared what they would find once they returned. They would expect to see the same family and friends, and yet it would not be the same. Their parents would be aged beyond their years by the stress of having a child in harm's way. Their sweethearts would not feel the same, and their children would not know them.

The soldiers themselves had become a part of a foreign family. They would no longer be told what to do every minute. Now they would have to make their own judgments and live with the results. The things that gave them joy before would now be childish. The worst part was that no one at home would understand what they had experienced, and none of it could be explained to an outsider. Perhaps that's the word—"OUTSIDER." They would forever be an outsider to all but their own.

Any fear was overridden by the consuming desire to go H O M E.

As the coast of America began to rise out of the ocean, the din of thousands of men grew still and reflective. A few cheered, and then they just watched as it came closer and closer. The ultimate goal of these men had not been Tokyo, for the American GI is not part of an imperial army but rather a liberating force. Their ultimate goal was a place called Comanche, Texas, or Worchester, Massachusetts, or Simpsonville, South Carolina, or Elwood, Indiana, or Franklin, Tennessee, or De Smet, South Dakota.

The Golden Gate Bridge was to the returning men of the Pacific what the Statue of Liberty had been to the men coming home from Europe.

When Mike's "magic carpet" returned there was a large American flag hanging from the Golden Gate's deck and some now fading and wind-damaged banners welcoming the troops home. A lot of men on that ship remembered the conversations they had shared with a buddy when they passed under that same bridge on their way to war. The sentiment then was speculation on whether they would ever see that bridge again. A lot of fellows with names like Sam, and Buddy, and Jimmy, and Lew, and Ray, and Mark, and Bobby were about to cross under that great gateway again. This time it would be only in the thoughts of the Joes who had survived their friends and may have borne witness to their buddy's untimely death. The men stood silent in their memories.

A Marine corporal by the name of Luis Calderon from Albuquerque had intentionally stowed his dress blues in his sea bag for the express purpose of having them for just this occasion. Normally the dress uniform would have been sent home when they were deployed, but Corporal Calderon had made it his goal to pass under that bridge with full-blooded Marine reverence for his country. He stood in his pressed dress blues at sharp attention on the tip of the flight deck and saluted the flag on the bridge until they had passed. It really put a lump in the throat of any man who saw it, and several of them assumed his stance in their own way. One soldier from the 96th was standing there saluting his country in his underwear, but his attitude was such that you would have thought he was in full review before the Commander-in-Chief.

After a long silent pause, and several yards beyond the bridge, a shout went up from the men on board. They were finally home!

When the carrier berthed there was an organized rush to touch American soil. Some had family waiting for them. Most did not. Some walked off like it was another day at work. Some kissed the dock. Some kissed the sidewalks once they made it to dry land. The lucky ones found a willing patriotic girl to kiss.

A well-used bus gathered in several marines including Mike and headed south towards Camp Pendleton, just north of San Diego. Mike wondered why they hadn't docked in "Dago" to begin with, but the enormity of the Magic Carpet operation had overwhelmed the entire West Coast system of harbors, and they had to adapt with a little extra land transportation.

Luis Calderon really stood out on that drab bus with his dress blues. He sat next to the window in the sixth row on the driver's side. Mike sat down next to Luis and started to strike up a conversation, but Luis kept his head turned toward the window. Mike was offended at first. Then he noticed that the window was getting steamed up. He quickly realized that it was time to give Luis a little room.

When the emotions simmered down, Luis turned to Mike and said "Welcome home, Marine." The words caught in his throat a bit, and Mike could feel a lump as he tried to reply.

That introduction turned into a good friendship. Over the next few days they were both assigned light duty and were usually finished with work by 1300. They spent a lot of time together in town and had some good times with several of the local girls. Mike was never serious about any of the women they enjoyed, but Luis fell pretty hard for a girl named Jane. Back in the barracks Mike would tease Luis and call her "plain Jane," but she was really quite a doll.

Luis was thinking pretty strong on marriage by the time his discharge came through. However, cooler heads prevailed and he returned to Albuquerque, where he married his high school sweetheart. Rosa was a great wife and life was good until they lost their four-year-old to spinal meningitis. Rosa herself took skin cancer when their oldest girl was thirteen. She left Luis with a seven-year-old boy and a teenage girl. It was pretty tough on the surviving family but in general things worked out.

The boy, Raul, got into a little trouble when he was in high school, but he was otherwise a very good student with a lot of drive. His baseball coach, Mr. Erskine, was a great influence in channeling some of that strong will and energy in the right direction. Raul graduated with honors and a scholarship to Anderson College in Mike's hometown. Unfortunately the Pencil Man was long gone by then.

Luis' girl Elena stayed in the Albuquerque area and married a boy named Sam. The two of them bought into a grocery store and did very well. It was hard work, but they partnered in the enterprise and it made for a good family situation. They had one girl, who owned her Grandpa Luis. When little Rose was school age she looked so much like her Grandma Rosa that it melted her grandpa's heart.

Luis did not remarry for several decades. He was too busy working and rearing his children. A few years after Rosa died he tried to get in touch with Jane, but he couldn't quite make the connection. When he was eighty he did catch up to Jane in a nursing home in Bernalillo. He actually married Jane and enjoyed her company for five months and thirteen days before he died from a massive heart attack. By that time Luis' granddaughter Rose was a nurse at the home, and she took the best care of Jane until she too died two years later.

It was a sad day when Luis was discharged and left Mike. It would be several more days before Mike would get his release. He didn't bother to make any new friends to replace his companionship with Luis.

With the time drawing near for his return to the foreign world of civilian life, Mike began to worry. He had talked by phone to his parents and to Veronica. They all seemed anxious to see him again, but Mike wasn't sure he was ready. He couldn't wait to see his mom and dad, and he was fired up about putting the squeeze on Veronica again. Still there was a force holding him back. Leroy was still out there. Bob Frazier was still out there. Jim Lester was still out there. Okinawa and Peleliu and the Canal were still out there. Tony was still out there.

No one had heard Tony's fate for sure, and Keku didn't want to tell Mike over the phone about her experience in the church that day. Having heard Mike's voice, she was relieved that he was alive. She was also not surprised when he described his wounds, as she had felt great pain in her left side in the ordeal of the spiritual warfare during the Mass.

A stranger arrived at the door about the time that Mike called to say he was coming home. He hadn't stated his business yet when the phone rang. Keku answered the phone and was torn between the thrill of Mike's imminent return and the news she sensed she was about to hear. Joe looked in the stranger's eyes, and his military experience told him right away the nature of the stranger's business. When Joe picked up the phone he made a strange request. "Mike . . . I want you to do something . . ."

Joe spoke in a strange meter as he tried to compose both himself and his words.

"Your mom and I both want you home so bad we can hardly stand it . . . but I remember how it was when I came back . . . from the Argonne . . . I wasn't ready . . . I needed some time . . . I want you to be ready . . . Take your time, son . . . hitchhike home . . . see your country . . . take some time . . . and when you're ready . . . you'll know . . . am I making sense?"

"Yeah, dad . . . it makes a lot of sense . . . thanks . . . I love you guys."

When Mike hung up the phone Joe turned to Keku, who looked so sad. She nodded her head at Joe in agreement. Still it was hard not to have her boy home. Joe took Keku and led her to the sofa. There he sat her down and held her close as they waited for the stranger to speak. He himself struggled to meet their sad eyes and he had to work on a lump in his throat before he began. The stranger reached into a paper bag that he had brought into the house. His lips quivered as he pulled out an unusual flag.

He began with "My name is Dick Brown . . ."

CHAPTER 16

Life in Death Valley

Once a Marine always a Marine. Nothing separated a Marine from the Corps—especially a Marine who has seen combat. Still there is a time and place for everything, and this was Mike's time to find his way home.

As he walked out the gates of Camp Pendleton for the last time, he bypassed the bus that was taking a load of now-former Marines to the train station. Instead Mike just started walking east. For easier travel, Mike had exchanged his sea bag for a lighter backpack with just the essentials and had shipped the rest home. About a mile outside of the base his adventure began when a fellow in a produce truck picked him up.

The driver's name was Thomas. Mike didn't know if that was his first name or his last, and neither fellow cared enough to settle the question. Thomas had been in the Army and didn't have much use for Marines. Still he had enough G.I. in him to want to pick up a hitchhiker in uniform. Thomas had been wounded in the battle for Metz. It was one of those "million dollar" wounds that got him home but didn't do any lingering damage. It would add to his problems with arthritis in his later years, but for now he was young and making his way with some good old American hard labor.

Thomas was running a load from his father's farm north to Barstow. It was a hot day and the truck smelled like cauliflower. They didn't talk much, but when they did it was about the old truck or some hot girlfriend. Thomas asked Mike where he was heading and he didn't seem too impressed when Mike said "Indiana." He told Mike about a guy he knew in service who was from Gnaw Bone, Indiana. He drew out the name and said it like Indiana was some kind of a lame joke. He seemed to take a greater interest in the Hoosier state when Mike showed him a picture of Veronica. "Do you think she's been faithful to you?" Thomas asked. "I doubt it," Mike replied, "but I can make 'em scram when I get home."

When they got to Barstow Mike found a diner and stopped in for a sandwich. The waitress talked him into a cup of chili as well, even though it was a hot day. When she offered him a piece of pie Mike said that he couldn't afford to spend too much. That's when the owner/grill cook came over and said "Take the pie. This meal is on me." Mike noticed a globe and anchor tattoo with Semper Fi on the man's stump. Mike gave him a conversational "hoorah," and shook his remaining hand. Then the owner said "Tarawa." Mike returned with "Canal, Peleliu, and Okinawa."

An old geezer at the other end of the counter stood up ramrod straight and added, "San Juan Hill." He said it with chest out pride and as three distinct words for emphasis. Mike stood at attention and gave the old soldier a snappy salute, which the old man just as proudly returned.

"Where ya headed, son?"

"Home to Indiana."

"Hitchhiking?"

"Yes, sir. Wanted to take my time and see some of the country first."

"Have you ever been to Death Valley?"

"No, sir, but I always wanted to go there."

"I live in the valley. Come home and visit for a few days. We'd be glad to have you."

"I'd like that, sir."

This was the kind of experience that Mike was seeking on his journey home. The stark beauty of America and its people was the kind of thing that could scrub off some of the blood and anguish of war.

The old man's name was Arthur Lilly. He and his wife Campbell had lived in Death Valley since the start of World War I. Like so many combat soldiers, Art just wanted to get away for a while, and boy did he get away! Art and Belle lived miles from the nearest of anything that could be called civilization. Their home was in a place they called Lilly Valley, which was so high in the rugged hills that it could hardly be called a valley. It was at the end of a hundred miles of a winding dirt road that couldn't have passed as a cow path in some places.

Art had loved and cherished Belle since the day he met her in '99, but there were times when he "couldn't stand it no more," so he'd head off to Barstow to "get a cup of coffee and a good look at that waitress."

Belle was a nurse at an Army hospital in Florida where Art had gone after sustaining battle wounds in Cuba. He was a pretty good-looking fellow in those days, and it didn't take much for him to convince her to marry him. Art said it had something to do with all of those sponge baths she gave him, but he didn't go into any more detail, and Mike was glad to leave it there.

While Art was recovering in Florida, his buddy in the next bed was a fellow from West Virginia by the name of Frank Howard. Frank seemed to know a lot about just about anything you'd want to know. One day Art expressed that he would like to marry Belle and go off to some place as far from the world as he could. Having looked into the eyes of the "Spanish boys" he had killed, Art was pretty disillusioned by it all. Frank told him that he had read about a place called Death Valley in California, and that it was as far from the world as one could get.

Belle and Art settled in the Valley with the help of their neighbors Ira Sweetman and her cousin Adrian Egbert. The word "neighbors" is relative, for they lived more than ten miles away in a place they called Cave Springs. It was just as it sounds. They lived in a home that was mostly a cave and it had a good cool spring for their water needs. The caves themselves were part natural but mostly carved out of the rock by Mr. Egbert himself. Adrian had been a miner since '94 and had found the spot looking for gold. It was such an interesting place that Ernie Pyle wrote about it in one of his pre-war columns and his book *Home Country*.

It was 1914 before they could pull it off. When they did, Art befriended Mr. Egbert, and Adrian led Art to the place they now called Lilly Valley. There was a spent gold mine shaft there that Art and Belle used for a home until a proper one could be built. Most women wouldn't have anything to do with such a life, but Belle loved it. "There was a clean-air freedom about the place," she said, drawing a deep breath for emphasis.

At the end of the dusty trail there was indeed a suitable home overlooking the desolate beauty of the hills that surrounded it and the valley below. Art surprised Belle with his guest, and she didn't seem to mind the unexpected intrusion at all. Belle herself was a bit worn by time, but it was obvious that she had been quite a beauty in her day.

Mike stayed with them for two weeks and loved every minute. One could stand outside and see for miles and hear nothing but the whisper of the breeze, when there was one. The sky at night was a stunning shower of stars. Crickets and coyote sounds replaced the screams of dying men, and the incoming rounds of battle.

One day Keku couldn't stand it anymore. She just had to know that her only surviving child was okay, so Kikthawenund sent Mamalis to check on her brother. She found him at the dinner table with Art and Belle. It was Belle who noticed her first. "Who's the Indian gal?" she asked. It was only the second time that someone outside of Mike's family had seen the spirits. Years of living in the desolation of Lilly Valley had cleared the minds of Art and Belle, and they could sense and see things that would otherwise be cluttered by the stress of "civilization."

Mike turned and smiled at his sister. She read in his expression all that she needed to know. She thanked the Lillys for their good care of her brother. "Been our pleasure," Art said. Belle added, "Can you sit a spell?" Mamalis shook her head "No" and laid her right hand on the side of Mike's face. An indescribable feeling of coolness and peace came over him, and then she left.

Mike talked to the Lillys for some time that night about the spirit side of his family. He told that them that he wished more than anything that he could physically hug his sister whom he had never known in the mortal realm.

Keku rested well that night.

CHAPTER 17

Bert T. and the Grand Canyon

When the time came for Mike to move on, it was with the help of one Bert T. Owens. The folks in the Valley would talk about him using his full name or just Bert T.—and always with a hard emphasis on the "T."

Art spotted Bert T. passing through Lilly Valley and flagged him down. Bert T. waited for Art and Mike to catch up as they rode down the slope on mules to meet him. It was the first time Mike had ridden a mule, and while it would not be his last, he made a mental note to not do it very often.

Bert T. was driving his old mining wagon to Fred Utt's place. Fred was the only mechanic/blacksmith in all of Death Valley. Fred could have taken advantage of that, but he was always fair with his prices and was an excellent mechanic.

He had a machine shop and a forge, and he could generally make any parts that he couldn't buy. There weren't a whole lot of buckboard supply stores in those days, so he would have to machine any parts that Bert T. needed.

Bert T. had been a bauxite miner and mule skinner in the twenty mule team days. He wasn't much of a talker, but when he did it was about mules, mining, and a "red-haired gal from Sausalito," who was probably a gray-haired gal by now if she was alive at all.

The wagon itself was a heavy-duty freight wagon that had been used during the twenty mule team days. It required a team of four mules even when it was fairly empty. Bert T. drove it with a six mule team that day and Mike wondered if even that was enough. The lumbering old wagon had a busted spring on the passenger side. Mike had to hang on to the end rail of the seat all the way. Every rock and crater was magnified by the broken spring, and the mules sent up a pretty heavy cloud of dust as per the surface of the terrain.

Bert T.'s inculcation of how to work with mules would come in handy in a few days. His talk of the old days was a tonic to Mike. Those were days of hardscrabble living and tough men, but there were solid friendships as well and the opportunity to earn abundant freedom by the work of a man's back and hands. Bert T. spoke of things that were as far from war and the strife of Twentieth Century living as one could get.

When they arrived Fred looked over the situation and said, "Two days." He told Bert T. to go get a drink and "See the missus. She'll show you where you can bunk." It was assumed on all fronts that anyone who came to Fred's place would at least stay the night and longer if the repair warranted the time. Just about anybody who came to Fred's garage would have traveled a long way, and it would not be wise to make the trip back in the same day.

While Fred went to work, Bert T. and Mike headed for the "cola machine." It was one of those machines that opened from the top. Fred had reconfigured it so that the bottles were loose and easy to retrieve. It was cooled by spring water, and the drinks were as cold as if they had been on ice or refrigerated. It surely tasted good to Mike. It had been a long and dusty trail, and colas were still a rare treat to a fellow who had spent the last four years in the Pacific war.

Fred also had a stable for the few horses and mules that were used by fellows like Bert T. It was Bert T.'s job to keep the animals fed and the stalls clean in exchange for the "rent" on the barn and bunkhouse.

After two days and several good meals, Bert T. was ready to head home. He was glad, too. The noise was driving him crazy. Fred's place was only a dozen miles or so from the edge of Death Valley, and once or twice a night one could faintly hear a truck doing a Jake brake through "nearby" Beatty, Nevada. The sound really carried through that area.

Mike stayed with the Utts for almost another week. He loved to watch Fred work. The man was more of a surgeon than a mechanic. Mike "helped" as Fred worked through the "anatomy" of a '34 Plymouth that belonged to a couple who were honeymooning their way from Lone Pine, California to the Grand Canyon. Mike stayed in the stable to let the couple have some privacy in the bunkhouse. Even then, at least from a noise perspective, it wasn't very private for anybody trying to sleep outside of the bunkhouse. They were surely enjoying their honeymoon, while all Mike had was an itchy bed of hay and the leftover smell of Bert T.'s mules.

About noon the next day Fred determined that he would need a part to complete the job, so he asked Mike if he wanted a ride to Vegas. Unlike Bert T., Fred was a really personable guy and good company for the trip. Fred was just a few years older than Mike and had served at the Naval Assembly and Repair facility at Corpus Christi, Texas. When Mike told him that he was from Anderson, Indiana, Fred asked if that was close to "Alexander, Indiana."

"You mean Alexandria?"

"Yeah that's it. I always remember it by that Tyrone Power movie "Alexander's Rag time Band." Did you know he served in Corpus Christi? Well anyway there was this fellow from Alexander named John Prieshoff. He was a real nice guy."

Mike didn't correct Fred on the town name. He shared what little he knew of Alexandria and said that he didn't know John. The funny thing was that Mike would be working with John a few months later.

Las Vegas was just on the cusp of becoming the town we would later know. Most of the gambling joints were still of the Old West style. The flamboyant Flamingo was just coming into play. The place that impressed Mike the most was the Plymouth dealership—but in a bizarre way. It was nearly devoid of any new cars, which was like walking into an empty grocery store that was somehow still in business. Most of the cars the dealers had on hand in those days were few in number and pretty beat up. No cars had been made during the war. The automakers were just starting to changeover from war production. All of this was capped with a big autoworkers' strike, so it was hard to get a car anywhere in the country.

Mike didn't stick around Vegas too long. He had his sights set on the Grand Canyon. He had always wanted to see the place and figured he had better get there before the noisy honeymoon couple showed up and caused an avalanche.

Once he was there he hooked up with a fellow named Lee, who ran the mule concession for the park. Mr. Lee was always in need of fellows to care for the mules and, if they were good enough, lead the mule excursions to the canyon floor and back. With the information that Bert T. had shared with him, Mike was able to muster a passable interview and worked there for about a month.

It was the first time that he had had enough extra cash to purchase some civilian clothes—and the first time he had been out of uniform since 1942. It felt strange, but good.

Lee's mule concession wasn't a very fancy operation, but he knew his business. He had been trained by an old-timer who had originally come from Willow Hill, Illinois and had worked the mules since the days when Mark Twain was traveling around the West. The old-timer actually knew Mr. Clemens when he had lived for a while at the Canyon. He had described the now famous author as a "bum," which he pretty much was at the time.

Over the course of his month's stay, Mike became proficient with the mules. He didn't mind the work, and he fell in love with the magnificent masterpiece of God before his eyes. Mike explored as much of the canyon as one could in a month. It was so long, and so wide, and so deep, and so vast. The colors of the changing day fell upon its walls like a God-sized artist's brush and dazzled the observer. It was good for the soul.

A few days before Mike moved on, he led a party down into the canyon. Two of the riders were the honeymoon couple. It was a hot day and by the time they returned to the top, those two were really lighting into each other. The rest of the evening it was plenty icy between the honeymoon couple. The other guests at the lodge finally had a quiet night's sleep.

On his last day at the canyon, Mr. Lee expressed a little sadness to see Mike go. "You're a good boy and a good worker, son. I wish you could stay." Mike told Mr. Lee that he had been a great boss and that he appreciated the job.

Alone in the stable Mike got a little misty eyed for a mule named Buttercup. Buttercup had been a little, well, "mule headed" when Mike first worked with her, but with some of Bert T.'s advice she had become like a faithful pup to Mike. Mike would put a carrot in his back pocket, and Buttercup would come right up and take it out. The tourists got a kick out of that one. In turn Buttercup never flinched anymore when Mike saddled her, and she had become the most requested mule in the pack. She was always given to any child or rider who was uneasy. In the evenings Mike would give her a good grooming, and Buttercup would try to lick him while he brushed her down.

The night before Mike's departure he sat on the canyon rim and took it in. Even with the "painter's brush" put up for the night, she was magnificent. Her deep dark cut only served to enhance the profound darkness of the night. Stars filled the sky and blazed between the openings in the rocks. The few campfires in the canyon floor could be seen for miles, and the sounds of the nocturnal animals amplified off the canyon walls.

As Mike was taking in the beauty of the moment, Kikthawenund came and sat next to his grandson. The old chief said nothing, nor did Mike. Each was pleased to share the wonders of that moment with the other. Mike thought of home. He thought of his mother and how Keku would end each Mass by thanking Jesus for his sacrifice, God for his universal creation and love, and her brother and sister trees for giving her a comfortable place to sit and kneel.

Mike thought similar thoughts as he sat with the grandfather he had loved so much and known so well without ever being able to feel his physical touch. He thanked the God of all creation for this sight before him.

Grandfather smiled.

CHAPTER 18

Summer in Texas

Mike's next destination would be in Texas, where he had a solemn duty to perform.

Mr. Lee drove Mike to Flagstaff, where Mike was able to hitch a ride with a trucker named Duke, who was hauling a load to Dallas. Duke was sullen and downright spooky. It was weird that Duke had even pulled over to pick up Mike in the first place, because he never spoke so much as "Hi" after Mike climbed into the cab. He just stared ahead as if he were planning a murder.

Mike got out of the truck at the first truck stop, near Winslow. He made another connection with a driver by the name of Miller. Miller was just the opposite of Duke. He was personable and talked incessantly. The man hardly inhaled between words. By the time they had made Gallup, New Mexico, Mike knew the intimate and complete details on each of Miller's three wives and all sixteen of his children, and his seven grandkids plus, every experience and close call he had seen on the road, and everywhere he had worked, and every load he had hauled, and the time he had jack-knifed the rig in Indianapolis and how the road was covered with ladies brassieres, and on, and on, and on, and on, and . . . . By the time they reached Albuquerque, Mike was climbing out of his skin and wishing he had stayed with Duke. At least if Duke had killed him he would have had some peace.

In Albuquerque, Mike spent a few days with Luis. It was a good reunion. In the short time they had been separated Mike had seen some rare and special places. Luis had started things up again with Rosa and was settling into a good life. Mike took an instant liking to Rosa. She was sweet of spirit and stunning in her beauty. Rosa was a great cook, and she adored her handsome Marine. Luis just glowed when he was with her.

It would have been good to stay a while longer, but three is still a crowd and both Marines needed to get on with their lives.

Rosa worked in a diner and knew of a fellow who worked for the phone company and was traveling to Midland, Texas. Dick Courtney was the kind of guy who could sell ice to an Eskimo. Before you knew it you were signing on the dotted line. It wasn't that he was a shyster—Dick was just a really nice guy and had a knack for knowing just what to say and when to say it.

It was a good trip to Midland. Dick had many interesting stories of the people he had met in life, and he listened intently to what Mike had to say. I guess that was the real reason Dick was so successful. He made people feel important because he really did care about them.

This quality was inherited from his parents. Dick told of some wonderful acts of generosity his folks had given to the down-and-outers who came to their door during the Great Depression. They were a large family and not well off themselves, but there was always enough for a needy stranger, "Even if Mama and Papa did without." Mike remembered similar acts of kindness in Anderson. It seemed those awful times revealed the true wealth of Americans.

They traveled through the night with one driving while the other slept. As they passed by Roswell, New Mexico, the car died. The entire electrical system failed right there in the road. He and Dick pushed it off to the side, but it wouldn't have mattered. They hadn't seen another car all night.

While they sat there trying to figure out what to do, six strange lights came near them in the sky. They danced and moved about as nothing either man had ever seen. The lights hovered and darted and stopped on a dime. They became very bright and fused into one expanding light, and then they split apart like a shotgun blast and vanished.

The moment the lights were gone, the headlights came on and the radio kicked on in the middle of a Bob Wills song. Dick got in and the car started right up. They drove on for some time in silence before they began to assess the situation and what they should do. They decided it would be best keep what they saw to themselves.

From Midland Mike caught a ride with a farmer named Bill Rankin. Mr. Rankin was maybe sixty and had an air about him of being a college professor or perhaps a banker. He was soft spoken with a vocabulary that was very well developed. He was wearing a suit and tie with a nice hat, and yet there he was driving a '38 flatbed to his farm just east of San Angelo with a load of milo seed.

Mr. Rankin was a Quaker and therefore a pacifist. He had skipped the First World War over just such convictions. Having recently gone through the slaughter of combat, Mike felt a little uncomfortable in Mr. Rankin's company. That being said, Mike detected not the slightest note of personal judgment against him from the elder farmer.

Deep in this bastion of Baptists they spoke of crops in Indiana and crops in Texas, of Mike's mixture of Lenape-flavored Catholic spirituality and of the Quaker faith. By the time they made Mr. Rankin's farm, there seemed to be no consensus of preference on crops or religion, but it was a good experience for both men.

Mike spent the night at Mr. and Mrs. Rankin's home. The next morning Mrs. Rankin fixed Mike a hearty breakfast including Quaker Oats, which he thought was pretty funny. As he walked down the lane to the highway Mr. Rankin called to Mike, "I hope you find it, son." Mike started to ask "Find what?" but stopped his reply as they both knew what Mr. Rankin was trying to say. Instead, Mike just waved and left the Rankins in peace.

It was a warm day—a good day to be alive. Mike walked down U.S. 87 for some time and several miles before he found another ride. He didn't mind at all. In fact he could have gone on down that road all day as far as he was concerned. The Texas hill country is absolutely desolate to many people, but if it suits your state of mind there is no greater balm for the soul. The sky is broad and blue. The land stretches and undulates for miles in every direction. It is so quiet that a man can shed his every worry and make peace with God.

Just past Vick, where the road turns more south, and not quite to Eden, Mike felt the presence of another walking beside him. He was startled at first. It had a vague form that drifted in and out and swirled about. At first Mike thought it was Kikthawenund. Instead, he was shocked to see Jim Lester in the flesh—or was he? Jim had an appearance that was sometimes solid and sometimes like a vapor. He was dancing and jumping and sometimes walking backward in front of Mike like a school kid whose team had just won the big game.

"Hey, Mike, where are you going?" Jim didn't wait for an answer. He was too antsy. "I'm going home, Mike. I'm almost there. I'm gonna see my mama, and my daddy, and sis, and my dog Butch, and my cousin Billy, and my girl. Are you coming? Are you coming? Are you coming? . . ."

Jim's voice echoed as he twisted and faded away and out of sight. A few minutes later a rancher pulled up alongside and called out, "You want a ride?" It took Mike a moment to answer as he shook off the shock of Jim's crazy apparition.

The rancher's wife was in the cab, so Mike had to ride in the bed with several feed sacks and their children, Rachel and Bucky. Rachel was a little older, perhaps eleven. Bucky said he was nine. They both thought it was pretty swell when they found out that Mike was a Marine and had fought in the war. Bucky and Mike hit it off like big brother and little brother. Rachel thought Mike was cute and tried out her budding charm on the handsome Marine.

Mike didn't want to burst her bubble, so he played along with her to a degree. He did think that she looked a lot like her mother—the rancher's wife was awfully pretty. He was sure the rancher would have his hands full in just a few years when the other ranchers' sons started to take notice.

Bucky was all boy. He was tanned and strong from working with his dad. He asked all sorts of questions about the war as though it was a great game to be played. Mike did his best to downplay the glory without traumatizing the children with the gruesome details. He finished by saying, "Your mom and dad work hard every day to feed people all over the country. If you're looking for heroes, they're right there," and he pointed to the cab.

The rancher dropped Mike off in Melvin. Before Mike made it to Brady, Texas, a sailor, who had been separated about the same time as Mike, picked him up on an ancient Indian motorcycle. It was pretty hard to hear, but he managed to pick up that the fellow's name was Ronson, "like the lighter," and that he was headed to Comanche to get a loan from a buddy who had served with him on USS Indianapolis.

Ronson and Mike stopped to get the noise out of their ears and to eat lunch in San Saba at a diner called Bill's, just across from the Doner Pecan Company. Bill ran the grill. His wife Veneda was the best waitress in all of Texas. She was a great one on several fronts. First of all, Veneda was a strikingly tall, slim blonde with an infectious smile. She listened well and was perfect with the details of the customer's order.

Veneda had the habit of singing while she worked. No one minded. She had a beautiful voice, and when Mike complimented her to that sentiment Bill spoke up with pride and said, "You ought to hear her play the piano." There was a lot of love and pride between the two, and it lent a pleasant air to the place.

The diner itself was as much a social gathering spot as it was a place to eat. The fact that the food was good was just the icing. There was no separation of "my table" versus "your table" or customers versus service staff. Everybody talked freely and strangers were warmly welcomed, as it kept the conversation fresh. Inevitably it turned to the two boys and if they had been in service. That's when Mike learned the rest of Ronson's story.

Ronson had served on USS Indianapolis until it was hit by a kamikaze off Okinawa. It had to return to San Francisco for repairs. While they were in port the atomic bomb was loaded aboard and she was rushed off to Tinian with the deadly cargo. While on liberty in San Francisco, Ronson had broken two fingers when a drunk Marine private smashed Ronson's fist with his nose—or so that's how Ronson told it. As a result he missed the sailing and the five days his buddies would soon spend in shark-infested waters.

While he missed the most dramatic part of the Indianapolis story, Ronson was no stranger to the same action. In the early part of the war his destroyer, USS Porter, was sunk by a torpedo that they bravely cut off en route to one of our big carriers. He only spent a few minutes in the deep Pacific that time, but it wasn't a pleasant experience.

After the Porter sinking he was assigned to an LSM. The LSM was an interesting piece of work. It looked like a big bathtub with a conning tower for a bridge. It was the smallest ocean-going ship in the Navy and could sail in shallow water or deep seas.

Ronson's LSM had the dubious thrill of sailing alone in the Solomons when a Jap plane from Rabaul bombed and sank the ship. This time they were in the water for two days before being rescued. They may never have been seen then if it wasn't for a Japanese destroyer that was passing their way and was shooting at the helpless swimming sailors. Two Marine wildcats from Guadalcanal spotted the destroyer firing and dove for a strafing run. As the planes drew near the pilots saw our guys in the water. The next morning another LSM and two PT boats came out to pick up the survivors.

"Them two days and two nights in the water was pure hell."

"Sorry ma'am."

"It was hotter than blazes all day and colder than . . . well, it was cold all night. There were sharks everywhere. Twice I felt one brush my feet and I thought to myself, 'Well, that's it Ronson,' but both times it got another fella instead. I felt bad about bein' glad it wasn't me, but I was. There ain't nothing like the scream of a guy being taken by a shark. We stayed together as much as we could. The guys who got scared and swam off by themselves didn't have a chance, but there wasn't anything that really made a difference. I swore that when I came home I was gonna find a place as far from the water as I could. That's why I came to Texas."

Mike asked Ronson where he lived and he said "Big Lake." Mike thought that was pretty weird, but when he looked it up later he discovered that there wasn't a lake anywhere near Big Lake.

After lunch they headed up Highway 16 toward Goldthwaite. Ronson let Mike off at the corner of 5th and Fisher streets. They shook hands and wished each other well, and Ronson rode off to his business in Comanche.

For the first time since the war, Mike was scared. His heart was about to beat out of his chest and his throat constricted. He was nearly sick to his stomach over the task he would have to do at this place.

He put his pack in his hand and walked into the sheriff's office. The sheriff was sitting behind a worn desk and was working on a sack of pecans, his paperwork, and a half-filled cup of cold black coffee. When Mike drew his attention he asked, "What can I do for you, son?"

"I'm looking for the folks of a Marine by the name of Jim Lester."

It wasn't hard for the sheriff to decipher why the boy with the somber expression was standing in front of him. He looked Mike squarely in the eyes and said, "Jimmy was a good boy. I used to coach his baseball over at the school. Jimmy was a fine boy."

Then he picked up the phone and when the other party answered he said, "Hey, Sara Lou . . . No, no, nothing serious . . . No, no, let him finish the yard. I just had something I needed to pass along. You can do it when he gets in. Well, now you're makin' me hungry . . . well, sweetheart that sounds fine . . . about 6:00 if we don't get any business . . . just tell L.D. that I'm gonna be out of the office for a spell and if he can't reach me here just have him call over to the Lesters. Thank ya, sugar . . . uh huh . . . well, you too . . . bye now."

The sheriff hung up the phone and led Mike out the door to the patrol car. He drove over to a single-story white house on Front Street that had the look of a Texas homestead. There a small woman in her forties met them at the door. Mike meekly introduced himself and told her that he had served with Jim, and was with him at the end. She just stood there for a moment with her hands on her face. Then she reached out to Mike like he was her own Jim and held his hands for the longest time in the doorway.

She introduced herself as Jo and asked Mike and the sheriff to come in. The sheriff sat and visited for a while until Dennis came home from a trip to the drug store. When he was sure everything was on the up-and-up, he tipped his hat and bowed out. Dennis asked the sheriff to go find Shirley and to send her home if he would, which he did without question.

There was a bit of awkward small talk among the three, and a general unspoken agreement in their conversation that Mike should keep the "news" for Shirley's arrival.

In a few minutes they heard a car drive up and the screen door squeak and snap shut behind a living vision. Mike was a little ashamed at what he was thinking when he first saw Jim's sister. It didn't seem the right time to notice, but she sure was pretty. Shirley was about seventeen and still had that youthful spark that makes us all dream of our summer days. Her hair was shoulder length and light brown with a bit of blond and red from the Texas sun. Her features were petite, and she was dressed just right. Mike was sure she made her daddy a nervous wreck, but she was a very sweet girl and he was convinced that Shirley had made them proud as well.

Mike stood as Shirley was introduced, and they both smiled at each other as though this was a sock hop and they were working up the notion to dance.

Mike decided that it would be best if the Lesters asked the questions they wanted answered and he would answer them as honest as he could without brutalizing them. It's hard to talk about combat to someone who has never been in it. It's even worse when you are trying to tell someone's family the awful truth. Mike shared with them the details that no stateside officer would know—or reveal if he did.

Jim's family hadn't opened Jim's bedroom since they received the word of his death, so one can imagine the tears that fell as Mike told the story. When the questions had been answered and the dust settled, so to speak, Jim's mother took Mike into the room and showed Mike Jim's baseball trophies, his school papers she had saved, and his model airplanes. Then she sat on the bed next to Mike and put her head in his chest. Mike held her as Jim would have held his mother. She cried and she cried as she finally "buried her boy."

It was decided that Mike should spend a few more days in Goldthwaite, and Mike agreed. Jo needed more time to be a mother. She needed to feed a growing boy and make his bed in the morning. Dennis needed to show Mike where Jim had tinkered in the garage on various projects. He took Mike to the school ball diamond and the wild places of Mills County where boys and dads go fishing or hunting for an excuse to be together as boys and dads. Sometimes they would just go for a walk to kick up a little Texas dust and listen to the wind. Mike liked Jim's dad. Dennis was a quiet man and very polite, and yet very strong and able in his demeanor. Mike recognized the traits of both parents that he had seen in Jim.

Shirley would be a high school senior in the fall, but this was summer. They went swimming one day and to a movie one night. She would introduce Mike to her girlfriends, who would be jealous as heck. They were a "nice looking couple." Miss Dorothy said so to their faces when she saw them walking along Fisher Street.

Mike and Shirley walked a lot. She wanted to know more about her brother's "missing" years. Jim had talked a great deal about his little sister and several of the guys had asked Jim to "fix them up" when the war was over.

They talked and they walked. It was summer and they were young. As the days passed they walked ever closer and drew ever closer. Was it love or was it just summer? Mike was confused and more than a little angry with himself. This wasn't the reason that he had come to Goldthwaite. What about Jim? What about Veronica? This was wrong.

Years later the Pencil Man would sit on Meridian Street with his board and pencils. It would be summer. A pretty girl would pass by and he would think of Shirley and wonder if he should have stayed in Goldthwaite.

CHAPTER 19

Waco

In his own mind Mike had overstayed his welcome. The Lesters were sorry to see him go, but go he must.

From Goldthwaite Mike followed U.S. Highway 84 toward Waco. Again it was peaceful country, and Mike didn't care if he caught a ride or not. The days revealed majestic vistas of the Texas hill country, but they were also so blasted hot. He wondered why he hadn't noticed the heat while he was in Goldthwaite.

"Because you were in L O V E, little brother." Once again Mamalis had popped into Mike's mortal life. "I like Shirley. She's much better then that old Veronica."

"Mind your own business, you little spook."

Mamalis laughed and slipped away. Mike thought about the close relationship between Jim and Shirley and wished again he would have had the chance to grow up with his sister.

He found a small stand of trees that provided enough shade for a good nap, so he decided to sleep the rest of the day and do his traveling after the sun went down.

That night as Mike traveled in the cool air beneath millions of bright Texas stars, Kikthawenund appeared and walked by his side.

"It is a good night for a walk, Grandson. Have you learned anything from your journey?"

"I've learned this is a great country. I've learned that I miss my mom. I've learned that my dad is a wise man. I was so tied up in knots when I was in California. Now I feel a little more relaxed."

Mike paused and then he said, "I've learned that love stinks. Sometimes you're out in the cold, and other times you have too many opportunities and can't decide which one to go with. What if I chose the wrong girl and I'm stuck for life?"

Kikthawenund laughed. "Men have killed for love, and yet without love there would be no life. I'm glad that I am an old man and dead." Mike laughed and thanked his grandfather for sharing the night with him.

"Young men have many choices and not much experience to make wise decisions."

Kikthawenund grew very solemn, as if he knew what lay ahead and was trying to warn Mike of something he was not privileged to tell. "There are many spirits in this world, Grandson. Some of them are strong and wish you ill. My spirit may not be able to reach you in some times of need, but my wisdom will be with you always. Choose wisely, Grandson—choose slowly, and remain close to the Great Spirit."

They walked side by side for another hour, and neither man spoke. Kikthawenund disappeared again with the coming of dawn.

A mile east of Arnett, Texas, Mike wrangled a ride with a fellow by the name of Hunt. Mr. Hunt was a man of about fifty who had a dream. He told Mike that there was oil near Waco. It hadn't been discovered yet, but he was "just sure" he could find it. He wasn't a ragged man, but he certainly didn't look like an oil tycoon either. His '38 Packard must have had more than 100,000 miles on it, and Mike thought that it probably used more oil than Mr. Hunt was likely to find.

Mr. Hunt had a dream for sure, but it didn't seem so much for riches as it was to prove that he was right. By the time they made Waco, Mike had heard every nuance of every plan that Mr. Hunt had ever developed. He was nearly convinced to join Mr. Hunt in this Quixotian quest, but he let the thought pass. By that time in the journey Mike's overriding desire was just to go home. Later, in his Pencil Man years, a newspaper page drifted up against the foundation of Clair Call's store. When Mike picked it up he saw where H.L. Hunt had indeed struck oil and was becoming one of the wealthiest men in America. With a smile on his lips the Pencil Man thought, "Way to go, Mr. Hunt, way to go."

Waco was a fine town by any standard, but it was one of the larger towns Mike had encountered since he began his walk home. Things were starting to close in as they do when one travels from the vast expanses of the West to the more developed East. It was mid afternoon when they arrived and he took his leave of Mr. Hunt. They shook hands and wished each other well.

Without much thought to what lay ahead, Mike decided to move on. Near the edge of town Mike hitched a ride with a fellow hauling a load of tomatoes from his small farm to market. The driver was a Mexican named Pablo. He was a very nice fellow—about the nicest man one could ever hope to find. It was evident that Pablo was humble in both means and spirit and a very hard worker. Mike took a quick liking to the man, but the poor guy had the luck of Jonah.

They headed up Texas 31 for Tyler, but just short of Dawson the truck broke down. The nearest town of any size, Corsicana, was about twenty-five miles away. Luckily that was where Pablo's brother lived, but every chance they had to call, he didn't answer his phone.

The traffic was unusually light, and one couldn't hitch a ride to save one's soul. By the time they walked to Silver City, Mike was hungry so he offered to buy Pablo supper.

Despite its prosperous name, there wasn't much to be had at Silver City. There was one gas station/diner/post office/city hall/bar. They went in and Mike ordered a barbeque sandwich with coffee and a piece of apple pie.

Pablo had had barbeque for lunch so he ordered the chicken and noodles, coffee, and peach pie. The waitress came out a few minutes later and told him they had just run out of chicken and noodles, so he ordered the beef stew instead. She came out with the two coffees and Mike's apple pie, but they were out of peach pie. He sent her back with an order for the apple pie, but when she returned she had the bad news that the other waitress had taken the last of the beef stew and the last piece of pie.

Pablo told her that he didn't need the pie and that he would settle for the barbeque. She came back with Mike's barbeque and the sad news that the other waitress had taken the last of the barbeque and that Mike's was a smaller portion than what they usually served. In the end Pablo settled for a cheese sandwich that was more stale bread than toast. When he asked for a second cup of coffee, they had just run out. Mike gave Pablo half of his pie to help compensate, but without the coffee to wash it down Pablo left the restaurant with his mouth as dry as Texas dust.

He needn't have worried about the dry mouth. When they were two more miles down the road and another twelve miles from Corsicana, it began to rain. It seldom rained in that part of Texas in that time of the year, but it did that night. It was a real gully washer and cold to boot. Pablo had a jacket, but it was ten miles back in the truck. Mike looked for something in his backpack to help, but all he had was a cotton shirt. About six miles from Corsicana the sole of Pablo's left boot came lose from being soaked by the rain. From that point it went FLAP, FLAP, FLAP with every step.

They dragged into Corsicana around midnight, but Pablo's brother wasn't home. In desperation and soaked to the bone, Pablo let out an insane shriek that drew the attention of a neighbor's Doberman pinscher. The dog completely ignored Mike and chased Pablo up a tree.

Pablo hung there for a minute or two. The rain was making the bark slick and the dog was making his bark loud. Pablo could feel the dog's hot breath as he jumped within a few inches of Pablo's leg with every leap. Lightning in the air gave a slight tingle to the wet surface of the tree.

Finally the tree limb broke, dumping Pablo with a loud bang onto the tin roof of a neighbor's garage. When they heard the noise they called the sheriff, who mercifully arrested Pablo and kept him in jail until the mess could be straightened out the next morning.

The story goes that when Pablo's brother Ernito, who was a very respected and successful businessman in Corsicana, found out about the incident he came to the jail to vouch for his brother. They got into Ernito's Cadillac and drove back to Pablo's truck. When they arrived they found hundreds of birds picking through his load, and somebody had stolen the wheels.

Pablo gave up. He sold his farm just outside of Waco, which hadn't been that productive in the first place, and moved back in with his mother in Chihuahua.

A few months later Mr. Hunt purchased Pablo's old farm and struck his first oil well in what had been Pablo's back yard.

CHAPTER 20

Women, Cars, and Love

When Pablo was arrested, Mike decided he had had enough. Besides, there wasn't anything he could do for Pablo except get himself arrested, so he relieved himself behind the First Baptist Church, apologized to God, and headed out of town.

A mile east of Corsicana it stopped raining, and a warm breeze commenced from the southwest. By the time he made Kerens, Texas, Mike's clothes were getting fairly dry. A mile or so east of Kerens there was a small lake near the road and a roadside picnic area. Mike decided to settle in for a little sleep on one of the picnic tables, using his pack for a pillow.

He must have been exhausted, because the next thing he knew it was 9 a.m. To his immense surprise, there was a young woman standing over him, a real looker. Before Mike could ask himself if he was dreaming, she anxiously blurted out, "Oh, I'm so sorry to wake you. Would you please help me? My tire is flat, and I'm late for work, and this is my evaluation day!"

Mike, of course, was more than willing to assist. Besides, he didn't have anything else to do, and she might return the favor with a ride. The day was already promising to be a scorcher, so he asked her if she would mind if he took off his shirt. She said she didn't mind and almost bit off her lip when he did. Let's face it—Mike was one young fit and strong Marine in those days. He in turn didn't mind that she stood next to him in that smart dress and high heels while he bent down to fix the tire. Even if he didn't get a ride, this was already shaping up to be a better day than yesterday.

Her name was Violet, she worked in a bank in Tyler, and she had the longest legs Mike had ever seen on a woman. Violet must have been all of six feet or more, and carried it well.

After the flat was fixed she did indeed offer Mike a ride. She asked him where he was headed, and when he said "Indiana," she told him that she could at least get him as close as Tyler. Mike must have had her rattled because when she pulled back on to the road she was headed back home instead of toward Tyler. Violet blushed like a rose and turned the car around.

On the trip to Tyler, Mike found out as much about Violet as a man could in such a short time span, and she asked a lot of questions about his life story. Violet was very impressed by all Mike had experienced. She also made it quite clear that she wasn't seeing anybody, which was just fine with Mike. Somehow he managed to forget all about Shirley and Veronica.

Mike observed more detail of this comely lass as they rolled down the highway. Violet had beautiful hair and eyes. Her dress was perfect for her shapely frame. Her voice, her fragrance, her smile, and even the grace of her hands made his heart beat faster and faster.

For her part, Violet had never seen a man she had found more attractive. Thank goodness she was driving in the wide open country of East Texas, for she kept her eyes more on Mike than the road.

Things were getting pretty steamy with every mile, and then it really heated up when they spotted a sign for a roadside motel between Malakoff and Crescent City. Mike's heart jumped when Violet blurted out, "I don't suppose it matters if I'm a little bit later."

"Where did that come from?" he thought. When they saw the motel sign they both mouthed "vacancy." Violet slowed the car way down. On impulse she pulled into the motel drive and stopped with her foot on the brake and the car in first.

"I'm getting really hot—I mean it's getting really hot."

"Do you want me to drive you? I mean the car?"

"Yes—no—I don't want to be late—to work. Do you want me to be late?"

"Yes—no—we should go to work—you should go to work."

Mike had his hand on the door handle when Violet let her foot off the brake. The car lurched and nearly hit the motel sign, which helped to break some of the spell.

As they drove down the road they both exhaled in unison. Mike wanted to touch her so badly he could hardly stand it. He'd been in the Marines way too long. If he had touched her she would have driven right off the road.

They didn't dare to speak to each other the rest of the way to Tyler.

Man, it was hot!

When she pulled into the bank parking lot, Violet couldn't stand it any longer. She threw her body across Mike. He could feel her heart pounding against his chest as she nervously said, "Thanks for fixing my flat, Mikey. I wish I could see more of you."

"I wish I could see more of you, Violet. I REALLY enjoyed the ride."

"Well, I guess I should go?" She said it like a question.

"Yeah, me too."

"Do you think I'll still get a good evaluation?"

"Is your boss a man?"

"Well, yes."

"You'll get a great evaluation, Violet."

Impulsively, Violet gave him a wild passionate kiss that made Mike dizzy. She rolled over his body and ran for the bank—mostly on her toes with the tiny heels tap tapping a funny tune on the sidewalk.

Mike grabbed his pack and stumbled out of the car. He walked down the street like he had been hit by a truck. As he walked past a woman who was washing the outside of her store windows she tossed her spent water toward the street and hit Mike squarely. Still in a daze he walked over, kissed her, and wandered on.

By contrast, the afternoon of that same day could not have been more different. Mike was approaching Swan, Texas, when a frantic woman in her mid forties slammed on the brakes and shouted, "Do you know how to drive?" Mike acknowledged that he did, and she cried out, "Please get in! Drive me to Paris!"

Mike got in and started to drive. "Please faster—as fast as you can!" Mike roared down the highway with the pedal to the floor. As they raced through Texas on U.S. 69 the woman regained some composure and explained that her husband had suffered a heart attack and that he was dying. On hearing herself say this, she understandably lost control again. After crossing this hump and settling down a bit, she explained that she was visiting with her mother in Tyler when she got the call from her brother-in-law Tom, who worked in a Paris civil engineering firm with her husband Willis.

Over the miles she let out more of the story. Her name was Marjorie. She and Willis Blocker had been married twenty-eight years and had two children, a boy and a girl. The girl was a senior in high school in Paris. The boy, Willis Blocker Jr., had been killed in the battle for Kwajalein. The whole company was wiped out when they climbed a hill, not knowing it was a bunker filled with high explosives.

"The Japs set it off with them standing on it. They knew the battle was over. They knew it was no use to fight on. It was just plain murder. They murdered my boy, and now they've killed my husband. Willis grieved himself into this—I just know it."

"Sir, I just want to get to my husband to tell him I love him just one more time. Can you understand that?"

Mike could indeed understand that sentiment. He thought of the friendship he had struck with Bob Frazier and how he had been killed on Guadalcanal without the chance to tell him goodbye. He understood all too well. He thought about the Canal. Had it really been four years? Why not eons ago? Why not yesterday?

They blasted through Lindale, Mineola, and Alba without slowing down. A state trooper began a chase near Ginger, but Mike kept it floored until they had to stop for gas in Emory. When they did, the trooper roared in behind them and drew his weapon. Mike didn't pay any attention to him as he grabbed the hose and started pumping the gas. Marjorie jumped between Mike and the trooper and urgently explained the situation. It turns out that he recognized the name Willis Blocker and asked if she had a son by that name. His son had been good friends with Willis Jr. and had died in the same explosion.

The trooper called ahead to set up a series of roadblocks at the danger points. The gas station attendant came out in a hurry wondering why Mike was pumping his own gas. Mike assured him that he knew what he was doing as he had worked two summers at Nuce's Texaco in Anderson. Mike pumped in twelve gallons, all she would hold, and shoved three dollars into the station owner's hand and told him to keep the change. Then they jumped back in and sped away with the trooper leading the way.

Running low on gas, the trooper handed off the escort duty to another trooper near Prattville who led them straight to the front door of the hospital in Paris. Marjorie jumped out and ran into the building, where she collared a unit clerk who led her to her husband.

He was still with it but very weak. They exchanged kisses, "I love you's," and goodbyes for maybe ten minutes and then he lapsed into a coma.

Mike parked the car and came up, but by then Mr. Blocker was unresponsive. Marjorie, her daughter May, their pastor Reverend Farris, and Mike stayed at his bed for a few more hours, and then he was gone.

When Willis died there was of course a great outpouring of grief. Mike stood in the back of the room as Marjorie, May, and Reverend Farris held each other and cried. One had lost a husband, one had lost her daddy, and one had lost a dear friend. Then Marjorie went over to Mike and said over and over, "Bless you, bless you, bless you. You got me here on time to say goodbye."

Marjorie's last statement cut Mike to the quick. What if he had gone to that motel with Violet? That kind of love was like a melting Popsicle on a hot day. This was real love. This love mattered, and he had almost made Marjorie miss her last goodbye for a meaningless fling.

Mike was ashamed. He sat on a bench in the corridor, and buried his face in his hands.

CHAPTER 21

The Saddest Man

Mike stayed for the funeral. It seemed to be the right thing to do. Tom, the brother-in-law, put Mike up for the few days before the funeral. Several members of Marjorie's family came up to Mike to thank him for driving her to Paris so quickly, and any number of them asked him to stay in Paris for a while.

Paris, Texas was a boom town. It had an atmosphere that seemed to raise a new building or open a new business with every breath. The subject came up one evening, and the answer seemed to lie in the fact that the people of Paris earnestly believed in the city and each other.

"Success is ninety percent pride," Tom postulated. "You have to believe in yourself and be excited about what you are doing. It's an unstoppable force, Mike."

Mike thought about how pride had almost perished during the Depression, and how this very growth he saw in Paris was one of the things he had fought for in the Pacific. Mike had seen so much destruction and futility on the islands. Now it was time for people to cheer, and work, and build. He wondered what would happen if Paris would ever lose its pride. He wondered if a thing like that, once lost, could ever bloom again.

The morning after the funeral it was decided that Marjorie's nephew Walter would drive Mike to Texarkana to make up for the good deed he had done for Marjorie and the extra time he had spent with the family.

He introduced himself to Mike as Wally. Wally shared some interesting thoughts during their time together on the road. The drive itself wasn't out of the way as Wally was heading to Atlanta to visit a friend and then to his home in New Jersey.

He was about the same age as Mike, but his war years had been spent in engineering school at the Naval Academy, with a direction toward naval aviation. Wally had all sorts of wild and visionary ideas. He was a lot like Mike's favorite author, H.G. Wells, in that regard. He actually believed that he would someday fly to the moon and "walk around." He also believed that humans would someday live in space, "Just as people do today in Chicago or New York."

It all seemed pretty far fetched to Mike, but he enjoyed the ideas and the enthusiasm with which Wally shared them. In his Pencil Man days Mike would sometimes watch the moon at night and imagine Wally waving back. Then he would imagine himself running on the moon.

They arrived in Texarkana a little past 2 p.m. Wally let him out at 7th and Hickory where Mike headed north along U.S. 67 and Wally went south to Shreveport. Mike felt funny and almost melancholy when he stepped out of the car and into Arkansas. Texas had been a large slice of life, learning, love, suffering, and humor. Texas had been a world unto itself, and Mike was uneasy with stepping into the unknown, as though a state line was some sort of portal to a different world.

A little south of Clipper, Arkansas Mike caught a ride with a long-haul driver who was moving a load of six-inch pipe. The driver's name was Adolph, and he was the saddest man Mike had ever met. Adolph was in his early to mid thirties, but he looked much older. He had lost his five-year-old daughter, his three-year-old son, and his wife of seven years when a tornado hit their home in Bristow, Oklahoma. Adolph had been a long-haul trucker even back then.

He was on his way home from Seattle and was less than a day from home when the storm hit. Adolph could see it ahead all night, as one can see distant storms in Oklahoma. When he rolled into Bristow he found busted studs, twisted metal, and shattered glass where his home had been. He also found a broken doll named Margaret, a teddy bear named Benny with a nail in his heart, and the locket that he had given his wife because he couldn't afford a wedding ring. To make things worse Adolph had to identify the mutilated bodies of his baby boy, his little princess, and the only woman he had ever loved, or ever would.

When Mike climbed into the truck Adolph didn't say a word. He didn't even look at Mike. He just listened for the door to shut and then he pulled out. Mike asked where he was headed and the driver said, "Little Rock." That was all he said for the rest of the trip. For the next hundred and twenty-eight miles all Mike heard were the sounds of the engine, the wheels, and the odd music that played as the wind passed through the pipes behind them.

When they arrived at a truck stop in Little Rock, Mike said "Thanks." Adolph didn't acknowledge. The whole atmosphere had been ominous and other worldly. In the truck stop diner Mike sat down with a cup of coffee to steady his nerves.

Another trucker walked over and sat down in the booth with Mike. "My name's Bill. His name is Adolph. I saw you get out of his truck."

Bill continued his story between sips of strong coffee.

"Adolph and I started trucking the same year. He lived next to me in Bristow. I was behind him the night of the big storm. We followed that storm all night across Oklahoma. We weren't sure what we would find when we got home."

Bill paused. He had a distant look. He took a sip, and continued.

"Of course you worry about the worst, but you don't really expect to see anything but your family scared and waiting for you. My house was right next door to Adolph's—hardly a scratch. The missus was shook and all, but she and the kids were fine. Adolph's home was a different story."

Bill went on to tell what Adolph found when he got home.

"It was the hardest thing I've ever seen. Adolph was my best friend, and here I couldn't do a thing for him. He just fell in on himself and sort of died.

"He never remarried. He never even looked at another woman. Even before—you know how it is—there's always some woman throwing herself at us guys. Most of us don't mind. Here we are far from home. Nobody will find out. You know what I mean? Not Adolph—he loved Mary Ann all the way—never a doubt.

"That day he just shut out the world. He doesn't speak to or look at anyone—not even me.

"During the war people treated him bad because of his name. They called him all sorts of stuff. Sometimes they'd give him one of those sieg heil salutes. They even slashed his tires once just because of his name. He took it all and said nothing.

"Now he just lives on the road like some ghost. He never bought another home—he doesn't have a home. If he ever sleeps, he sleeps in his cab. He just drives."

Mike thanked Bill for sharing the mystery. Bill stood up, took one last drink of coffee, and set the mug on the table.

Then he looked at Mike with a deep sad expression and finished with, "Someday Adolph is gonna be on one of those mountain roads and he'll fall asleep or something. He'll go right over. He won't do anything to save himself. He'll just keep driving."

Mike left the diner. As he walked across the parking lot a hooker tried to pick him up. Mike turned to her and yelled like a mad man, "GET OUT OF HERE!" Then he walked into the empty night, deep in his thoughts.

CHAPTER 22

The Free Man's Son

Mike was bone weary as he walked in the dark toward Memphis. He was so tired, but he couldn't sleep, too upset by Bill's midnight revelations and his experience with Adolph. Mike's mind was focused again on his only partially buried thoughts of dread.

For the first time in a while Mike bore his thoughts on Tony. Why didn't his mom and dad say something the last time Mike called? The war was over. The prison camps had been emptied. Surely by now Tony was either dead or at home. Maybe dad had encouraged Tony to walk home. Maybe Tony was messed up and needed to get his thoughts cooled down. Mike was worried for his brother, but he also had it fixed in his mind that Tony would beat him home in one of those old boyhood rivalries. This was quickly smothered by the vision of Jim Lester's body sliding, in slow motion, into the sea.

Suddenly Mike was jolted to his senses by the roar of a truck engine and the blast of an air horn. In his weariness and his disjointed thinking Mike had wandered too far onto the road. Mike jumped to the shoulder. The trucker slammed on his brakes and stopped a few feet ahead to see if he had hit the man.

The driver was the same Bill who had talked to Mike in the diner.

"Are you okay, boy?"

"I'm okay—I'm okay!"

"Well, get in here, son—you could have been killed! I'm going to Memphis. Is that okay?"

"Sure, that'd be great—thanks."

"You look beat, boy. I have a bed of sorts behind the seat here on top of my tool box. Crawl back in there and get some sleep."

It's hard to sleep in a noisy bouncing truck, but Mike was gone in seconds.

Three hours later they were approaching Memphis. The morning sun was starting to hit the eyes, so Bill stopped in West Memphis for breakfast at Big Ray's and to let the sun rise a bit.

Mike and Bill shared a good breakfast and a morning chat. They talked about trucking, war, and dames. Bill was no saint, but he was a good listener. He had wrecked his marriage with too many truck stop women, but he stayed clear of the drugs that some drivers used to stay on the road for longer hours. More than once he had turned a driver in for using uppers.

"I don't care if they kill themselves, but they make the road dangerous for everybody." The other drivers called him "Shep." Bill was kind of a shepherd, a real "go to" guy for the young drivers, and a long time friend of the veteran long-haulers.

After breakfast Bill drove Mike over the Mississippi and let him off on 3rd St. and headed east, hoping to make Knoxville to drop part of his load and sleep a few hours before moving on to Charleston.

Mike walked north looking for a way out of town. Several minutes later he paused just outside of a blues bar called Lena's. The whole bar was a tribute to Lena Horne, who had probably never seen the place. She was worshiped with photographs, old Lena Horne concert programs, and the standard and frequent toasts to "Miss Lena."

The big draw for Mike was the music. It pulled him off the sidewalk like he had no will. In the center of the room was a small brotherhood of musicians. They were all very old and accomplished. The keystone of the group was a musician named Aaron Wilkes, who was playing the saxophone so smoothly that one could skate on the notes.

After the set Mr. Wilkes looked over to Mike's table.

"You like the music. I can see it in your eyes."

"Yes, sir! I sure do. That's the best saxophone I've ever heard."

Mr. Wilkes replied, "That's not my best instrument. I play the piano too."

Mike was amazed. How could anybody play anything better than what he had just heard? Mr. Wilkes turned to the piano and made heaven sweat with a mellow version of *Stardust*. Mike was astonished, but Mr. Wilkes wasn't finished yet. He pulled out a violin and played a classical piece. Mike didn't know the name or the composer, but it was so inspiring his heart nearly stopped. Mike felt like shouting "Bravo!" but the crowd turned away in disgust.

"They hate it when I play like that. They come for blues or jazz—maybe a little Dixieland. I don't care. I'm ninety-five next month. I'm a free man. I can play what I like. My daddy was a slave. My twin brother Moses and I were named Moses and Aaron because we were born after he was free—in the Promised Land, so to speak. He used to work all day for almost nothing, but he'd come home and pull out that dollar or so that he had earned and say, "We might be poor, but we is free. Don't you forget that, boys.""

"That's why I play here. That's why we all play here. Lena's is off the beaten path. Down on Beale Street—that's where the tourists go. They go to be entertained. Here at Lena's they come because they can't help themselves. The music just pulls them in.

"See that little white boy over there? He's way too young to be in this place, but we let him stay. He buses tables for tips, but he'd do it for nothing. He has the music in him. He lives for it. It'd be cruel to send him away. His middle name is Aaron—just like my first name. I call him son and he calls me pop."

Mr. Wilkes laughed a satisfied laugh, and then he asked Mike where he was headed. When Mike told him he was hitching home to Indiana, one of the musicians named Stick pulled up his clarinet and started playing *Back Home Again in Indiana*. The others joined in for a set, and when they were finished Mike thanked them all and bade them farewell. He left a dollar on the table for the raven-haired kid, who returned the kindness with a shy "Thank you, sir. Thank you very much."

As Mike walked out of town he put a lot of thought into what he had just experienced. He thought a lot about the fate of a man. Mike thought about Bob Frazier. Why was he on that patrol instead of

Mike? Why was Bob killed and here he was following the Mississippi on a pleasant walk home? Mike thought about Freddie Alberts on Peleliu. A sniper's bullet whizzed past Mike's head—no more than an inch. Mike had heard the sonic crack and turned to see Freddie as the bullet took his life. "Why was Freddie killed and not me?"

"Why did I walk into that bar? Why wasn't I just one street over? I would have missed the greatest treasure if I had been just one street over and hadn't heard the music," he thought. "Why did I survive? When will fate's bullet strike me?"

It was heady thinking, and soon Mike would face a heavy dose of that fate.

CHAPTER 23

Peggy Lilac

Author's note: As I read the journal of my departed friend, I came across this section. I hesitated to add this part. It contains more evil than any other event of the Pencil Man's story, and I wouldn't blame you if you skip over this episode of Mike's life and just know, in the subsequent chapters, that something bad happened here.

This section involves the decision of a young man, far from home, who faces great temptation. Mike was a young man of stronger morals than most, but he was no exception to temptation's snares.

I do not wish to offend my readers, but I also see the need to include this section to explain Mike's later decisions. While it may show Mike's greatest failure, it becomes a lesson that eventually leads to a great victory in Mike's young life.

The day began on a comical note...

Mike took U.S. 51 north out of Memphis. It was a hot, muggy day. An hour or so later it began to sprinkle, which was okay with Mike. The rain washed away the sweat and cooled him off a bit. That would have been fine except that it picked up and began to downpour and wail. By the time he made Kerrville, Mike was soaked and miserable. It was nothing compared to the days of monsoon on Okinawa, but it wasn't like being home and curled up with a good book either.

At Kerrville Mike took shelter under the porch of the Kerrville Happy Pig Barbeque Restaurant, which was also a Sinclair filling station. The Happy Pig smelled delicious, but Mike thought he was too wet to go inside. He sat down on a bench outside next to an old geezer who called himself Checkers. Checkers seemed to be the "mayor" of the Sinclair station. He would run out to fill up the cars, wash their windows, and check the oil and the "tars," as he called them. He wore everyday bib overalls and had a Texaco hat that he thought made him look official. Mike supposed that Sinclair didn't mind as long as they got their money.

Checkers, of course, wanted to know all about this young stranger with the funny accent. This seemed to be another part of his job description.

The old man told a story of his wayward youth. "There was a bunch of barnstormers who came to Memphis one time. One of them was a gal, and boy was she purdy. Well, I got to bein' real smart-alecky with her—callin' out all sorts of things about her looks and all. Well, she come right up to me and she says, 'Hey, big boy, how'd ya like to go flyin' with me?' Well I puffed out my chest and said, 'Sure baby.' The next thing you know she had me loop-T-loopin' all over the place, and she even had me upside down fur a spell. Well, I sure learnt my lesson that day. Yes, sir, a woman will sometimes teach you things you don't want to know."

Mike laughed and thought about some of the "woman" lessons he had already learned on this trip.

The sun came out, so Mike stood out in its rays to help dry his clothes. When he felt sufficiently dry he walked into the Happy Pig and sat in a booth near the window. A waitress named Paula handed him a menu and asked what he wanted to drink. He ordered a cola, and when he saw the options he said, "Make that a vanilla cola." She smiled and when she returned with the drink Mike ordered a pulled pork sandwich and onion rings.

While the rings were frying Paula came over and asked, "Where are you headin', Sugar?" Mike explained that he was hitchhiking home from California to see some of the country he had fought for. She asked if he needed a ride and Mike said "Sure," kind of hoping that Paula was asking to take him herself. Instead she pointed to the "Singer Sewing Man" who was a Happy Pig regular and was heading north when he finished his lunch. Paula introduced the two and went about her business. The man asked Mike to join him, and when they were through Mike left Paula a good tip and departed with the "Singer Sewing Man."

The man's name was Carl Schleuder. He drove a big 1942 Chrysler Crown Imperial. Carl was a salesman by trade, but an engineer at heart. With every car that passed Carl would say the make, the model, the year, and the engine type and transmission. Mike didn't know but what he was kidding, but he sure sounded like he knew his business. Carl could even point out any defects based on the sound. Then Carl went so far as to tell Mike what day of the week the car was made. He said that he didn't have anything to go by on the older cars, but on the newer cars that were less likely to have any wear-related problems he had a system. He knew the normal sounds of each new car. If one of them didn't sound right he would say "Monday, Thursday, or Friday." He figured that everybody was in a bad mood on Mondays, they were planning their weekends on Thursdays, and they would do anything to get out the door on payday. Mike asked Carl about his own Imperial, and Carl said, drawing the response out with pride, "Wednesday." "They started her out at 9:45 in the morning and finished her up at 11:15—paint and all. I was there to watch the whole assembly."

Carl not only sold sewing machines, he could also field strip a Singer model 128 almost as fast as Mike could field strip an M1.

As they drove on the conversation drifted into family. Carl's talk of his mom and dad made Mike homesick for his own good parents. Then he showed Mike a picture of his wife Terri. Wow! She was a knockout. She was every bit as pretty as Veronica, and sounded a whole lot sweeter. Carl said how hard it was to be on the road so much, but that it was all the better when he came home to Terri.

It was probably the tone of Carl's voice as he talked of his wife that made Mike think of his own future. He began to wonder if he should hold off on Veronica and find someone more like Terri. He started to ask Carl if his wife had a sister, but he thought better of it and let it go.

Carl tried his best to sell Mike a sewing machine, but he couldn't override Mike's three best arguments. First, his mother had one; second, Veronica probably didn't know a needle from a bobbin; and third, how was he going to hitchhike all the way to Indiana with a sewing machine on his back?

It was closing in on 3 p.m. when Carl and Mike parted company near Eddyville, Kentucky. Carl drove on to Louisville and Mike started north toward Evansville on U.S. 641.

North of Repton, Kentucky Mike came across a county road that followed a creek. It hit him at a time that he was ready for adventure and its shade-lined path appealed to him on this still hot late afternoon.

Mike walked two miles or so without sighting a soul. Then he saw a jeep approaching, apparently heading for the highway. The driver stopped and offered Mike a ride. He said, "Thanks, but you're not going my way."

"I am now," she purred.

Her name was Peggy Lilac, but it wasn't her unusual name that Mike remembered. For one thing, she was driving a military jeep with all of the markings. For that to happen someone would have had to steal one from a military motor pool. However, Peggy had a demeanor that sucked the air out of any rational thinking.

Peggy was several years older than Mike, and a slight highlight of grey was mixing with her full carefree do of blonde hair, but she was the most sensuous woman he would ever meet. She wore a peasant blouse that hung over her shoulders and a skirt that had a varied and carefree length. When the road wind tossed her skirt about, she made no motion to control it like most women would. She spoke very little. Her movements and her smile were very seductive.

The road followed a creek and was heavily shaded. Obviously only the locals used this road, but the smell of the cool creek and the seclusion of the trees felt good on this hot day. Everything suggested pleasure—the pleasure of the scenic byway, the pleasure of the air, and the pleasure of Peggy Lilac.

A few miles from the highway Peggy turned sharply left, down a lane and over a wooden bridge. The lane wound deep into the woods to her home. She casually parked the jeep and invited Mike inside.

The home was an unusual design featuring a great room with a high ceiling and an open architecture that included the living room and kitchen. This was surrounded on three sides by an enclosed back porch, one bedroom, a utility closet, a storage closet, and a bathroom.

Peggy's ultimate goal was obvious. It was from the moment she picked Mike up, but she made no effort to rush him to bed. She pulled him in like slow-moving quicksand. She took his pack and his shoes and put them on the back porch, and then she eased him to the sofa and told him to take a nap while she fixed supper.

All during the meal she watched Mike like he was the main course. He was so nervous he could hardly eat. When they washed the dishes together they touched for the first time. The tension was unbearable.

After supper Peggy drew Mike a bath and left the bathroom. He got into the warm water—it smelled like lilacs. A few minutes later Peggy walked in with a smile and took all of Mike's clothes. She laid a towel and washcloth within reach and slowly walked out the door.

When he finished the bath he dried off. Having nothing else to wear, he wrapped the towel around his waist and walked into the great room. Peggy met Mike there and pulled him into her bedroom. "You'll sleep in my room tonight," she said in a provocative tone. Then she pushed him toward the bed, tucked him in with a soft kiss, and left the room.

Mike was confused. Should he chase after her? Was she coming back? Was she just an insufferable tease, or was she still setting the mood?

A few minutes later she came back. She took off her blouse and skirt and hung them up neatly on a rack attached to the wall. The backlight of the great room starkly highlighted her maddening silhouette. Then she walked out and locked the door from the outside.

"What is she doing? She's driving me crazy!" he thought. For the longest time she didn't return, and he couldn't hear her in the house. Mike became angry with himself. She was controlling him. This was wrong! What about Veronica? The room smelled like lilacs.

After the longest time Mike heard Peggy running water in the bathroom. She bathed herself with purposeful strokes. The sound of the water was smooth and seductive. His heart began to pound as she stepped out of the tub. She walked to the bedroom, unlatched the door, and crawled into bed with Mike.

For two hours or more she drove him mad till they were both exhausted. They each fell asleep with Peggy lying on Mike's chest.

Meanwhile, Mamalis was worried. She could sense that Mike was in trouble. She could hear his heart pound and feel his tension. She roamed the spirit paths to find her brother. Some evil force was holding her back.

When she did find Mike she was disgusted and angry towards him. "How could he do this? Who was this cheap whore with her brother?" Mamalis stomped her foot and shouted "YOU IDIOT!"

Mike, of course, was the only one who could sense his sister's presence. It stirred him just enough to feel Peggy tense up as she reached for something under the mattress.

Peggy raised the knife and plunged it into Mike's shoulder, while at the same time he moved just enough to avoid a life-threatening injury. From that point his anger and his Marine training went into action. Despite his wound he quickly had the knife free and Peggy down. He hit her once, twice, and a third time, until he was sure she was out cold. Then he took her neatly hung blouse and roughly tied her limp body to the headboard. Finally he took the bloody knife and threw it at the ceiling where it stuck high in the rafters—far beyond anybody's reach.

Searching the house for his clothes, he made a grisly discovery. His clothes were neatly packaged in his pack with his shoes near the pack and guarded by a shovel smeared with fresh mud. Mike quickly dressed and looked for something to compress his wound. He found a dish towel perfectly arranged on a rod in the kitchen. He folded the towel and pressed it to his bleeding shoulder, using the strap of his pack to exert added pressure to the gash. It smelled like lilacs and blood.

Mike ran from the house and down the long lane to the county road. The running made his heart pump the blood faster, but he had to get as far from her home as he could. No one knew he was there. If he passed out from his blood loss and Peggy worked herself free, he would be at her mercy—and he had already seen that in action.

The night was dark and terrifying. He could hear a pack of wild dogs in the woods and wondered if he might fall prey to them. He heard a scream of anger. Peggy was waking up. His heart pounded as he listened for the jeep to run him down.

Finally he made it to the road and ran for the highway looking for someone—anyone—to save him. Roughly two miles from the highway Mike spotted a sheriff's car parked along the road. His floodlight was pouring through the back window of an unfortunate teenage couple's car. The sheriff held his flashlight and had his hand on his weapon as he cautiously approached the front seat of the vehicle. Not seeing anyone in the car, he moved to the side of the road and shined his light down the hill on the couple, who were just getting a good start on a bad decision and blissfully unaware that they were rolling about in a patch of poison ivy.

The sheriff heard someone running on the road and spun around. He drew his weapon and caught Mike in his light. Mike shouted, "Help me! Please!" and then collapsed. The sheriff holstered his pistol and ran to the fallen stranger. Mike was able to give a brief account of what had happened before he passed out.

The sheriff growled to the teenagers, "Y'all get up here RIGHT NOW!" The couple did as they were commanded. The sheriff ordered them to take the stranger to Doc Kevin's house and to tell the deputy that he was going to Peggy Lilac's to investigate the attempt on the stranger's life.

The teenage couple carried Mike to the car. He was still bleeding, but beginning to come around again. The boy complained loudly that he didn't want the blood on his seats. The girl kept saying, "Shut up, just shut up!"

The young couple dropped Mike off at Doc Kevin's house and drove on to the deputy's home as the sheriff had ordered. After gleaning as much information as he could from them, the deputy escorted them home with a stern warning. He figured they would be punished enough by their parents and schoolmates. Then he rejoined Doc Kevin and called the other deputy to stand by for the sheriff's call.

The sheriff drove down the lane to Peggy's house. By now she had worked herself free and was heading for the jeep when she heard the patrol car. She hurriedly tried to clean up the mess. The sheriff pounded on the door and finally pushed it in when she didn't answer. There she stood—with a pile of blood-soaked sheets in her arms. The bloody knife was stuck in the rafters just as Mike had said.

Peggy had never gone after any of the local men. She drove them plenty crazy, but she knew that she would be caught if someone locally known came up missing. This time was different. She was found with the evidence in her arms. She had one weapon left. When the sheriff asked to see her bedroom, Peggy dropped the sheets and purred, "Gladly Sheriff."

When the sheriff failed to return, two deputies and a few men with shotguns formed a posse and went out to Peggy's house. They found Peggy, dead by her own hand, in the great room. The sheriff's body was in the grave she had intended for Mike. His clothes were neatly folded and placed between his legs. Over the next few weeks they found several more graves. They were all transients or strangers to the area. One of them was an Army corporal—probably how she came by the jeep.

Mike survived his wounds. After he had given his statement he was free to go. Doctor Kevin was amazed at how quickly the wound had healed. He didn't know that Mamalis had placed her hand on Mike's wound and had sealed it. She left the scar as a reminder, and then she hit Mike really hard to make it hurt again.

"Ouch! You little spook—that hurt!"

"Well, you deserve worse, you idiot! What were you thinking?"

Mike hung his head. "I wasn't thinking. I should have walked away, but I didn't. I've shamed my family. I've shamed myself. I've cheated on Veronica."

Mike welled up, as does a truly a repentant man. Mamalis wanted to comfort him, but she didn't. Mike was covered with poison ivy from being handled by the teenage couple. She didn't want to inadvertently heal him of that. She was mad at her brother and wanted him to suffer for a few more days.

CHAPTER 24

The Spittin' Baptist

Things were different now. Mike had stained his life with a deep dark sin. This was not a simple surrender to the impulses of youth. The incident with Peggy Lilac was different. It was like willingly giving his soul to the Devil in some satanic rite.

Mike was so close to home, and now he was ashamed to see his mother again. The pack seemed heavier as he walked up U.S. 60. There would be no more adventures on shaded county roads for him. In fact, Mike turned down several ride offers—especially the ones from women.

By the time he made Sullivan, Kentucky, Mike was tired, hungry, and broke. Peggy had stolen all of his remaining money. He thought of calling his dad, but Mike was too ashamed to go home yet. He decided that he needed a job for a few days to finish the remaining journey. Mike had no more thought this when an old man pulled alongside and shouted over the noise of the engine, "Hop in, son."

So started the adventure of the "Spittin' Baptist."

His name was Norman Peacock. It was a name normally associated with fine feathered elegance, but no one would ever link those thoughts with this man. To begin with, there was the truck. It was the ugliest truck Mike had ever seen. It had burlap feed sacks to cover the multiple holes and broken springs of the tattered seats. The outside of the truck was covered with rust, holes, and general oxidation. There wasn't a speck of paint or any hint of what the original color might have been. There was no muffler, there were holes in the floorboards, and a cloud of blue oily smoke rolled out of what was left of the tailpipe, obscuring the countryside for miles behind.

It may be cruel to say, but Norm was even uglier than the truck. His hair was sparse and scruffy. He had only slightly more teeth than the day he was born—and he had been born a long, long, long time ago. His most prominent feature was a four-star drool of home-grown tobacco, seeping in a constant flow from his mouth. As a result Norm did a good deal of "spittin'" as he called it. He had it timed so regular that one could nearly set their watch to the rhythm. As a rule Norm could make her fly a pretty good distance, but the inside and out of the driver's side door gave plenty of evidence that he didn't always hit the mark.

"Son, I could sure use some help for a few days. The crops need hoein' purdy bad, and my back is out again. I'll pay ya thirty dollars if you do a good job and can last a week."

Mike told Norm that he would be glad for the work. He explained that he had been robbed and that the thirty dollars should be more than enough to get him home. Norm held out his hand, and they shook on the deal. In addition he offered to let Mike stay with him and his daughter and promised to keep him fed.

Mike wasn't too sure what to expect on the second part of the deal. If the house was as bad as the truck it might not be safe to eat or sleep there. Still, he had to admit that on Okinawa he had worn the same clothes, slept in the mud, and survived on D-bars for weeks on end.

When they pulled into the farm it was in pretty sad shape. The house, the outbuildings, and the fences had the look of belonging to someone who was too old to maintain such an enterprise. To his utter shock, when Mike entered the house he found the extreme opposite condition. The inside of the farmhouse was neat as a pin. It was tastefully colored and decorated with simple lines, fragile antiques, and heirlooms. It had the clean smell of a well-kept home, mixed with the enticing fragrance of frying chicken and fresh-baked apple pie filtering in from the kitchen.

The centerpiece of this masterpiece was Norman's daughter, Norma June. Named after her father and her dearly departed mother, Norma June was an incredible piece of work. She was plain in her features—neither ugly nor beautiful. Her beauty welled from within, which made her plain features stunning. The words to describe Norma June would be peace, industry, welcome, tolerance, organization, and comfort. She would have made an excellent wife, or she could equally live as well on her own—comfortable in her own skin. She had had her share of beaus and could stir up another one if she chose, but her first love was her father.

Norman walked over to his daughter and gave her a kiss on the cheek that left a moist bit of tobacco juice. She smiled and waited till his head was turned before she discreetly wiped it off with a cloth that she carried in her apron pocket for such occasions. She would never embarrass her father for any reason of simple comfort.

She introduced herself to Mike with a warm smile, looking directly into his eyes as she spoke. In that instant Mike saw an angel. He had just danced with the devil and had barely escaped with his life and some of his soul. Here in front of him was the extreme opposite. He was humbled by her goodness and felt a twinge of love.

There was no hint that Norma June was upset with Mike's unexpected appearance. Neither was there any question but that he would join them for supper and sleep in the guest room. If Papa brought him home, that was enough.

Norma June excused herself to check on the chicken and the mashed potatoes. Then she came back into the living room and led Mike to his room. She told him that he had time for a bath and brought him a clean towel and washcloth. She instructed Mike to take a change of clothes into the bathroom and to feed his dirty clothes into the laundry chute that dropped into the basement near a fairly modern wringer washer.

Mike was a little uneasy with all that had just taken place. It was eerily similar to his experience at Peggy Lilac's house, and yet so different. Norma June's bath smelled like Pine-Sol and Bon Ami.

During supper Norma June noticed that Mike had some poison ivy rash. After she cleaned up the table and washed the dishes, she made up a paste for Mike to treat the rash. Her grandma had taught her a great deal about home cures.

When the evening chores were settled and Norman had come in from milking the cow, they sat in the living room and Norm spit out his chaw to read the evening scripture. They followed this with the hymn *There is a Balm in Gilead.* Despite his rough exterior, Norm had a golden tenor voice, and Norma June blended with a beautiful alto.

When Mike woke the next morning his rash was nearly gone, and he was ready to earn his keep. Norm showed him how to milk the cow and feed the animals, while Norma June fixed a generous breakfast of fresh eggs and bacon with pancakes and the best cup of coffee Mike had ever put away.

After breakfast Norm took Mike to the fields. He had a simple rotation of some twenty acres of corn, ten of tobacco, and fifteen or so of alfalfa for the horses and the cow. Norm still did his farming with horses, and Mike couldn't see how the old man kept up with it all. He supposed that was why the buildings and fences were in such poor shape. Norm already had all of the tobacco and about a quarter of the corn cultivated. Still there was plenty to do.

While it was hard labor in the hot sun, it was also good for Mike's soul. He worked every minute of daylight to get the job finished. One day he was working without his shirt when Norma June brought him a sandwich for lunch. She plainly saw his scar. The only thing she said was, "The corn is looking good. I see the poison ivy cleared up."

While Mike worked the fields Norm loaded up his chaw and spent his time caring for the animals, sharpening his tools, and mending his plow and planter. It took Mike just over a week to do all of the hoeing, but he didn't ask for any more money than the $30 he had been promised. On his last day he told Norm that he would scrape and paint the house for Norma June if Norm would buy the paint. There was no discussion of compensation from either man.

Almost another week passed before Mike was finished, but when he was Norma June was so pleased. She finally had a home that looked as nice on the outside as it looked inside. Mike in turn was thankful for all of the good meals and care. It was a pleasure to help two such fine people.

Mike finished around noon on Wednesday and told them that he was going to head home after he had a chance to clean up. Norm asked Mike to stay over till morning. He wanted Mike to join them for prayer meeting at the Baptist church that night. There was a special speaker that he wanted Mike to hear. Mike agreed to stay.

The preacher that evening was a fellow from England—Reverend James Beam. Reverend Beam was an interesting fellow and a great speaker. He began with some entertaining jokes and stories. He told about the revival in Georgia where the church sign said "Welcome all, young and old, for a faith revival gathering with the Reverend James Beam." The first night's crowd was disappointing.

"The next night some teenager changed the sign to say, 'Come get your fill of Jim Beam,' and we packed the house."

Then he made a joke about his home country. "I was visiting America and had to return to England sooner than I had planned. A concerned parishioner asked about my sudden absence, and the church secretary told her that I had unexpectedly gone on to the United Kingdom. The poor woman began to cry and asked if it was too late to send flowers."

He finished his introduction by telling the congregation that he had once been a doctor and had worked in Africa with Dr. Albert Schweitzer. While he was there he met a man who was working on a Bible translation in the Swahili language. In that culture the liver is considered the center of emotion instead of the heart.

"Come in to my liver, Lord Jesus," he shouted. The congregation laughed. "But you see, if they heard us say come into my heart, Lord Jesus, they would laugh.

"Both cultures are wrong. I am a doctor. I know that the emotions of a person lie within his or her brain, and that gives us a problem beloved. It is easy to believe that our emotions are controlled by our hearts, because we do not think with our hearts. We think with our minds.

"Therefore, when we are tempted by the Devil, or even when the Lord calls us, we respond not with the fickle mindless act of a heart. We do so with a conscious decision of our minds. We love to blame that benign unthinking organ we call a heart. We love to think that the Devil MADE us succumb to his temptation, but the truth is that we consciously decide with our own thinking minds to commit a wrong. We are not helpless victims. We are accountable for our choices and actions!"

Reverend Beam went on for several more minutes with arguments and examples to support his premise. Mike was frightened. All of his cover had been lost before this man's penetrating words. Reverend Beam was right. He was just as much to blame for the incident at Peggy Lilac's home as she was. In a sense he was more to blame than Peggy. It really was his choice and desire to succumb to her seduction.

When the altar call was given, Mike did so want to go forward, especially when they sang the verse that said, *"Just as I am and waiting not to rid my soul of one dark blot . . ."*

Still he did not step out and move to the altar. The next day the pack on his shoulder was just as heavy as the day he had first met the "Spittin' Baptist."

CHAPTER 25

Crossing Over

In the morning Mike woke up and helped Norm one last time with the feeding and the milking. Norma June outdid herself with the breakfast, prompting a bit of humor when Mike said, "I ate too much. I'm going to have to walk this off."

At the front door Norma June gave Mike a prolonged hug and thanked him for painting the house, but Mike thought there was more to the hug than that. They looked into each other's eyes one last time. Mike wondered if Norma June would ever find her true love, or if she would live out her days alone after Norm was gone. He also wondered for a long moment if he should stay.

Norm drove Mike back to the spot on the road where he had picked up the lost boy. He gave Mike thirty dollars in cash and a twenty dollar gold piece that he had buried when FDR was calling in all of the gold dollars. They bade each other well, and Norm drove off in an otherworldly cloud of blue smoke.

Standing alone in the silence of a Kentucky summer day, Mike felt very lonely. He wondered if the past few days had been only a dream—but then dreams never gave a fellow calluses.

Again Mike didn't have many opportunities for rides. The few drivers who did pass stopped, but he politely turned them down. Mike didn't feel like he would be good company. At Morganfield he stopped in a restaurant and ordered a sandwich to go and asked that they fill his small canteen with a cola. He already had a bag of peanuts that he had bought at a roadside stand in Tennessee.

Just north of Morganville is a large cemetery. Mike stopped there and had lunch with a man named Haywood. According to his headstone, Haywood had been dead since 1922. Mike figured that Haywood was about the same age as his dad, so Mike decided to spill his soul as he ate his sandwich, drank his cola, and shelled his peanuts.

Mike talked about the war, the men he had killed, and the friends he had lost before his eyes. He talked about the people he had met along the walk home. He told Haywood about Tony and asked if his brother was alive or dead.

Haywood didn't say either way.

Mike told Haywood about Shirley, and Norma June, and Veronica. He asked Haywood which one he would choose, but Haywood's wife was next to him, and he obviously didn't feel free to talk.

Finally he told Haywood about Peggy Lilac and what the preacher had said about making conscious choices even in the presence of strong temptation.

"I'm afraid to go home, Mr. Haywood. I'm afraid I've seen too much evil and didn't fight it enough. I'm afraid that I'll be a weak and unfaithful husband. I already feel like I've disappointed my parents. It's going to be hard crossing that river."

Haywood just listened. He didn't condemn. He didn't scold or give advice. Sometimes you need that in a friend.

Mike started to gather up the peanut shells from Haywood's grave, but they blew over to the next grave. He figured if Haywood wasn't getting along with his neighbor then that was between them.

As Mike passed through the double brick pillars of the cemetery entrance and back onto the road, he heard a voice in the wind, "I hope you figure it out boy."

When Mike reached Uniontown, he turned left onto Kentucky Highway 360. A half mile west of Uniontown Mike found a path that took him to a small wooded area on the bank of the Ohio River. As the sunlight dwindled he looked across to the southernmost point of Indiana. He could not physically or mentally cross that river.

There was enough sand on that part of the bank to make a good bed. Mike put on an extra shirt and used his pack for a pillow. There was nothing else to do, so he went to bed early. In the morning he would decide to either find a way across the Ohio or to walk away from home forever.

As he slept he dreamed he was in a cold place and couldn't get away. No doubt it was the night chill from the river that fueled his dream. Then the dream changed. He heard a crackle and smelled smoke. Mike began to feel warm—so much so that it woke him up. When he did he saw an inviting camp fire with the spirit of an old Indian chief warming his hands and facing Mike.

"You are troubled."

"Yes, Grandfather. Do you know why?"

"I know that your sister has a temper."

Mike rubbed his shoulder wound and laughed.

"The river is deep, and swift, and wide. How will you get across?"

"I don't know, Grandfather. I don't know if I want to go across."

"Because you fear an answer does not mean the answer will change. Do you have a better answer?"

"I have a lot of fear, Grandfather."

"A man's fears are always larger than his enemies. Have you ever been afraid to fight your enemies?"

"Yes, sometimes, but I fought them anyway."

"A good answer, Grandson."

With these words the fire died and Kikthawenund disappeared. In his place Mike saw a huge man in a rowboat facing the shore. The man in the boat said not a word nor did he make any gesture, but Mike knew that this was the time to make his decision. Mike gathered his things and stepped into the boat.

The man stunk to high heaven and appeared to be a hermit who lived on the river. As they crossed they did so at a bend of the river that was laced with powerful cross currents. A normal man would have struggled, but this man seemed more powerful than the river. He rowed, and rowed, and rowed. At one point a large tree trunk, which had broken off during a flood, came hurtling toward them. The man turned the boat just enough to miss being crushed. On the

Kentucky side of the river Mike heard the sound of a pack of wild dogs where he had just been. He heard the angry scream of Peggy Lilac—just as he had that night. Were these some demons that were barred by the river from stealing Mike's soul? All the while the hermit rowed and rowed—speaking not a word—showing no emotion.

When they reached the Indiana side the man turned the bow toward the bank and Mike stepped out. Mike said, "Thank you," but the hermit did not respond. He rowed back into the river and vanished.

Mike was home again in Indiana.

Now what?

CHAPTER 26

Landis and Lincoln

That last toe of land in the southwestern-most part of Indiana is more swamp than anything, but one can still find sporadic fields of corn on every tillable square foot. How the farmers get to the fields, however, is a mystery. This is where the mighty Wabash River meets the mightier Ohio and flows to the mightiest Mississippi.

There is a narrow dirt path that leads north from the river to Old Dam Road, the first road of any kind. Old Dam Road is a slightly wider gravel road that loops in any direction to Hovey Lake. The area is very rural, remote, and scenic. Mike had the initial thought that this was either a sportsman's paradise or a good place to dump a body. Here the gravel winds among the wild weeds and scruffy trees to a point where one begins to pick up the pavement again and the first state road, State Road 69.

Indiana 69 bends its way north along the river to the first town of any size, Mt. Vernon. It was there that Mike looked for a place to eat breakfast. To that point he hadn't had a ride. The few cars on the roads were driven by early morning fishermen who were headed south to the choice spots along the river.

In Mt. Vernon Mike found a farmer's gathering spot called simply, "Restaurant." The food, like the name of the place, was average, but it was crowded just the same. The tables were full, and I mean every seat. There were only two spots at the counter, and that was on either side of the biggest and blackest Negro Mike had ever seen. His arms were wider than Mike's strong legs.

Mike sat down and ordered his breakfast from the menu above the kitchen serving window. Then he said, "My name is Mike," and held out his hand to the dark stranger. The man looked genuinely surprised and returned with "Landis. You are some piece of work, Mike."

"Why is that?"

"Most Negroes won't have anything to do with a man as dark as me. Why would a white stranger want to give me the time of day?"

Mike swallowed his coffee. "Why not?" Landis didn't know how to respond, so Mike went on to fill the gap in the conversation. "What do you do for a living?"

"I'm an accountant."

Mike looked surprised, and Landis said, "I didn't think you'd believe me."

"I believe you, all right. I just don't picture a big guy like you sitting behind an adding machine all day."

"I don't need a machine. All I need is a ledger to write down the results. Give me some numbers."

"Okay, how about 183 plus 945?"

"Chump change, boy. Give me some real numbers."

"All right, Landis—694,672,679 plus 78,643,901."

"773,316,580."

"Divided by 387."

"1,998,234.05685. Of course, that's rounded off a bit."

Landis answered almost before Mike could draw a breath. "Wow! That's amazing! Where do you work?"

"Mostly I work odd jobs in places like this. I saved them $1,000 last year in taxes. They feed me as part of the compensation. Not much of a perk, is it?"

"I'm surprised. Why aren't you part of some big accounting firm?"

"Would you pick me out of a line-up for your accountant?"

"I'd be a fool if I didn't."

"There be lots of fools in this world."

"How many?" Mike joked.

"I can't count that high."

They both laughed. Then Landis asked Mike where he was heading. Mike replied, "Anderson."

"Sorry, I'd give you a ride, but I have a job this afternoon at a tool and die shop in McLeansboro, Illinois."

A man at the cash register spoke up and told Mike that he was heading to Evansville and would be glad to give him a lift. Mike thanked him for the offer and quickly finished his meal. He started to pick up his bill, but Landis cut him off and paid it for him.

"Thanks, Landis!"

"The pleasure's mine, Mike."

They shook hands and Mike left with the stranger. The man was a chain smoker. He would smoke one down as far as it could go and light the next one before the first went out. When the first one was spent he threw it out the window and went into a miserable smokers hack before he could put the next cigarette in his mouth.

"These things are killing me."

Mike asked, "Are you okay?"

"Okay doing,"

Mike thought that was an odd response before the driver added, "That's my name—OK Dewing," then he spelled it out.

"What does the OK stand for?"

"Nothing, my mom and dad had a weird sense of humor. I don't mind. I've had a lot of fun with the name."

As they rolled east down Indiana 62, Mike told OK his name and asked what the man did for a living. He told Mike that he was a professor of sociology at the university in Evansville.

Dr. Dewing had some interesting ideas about the workplace. He asked if Mike had ever heard of a woman engineer. He could tell by Mike's reaction that this was a foreign concept, and he pursued his point. He said that men and women are different. Mike couldn't argue that. He went on to point out that most products in America were purchased by women.

"Take the kitchen stove for example. Women use stoves more than men, so wouldn't a woman know what features would attract the customers?" A man might be the dominant buyer for a car, but there are options that might appeal to the woman's tastes that could seal the deal between two like models. It's like mixing peanut butter and jelly. Together they have a whole new attractive flavor. Think of the benefit a company would have if it had a good mix of male and female engineers."

It made sense. Mike thought of the employers who had foolishly written off Landis because of his color or his size. Later, in his factory life, Mike would notice how some jobs were performed better by men and others by women. It was a good mix, as Professor Dewing had said.

As they rolled down the road, Mike rolled down his window. It wasn't all that hot, but the air was too thick with OK's smoke. Mike was one of those rare servicemen who had never taken up the habit.

Several times during the ride Dr. Dewing exchanged cigarettes, and each time he went through the same routine and said the same words, "These things are killing me." Mike figured that if the doc had a dollar for every time he said that he could buy himself a pretty fancy funeral.

They parted company in Evansville on Ohio Street near the river. Mike thanked Dr. Dewing for the ride and the interesting conversation. OK Dewing wished Mike well on the journey home.

Evansville was the largest city Mike had traveled through since the start of the journey. It took him a while to find the eastern gates, so to speak. When he did he hooked up with Indiana 261 and headed northeast. Indiana 261 eventually merges with Indiana 62 near Boonville. Just past Boonville Mike heard the sound of a jeep approaching from behind him. It was the same sound he had heard when Peggy Lilac came his way, causing Mike to tense up in terror. His immediate military response was to dive for the ditch and prepare for a fight, but he held his fear in check and turned to face the foe.

To his great surprise, his "foe" turned out to be a fellow Mike had met at the Grand Canyon. His time was Ted King, and he had been a national park ranger at the canyon. Mike felt like a fool as Ted pulled alongside and cheerfully offered him a ride.

In the first few minutes of their conversation Mike found out that if he had worked a month more at the canyon he could have caught a ride straight through with Ted.

"I put in for an assignment back here in Indiana so I could be closer to my folks."

"I didn't know there was a national park in Indiana."

"The Lincoln boyhood home is just a few miles from here. It's not as beautiful as the canyon, but there's a whole lot less walking, and the history is thick. You know how I love the history part. It's not actually a national park yet, but they've built a fancy new visitor center that leads me to believe that it will go national in a few years. The state of Indiana was sold on my national park experience, so it was an easy hire."

"It sounds like a good fit to me, Ted. Hey, did you bring your trumpet?" Ted was great on the trumpet. He'd go to the edge of the canyon in the evening and play. It had the effect of a mile-wide concert hall. Ted's playing was magical, and the acoustic effect was incredible.

Ted had been in Indiana only a few weeks and had made a day trip to Evansville to buy a new pair of boots. It was just dumb luck that he came across Mike on State Road 62. They drove to where Indiana 62 and U.S. 231 merge and go north to the park. Instead Ted turned south on 231 to go to Chrisney, Indiana.

"It's a little out of the way, but it's the nearest place to eat supper. You'll love it, Mike."

"Good food?"

"Have you ever known me to frequent a place just because of the food?"

The place was called the Billafare. It was run by a doll named Marianne. Every guy in the place had his eye on Marianne, but she had a wedding ring the size of a brass knuckle and a boilermaker husband. There wasn't an ounce of fat on the man, but he had plenty of muscle.

On the plus side, Marianne had a cousin named Mary Jo who was a real heartbreaker and the waitress who earned the biggest tips in the place. She was fair game, and needless to say, Ted quickly became a regular.

Mike spent the night with Ted in his quarters at the Lincoln Boyhood Memorial. A park ranger's housing is somewhat sparse, but the neighborhood is top Jones. Mike and Ted had a good talk that night. They caught up on some of Mike's trip and the goings on at the Grand Canyon. Like the canyon itself, things never really changed much. Mike's old mule concession boss, Mr. Lee, had his ribs broken by one of the mules again. It was his eleventh time. Each time he would complain "I'm getting too old for this," but he wasn't likely to quit his job till the mules sprouted wings. Mike didn't bring up the incident with Peggy Lilac.

The next morning Ted showed Mike around. There was a small museum and the Lincoln home site, with a mile or so of trail between them. Midway on the trail was the grave of Nancy Hanks, Lincoln's birth mother. It was a place in the woods that commanded solemn respect and a moment to pause. The home site wasn't much to look at if it weren't for the historical significance of the place. Ted said that there were plans to build it up to look like it did when Lincoln lived there. The most interesting part for Mike was the remains of the old buffalo trace the Lincoln family had used to travel from Kentucky to this place. Mike was also impressed with the story Ted told him about how the Lincolns had lived that first winter in a "half-faced camp," which was nothing more than a brush pile lean-to that was open on one side to a campfire for warmth. The whole place was thick with integrity. It made Mike feel very small.

After the personal tour Ted needed to get to his regular duties. They shook hands and parted company.

Walking east on Indiana 162, Mike thought about all of the things he would have been spared if he had waited to travel north with Ted. He also thought about all of the lessons he had learned. No doubt about it, his dad was right. But could he ever face his father again?

CHAPTER 27

Fr. Pelemon and the Sisters of St. Benedict

It wasn't long before Mike passed through the town of, believe it or not, Santa Claus, Indiana. It was just a spot in the road with an unusual post office. Mike stopped in for a drink of water out of sheer curiosity. He learned that the parents of children from all over the country would send their Santa letters here to have them responded to and postmarked during the Christmas season.

There was also a small amusement park with a giant statue of Santa Claus, a few small rides, and some "Santa's workshops." One of the rides was a miniature train with a shiny black engine. Another featured a circle pond with small boats for the kids. It was like a merry-go-round on water. It sure seemed like an odd out-of-the-way spot for an amusement park. It hadn't been open for more than a few weeks, but it was a nice place for families. Mike met the owner, Louis Koch, who was from Evansville and had nine kids. He figured that any guy with nine children had a pretty good idea of what families would enjoy, but would anybody come to such a remote place?

At the eastern edge of Santa Claus, Indiana 162 turns north. The road is fairly wide and is dotted with well-cared-for farms. This is a predominantly German Catholic part of the state, where the owners of the various properties show that typical German pride in keeping their places nice. This is also a place of big skies and rolling prairie. Like the hill country of Texas, there seemed to be but a thin layer of blue sky between God and man—a place good for the soul.

Mike walked seven miles and capped a hill to an amazing sight. Ahead and just east of the road rose an ornate "castle" on a dominating hill. He could see that it was located in the next town ahead. One mile more and Mike could see the town's name, "Ferdinand."

Once inside the town the view of the "castle" was obscured. Mike walked the main street north, looking up every eastbound street to catch a glimpse of the "castle." Finally he came to 10th St., where he could see an old cemetery behind an ornate Catholic church. Walking a block or so, Mike could begin to see the "castle" again. It was a very steep and fairly long hill, but his curiosity pulled him up like a magnet.

Mike's "castle" was indeed ornate, with fancy scrolled columns, stained glass, and a large dome. Spiral staircases, enclosed in brick towers, led from the lower level of the hill to a wide colonnade that surrounded the front of the structure and overlooked miles of beautiful Indiana countryside. There was a cemetery in front of the building that revealed the true nature of Mike's "castle." This place was the monastery of the Sisters of St. Benedict.

When he first saw the "castle," Mike didn't know what it was or where he was. He had never heard of Ferdinand or the monastery of the Sisters of St. Benedict. If he had not met Ted on the road from Evansville, Mike would have traveled more directly north on U.S. 231 through Dale and Huntingburg. He would never have seen Ferdinand from that route. If Ted hadn't gone to Evansville that day for a new pair of boots, Mike would not be in this place. It was as though God had called Mike to this, his mountain, and as if God were saying, "Sit down Mike—we need to talk."

For some reason there weren't any nuns on the grounds. They must have been inside doing whatever nuns do at that time of day. No one saw Mike—or so he thought.

Sister Basilia was on her way to the sacristy when she happened to glance out the window just in time to see Mike walking toward the grotto. It was a beautiful garden that had just been erected that summer. Everything about it was appealing to the eye and heart, so it was her natural reaction to look its way when she passed a window.

What Sister Basilia saw this time was a young man with a heavy walk and a troubled expression on his face. She had a very strong feeling that God wanted her to keep an eye on the young stranger, so she quite literally began to watch and pray.

Sister Margaret was a music teacher who had taught the children of Ferdinand for years. She was a favorite of all who knew her. She was very fun loving, and a good religious Sister. Over her service she had influenced many by her example to join the order. Sister Margaret's greatest asset may have been that she was also a good shepherd. She had an eye for the unusual and, passing in the hall, she quickly noticed that Sister Basilia was engaged in something very important.

Sister Margaret asked Sister Basilia if something was wrong, and Sister Basilia pointed out the troubled man in the grotto and shared her sudden urge to keep him in prayer. Understanding the situation, Sister Margaret offered to complete Sister Basilia's duties in the sacristy to free her up for this more immediate task. Then she went to Mother Superior and explained the situation so that Sister Basilia would be free to continue serving the young man's needs.

As Mike walked through the grotto, he noticed the beauty of the flowers and compared it to his life. It brought him more shame. He walked the stations and compared them to his own spiritual walk. Again he was ashamed.

Mike knelt and lit a candle for his brother. As he watched the flame flicker, Mike began to concentrate on Tony. He thought about the fact that he had failed to rescue Tony. He thought about how Tony had always been the better man. He wondered if Tony was alive, and was less sure that he was. Mike thought about how much he loved Tony, and his sister, and his mom, and his dad, and Grandfather, and especially Veronica. Mike felt so unworthy to be in their presence, let alone to feel their love as it had once been.

As he slumped on the kneeler in front of his brother's candle Mike heard a voice saying, "Light a candle for yourself." Mike hesitated, and then he lifted his hand to pick up the candle lighter. He lit it with the flame from Tony's candle. His hand shook as he tried to light his own candle. From the window Sister Basilia had watched Mike light the first candle and sensed that it was less a significant act than the second. Something told her that this was a candle that must be lit, so she prayed with an audible plea, "Light the candle!" Instead Mike slammed the candle lighter down and stood with his back to his brother's candle. He ran his hands through his hair and tore at his scalp. Then he kicked over a statue of St. Benedict, which plowed into the fresh soil of a flowerbed—destroying a stand of petunias.

From her vantage point Sister Basilia could see an afternoon thunderstorm gathering. She started to pray that it would spare the boy, but then she hesitated—sensing that this, too, was a part of God's plan. At first Mike just stood there and let it rain, but the human urge for comfort took over and he walked to the southwest stair tower of the colonnade, where he found a sheltered spot away from the flow of the water.

The rain set in for the night. Sister Basilia skipped supper and spent the evening at prayer in the sanctuary so that she could be physically closer to the young man in the tower. After dark, when she was sure he was asleep, she took her own pillow and blanket to Mike. Sister Basilia covered the cold troubled man and placed her pillow under his head. Then she kissed his forehead as a mother would a child and slipped back to her prayers. That night Mike dreamed of angels.

Mike awoke the next morning to the sound of a beautiful chorus of female voices. It was Sunday, and the music of the Mass was within range of his staircase shelter. Mike hadn't been to Mass in over a year, and that was a hurried arrangement in the middle of an Okinawa battlefield. It was led by Chaplain Paul Redmond, who was tougher than nails. The sounds Mike heard now were not tough. They were not of war. These were the sounds of peace—and right now he wanted peace.

Mike rose and folded the blanket. He cleaned himself up as best he could from a small puddle of rain water, climbed the stairs to the colonnade, and slowly walked to the doors of the monastery. Mike followed the singing to the sanctuary and opened the door. He crossed himself with holy water, genuflected, and sat as far in the back as possible.

Sister Basilia was near the door of the sanctuary. She was terribly haggard from the all-night prayer vigil. She had suspected that if the young man came into the sanctuary at all he would sit in the back. In line with this thinking, she had positioned herself to observe him from a discreet location.

The priest that day was a man from Jamaica who was studying at nearby St. Meinrad. His name was Father Pele, but the sisters called him Father Pelemon because he always called any man he saw "mon." He called the plumber the "plumber mon" and the gardener the "gardener mon." He even called the Bishop the "Bishop mon."

The gospel that day was on the story of Zacchaeus. His homily went something like this:

"Now that Zacchaeus mon was not a bad mon. When faced with the temptation of money, he CONSCIOUSLY chose to cheat people. No one made him do this but himself. Likewise, when he saw the goodness of Jesus he CONSCIOUSLY chose to repent of his evil ways and make restitution to those he had cheated. So you see, Zacchaeus was a good mon who had made bad choices. When he CHOSE to repent and to start living his life as he should, the bad that people saw was washed away like so much dirty mud. The good mon was always there, but the dirty mud of his sin covered him up so that people had only seen him as a bad mon. The devil did not make him a dirty mud mon. He chose to crawl in the mud. Jesus saw the good mon under all of that dirty mud, but he did not make Zacchaeus wash off the dirty mud. Zacchaeus made the CONSCIOUS decision to wash off the dirty mud and to live life as a new, clean, and happy mon."

Mike was shocked. This was exactly what the Baptist preacher had said. Sister Basilia saw Mike's strong reaction to Father Pelemon's words. She was sure now that the young man had some troubling sin to confess. As the Mass ended, Sister Basilia raced to Mike's pew and pushed him over one seat to block him from a quick exit. She quickly pulled down the kneeler, which forced Mike back into the pew, and started praying to buy time. When Farther Pelemon was halfway down the aisle, she abruptly stopped her prayers and asked Mike if he had slept well the previous night.

"Well, yes. Were you the one who gave me the blanket and pillow?"

Sister Basilia evaded the question and asked his name. By that time Father Pelemon was at the end of their pew, and she grabbed his arm and pulled him around saying, "This is my friend Mike. He's going to stay with us for lunch. After lunch will you hear his confession?"

Neither Mike nor Father Pelemon had a chance. The next moment Sister Basilia had a "mon" in each hand and was pulling them to the dining room. During the meal Sister Basilia, Father Pelemon, Mike, Sister Sylvia, and Sister Margaret sat around the table and swapped pleasantries and stories. Mike's story, of course, dominated the conversation after Sister Basilia asked him what had led him to the monastery. Mike's general account of his war service and his travels was fascinating enough, but he avoided the story of Peggy Lilac.

Knowing that he hadn't hit on the real reason for his actions in the grotto, Sister Basilia asked Mike if he had had any trouble along the way.

"In all of that distance there must have been a storm or something that caused you some sort of setback."

Mike lowered his eyes and said with a repentant tone, "I took a wrong turn in Kentucky."

That remark might normally have caused some laughter, but the pained look on Mike's face was a clue to everyone that Mike had a problem to unload. Mike fought hard not to break down in tears. Father Pelemon did his best to fill the awkward gap till the post-luncheon prayer was said. He then hurried Mike out of the dining hall and to a small room off the main parlor that was perfect for a private talk.

It was unheard of for a confession to be made face-to-face, but Mike had just had lunch with Father Pelemon, so it seemed funny to hide behind a partition at that point. They found the room off of the parlor and closed the door.

They sat at a slight angle to each other in two very comfortable overstuffed chairs, which seemed really strange for a confession. Mike started with the usual "Forgive me, Father for I have sinned."

Father Pelemon stopped him. "Let's just make this a talk, mon to mon. What did you do in Kentucky that was so bad?" Mike was a little taken aback, but he could see that Father Pelemon was a square shooter, so he told him the story of Peggy Lilac, and about the near miss on the road with Violet, and the war, and how he had failed Tony. Once he allowed the door to open a crack it just poured out.

Finally, when Mike had told all that he could, he said, "I wish there were a way I could ask God to forgive me for messing up the life he gave me."

"It's too late for that, mon."

Mike's heart sank. "You mean, I'm too far gone to ask forgiveness?"

"No, mon—it's too late—God has already forgiven you. Why else would he have brought you here?"

"Is that it? Isn't there some sort of penance—some Hail Mary's—some Our Father's?"

"Yes, there is a penance. It is the hardest one I will give to any mon."

"I'll do anything, Father. I owe him that. What is my penance?"

"Forgive yourself."

"Is that it?"

"Is there anything harder to do?"

"No, I guess not." Mike then unbuttoned his shirt and showed the scar from his knife wound. "But how will I explain this?"

"When a mon sins there is always a scar, but God forgives and has no time to look at scars. You can only make the scar deeper and uglier if you do not tell the truth about the scar. Do not say it was a war wound. Tell your mother the truth. If God has forgiven you, what right does your mother have to condemn you? Now go and make no more scars."

Mike went out to the grotto, where he reset the statue and washed the mud from St. Benedict's face. He replanted the flowerbed the best he could—taking a few petunias from the surrounding flowerbeds to fill in and hoping he wasn't going to have to do a confession on that act.

Then he knelt and lit a candle next to Tony's for Father Pelemon, and another for Sister Basilia—and one for himself.

CHAPTER 28

Thumbing to College

Mike stood up from his prayers, but before he could turn to leave he heard a voice say, "What is it like to sleep outdoors?" It was Mother Superior. "Sister Basilia told me that you slept in the stairwell last night. Do other people do this?"

"Well, yes. People who camp out or men who go to war sleep outside. You'd be surprised at the number of people who have no home. Most of them are hobos, but I've seen entire families on occasion."

"Then I must learn to sleep outside so I will understand their suffering."

"Well, it's not all suffering. There are things one can see and experience that can't be realized any other way."

"Show me."

Thus began Mike's boot camp for nuns. He explained that the first step is to find a place to sleep. This being her first time, Mike insisted that Mother Superior use a blanket for ground cover, another to keep the chill out, and a pillow. She in turn insisted that Mike would have the same to keep things even, so she left Mike and came back with four blankets and two pillows. "Now where should we sleep?"

Mike told her that he had slept in a number of situations. "I've slept in mud. That's nice because it's soft. Sleeping on a grassy hill is good too, but anytime you sleep on the ground you always have to put up with insect bites and ground moisture. Let's try for the colonnade tonight."

He showed her how to pick out a spot with potential cover and drainage in case it rained during the night. Then she asked about food. Mike explained to her that he usually ate at a restaurant, but that he always carried cans of hash and pork and beans in case he would need them. He showed Mother Superior how to find wood seasoned enough for a fire and how to start and build a fire suitable for cooking. This they did on the front lawn—much to the chagrin of the "gardener mon."

Word began to spread, and soon there were nuns coming out of the woodwork with blankets and pillows. For several hours Mike told them tales of his family, and the war, and his trip across America. The nuns conducted their evening vespers on the colonnade, the fire on the lawn burned out, and they all lay down for the night. In the rural darkness of tiny Ferdinand the nuns saw stars and shooting stars as they had never seen them. They heard the special sounds of the nocturnal animals. All was well in God's great world. The next morning they woke up terribly stiff and mosquito bitten, so they never tried sleeping out again, but they also remembered the "not all suffering" parts for the rest of their lives.

Mike ate breakfast with the nuns and attended a morning prayer service. Then he bade them goodbye with an exchange of "God bless you's" all around.

That day Mike walked with a renewed step. His pack was lighter on his shoulders, with the exception of a bag of breakfast rolls freshly baked by Sister Gustavia. Mike was glad these were German Catholic nuns.

Traveling north again on Indiana 162, Mike turned east when he reached Indiana 64 near Bretzville. A few miles east of there, near Kyana, Mike caught a ride with a fellow named Joe. Joe had driven his buddy's car to Jasper to buy a set of plugs and a distributor for his '33 Chevy. Joe was a nice fellow who seemed to always be struggling to keep his head above water. He was from French Lick, a town that was struggling to keep its head above mineral water. French Lick had once been a thriving resort based around its mineral springs, but it was now in decline along with the entire town economy.

On their way north to French Lick, Joe spoke of the Depression and how hard it had been on the family. He spoke of his wife and how proud he was of her. He didn't speak of any plans for the future. He was just trying to do the best he could on a day-by-day basis. Joe was the kind of guy you'd give a million bucks to if you could. He was decent, and honest, and a truly good man. It was hard to see the struggle—and the bit of fear—in his face. Mike quietly slipped a ten into Joe's sack of car parts. He still had fifteen dollars and his twenty dollar gold piece left to make it home. That would be plenty for his needs.

When they parted at French Lick, Joe gave Mike instructions for a more direct route through Orangeville to Orleans.

Orangeville wasn't more than a spot on the road, but Orleans was interesting. Orleans is an old Indiana hill country town that features a large town square and ornate architecture. Its best feature is that it is on Indiana 37, the main artery from southern Indiana to Indianapolis. Mike found a great café on Maple Street that had the best hamburger he had had on the whole trip. Maybe it was so good because Mike was in a part of Indiana that was more familiar to him. When he was a boy his family had traveled through Orleans to see Marengo Cave. In fact they had stopped at this very café for lunch.

From this point north Mike didn't need a map to find his way. The next town was Mitchell, Indiana. Mitchell is the heart of the limestone industry and the home of Spring Mill State Park—one of the great state parks in America. The limestone used to build the Empire State Building came from quarries in this part of Indiana.

On the north side of Mitchell, Mike caught a ride to Bloomington with one of the best-known men in Indiana. Herman B Wells was the president of Indiana University. He was returning from a business conference that had been held at the inn at Spring Mill Park. His car was nice but not new. The conversation was lively.

It was clear from the exchange that Herman Wells had the mind of a collegiate leader, but he was as common as a street sweeper. Dr. Wells clearly loved his students, and for that matter, young people in general. He was intensely interested in all aspects of Mike's story, but when Mike mentioned the state track meet he shouted, "Oh, I was there! That was the most electrifying footrace I have ever seen. I was hoarse from shouting when you boys crossed the line. Tell me all about it from your perspective. I want every detail." So Mike told Dr. Wells the inside story as I have told you in the early part of this account.

Dr. Wells went on to encourage Mike to take advantage of the G.I. Bill. Mike told him that his grades in high school had been only fair and that he had never considered himself college material.

"Nonsense, Mike. I can tell by listening to you that you have a great mind and that your life experience has made you more mature than most of our students. Please don't rule it out. If you change your mind please call me." With that he fished for a business card and handed it to Mike.

"The number on the back is my home phone number. You call me and I'll make sure you get admitted. I'll have someone from my staff guide you through the process, and I'll make sure you get a job on campus to help with the finances."

Later Mike did give it serious thought, but by that time he had his secure job and a family to think about, so he let it drop. One thing he didn't drop was his utter admiration for Herman Wells. He didn't think it was possible for anyone to hate the man. For that matter it was hard to just like the man—you had to love him.

Dr. Wells dropped Mike at the corner of Walnut and 3rd. "I'd take you farther, but I have a meeting in one hour," Dr. Wells said as he rolled his eyes. "Oh, to be a teacher again."

"It's been a great honor, sir."

"Well, Mike, it's been my pleasure. Your company has taken an otherwise mundane drive and made it very enjoyable. Good luck to you, son."

With that, Mike took leave of one of the greatest men in Hoosier history. He had to laugh. Here he had barely made it out of Anderson High School, and now he had been accepted into Indiana University merely by sticking out his thumb.

From there a guy in a garbage truck took Mike a short distance to Sample Road. Another two miles up the road a farmer named Oliver took Mike on board his truck loaded with sweet corn. Oliver was taking the load to a fruit stand just north of Martinsville. The location was good. Martinsville is the gateway town to the hills of southern Indiana. A lot of people would come down on the weekend to go to the state parks—Brown County, McCormick's Creek, or Spring Mill. Others would go to hear the country music stars at the Little Nashville Opry. Most people came when the leaves changed in the fall, but there was still good traffic before the schools opened after Labor Day. Some of Oliver's best customers came from the nearby Stines Mill Methodist Church.

"Those people are always having a church dinner. They pray more for their food than they do their pastor."

Mike stuck around and helped Oliver unload his truck, for which Oliver gave him a box of good Indiana-grown cherry tomatoes and an ear of sweet corn.

It was getting late in the day so Mike looked for a place to bed down. The very same branch of the White River that passes through Mike's hometown also parallels Indiana 37. He found a place just off of the highway where he could take a bath and fix up a campsite. There was also a high bank that was soft with sand. It would make a good place to sleep. That evening Mike made a meal of his last can of hash, roasted sweet corn, tomatoes, and some of Sister Gustavia's breakfast rolls. He was getting anxious now. One more day—maybe two—and he would be home.

CHAPTER 29

Back Home Again

Mike woke to the sounds of fish splashing in the river. It was still dark, but there was every indication that this was going to be a good day. Up the road a piece near Smith Valley Road, Mike hooked up with a farmer pulling an empty horse trailer. His daughter had won a blue ribbon at the Morgan County Fair and was showing at the State Fair later that morning.

The empty horse trailer was the interesting story. It seems that he had taken his daughter to the fair a few days before and they were planning on staying the week. His wife wanted to go too, but she was nearing her delivery for their fourth child—so far all girls. Then the news came that his wife was in labor and was calling for her husband. The daughter stayed at the fair with her horse and a family from Howard County whose daughter was a close friend and competitor.

The farmer made some hasty arrangements for his daughter and jumped into his truck with the trailer still attached. He was too far along to go back when he noticed the empty horse trailer rattle-t-banging through the streets of Indianapolis and down Highway 37. He drove straight through to the hospital in Bloomington and arrived in time to catch the last seven hours of his wife's wrath and her intense labor. A few minutes before dawn their fourth child was born. I know what you are wondering, but do you really need to ask? An hour later he kissed his wife goodbye and raced back up the road to arrive in time for his daughter's State Fair show.

Approaching Stop 11 Road, Mike could see the farmer drifting off to sleep, so he told the farmer to pull over and Mike drove from there. He had never towed a trailer before and it took a bit of driving to get used to the difference, but it didn't take too long to adjust. The trailer rattled like crazy, but the farmer quickly fell asleep and drowned out the noise with his snoring.

They drove north on 37 till they saw the giant IPALCO smokestacks, where 37 picks up Harding Street. Harding connected with Raymond Street, where Mike turned east to Meridian Street, the center north-south artery in Indianapolis. The corner of Meridian and Raymond Street looked like any intersection in any small town, betraying the great city just a few blocks north. Beginning at Merrill Street the buildings began to grow tall. At South Street and Meridian they passed the Slippery Noodle, the oldest blues bar in town, with its trademark "Dis is it" slogan.

Passing under the Union Station tracks, Mike could begin to see the Soldiers and Sailors Monument on the Circle. Just before the Circle they crossed the prominent east-west road of the city, Washington Street. The history there was thick. Mike's heart began to leap with his own memories.

Washington Street follows U.S. 40, which is the old National Road that opened up the "West" in the early days of our country. It passes by the Indiana Theater, a giant ornate palace of plays, movies, and big band music. Hoagy Carmichael, Glenn Miller, Tommy Dorsey—they were all regulars. Near the Statehouse on Washington there is a marker where Abraham Lincoln made a speech on his way from Springfield to the White House in 1861. Mike remembered that marker from a scouting trip he had made as a kid.

One block more on Meridian and Mike was back at the true heart of Indiana—the Circle. A person has to be there and see it, or go up in the Monument to look out across the city. Perhaps one just has to be a Hoosier to understand what it means for a Hoosier boy, long parted from his home, to see Monument Circle again.

Mike drove around the Circle three times, horse trailer and all, and then he drove north on Meridian toward the Fairgrounds. As he made the turn back onto Meridian, Mike thought of Bob Frazier and how they had planned to get a steak at St. Elmo's when they returned from the war. He couldn't have eaten anywhere at that moment as a big lump took possession of his throat.

His tears were gone and the excitement kicked in as Mike turned east again onto 38th Street and drove to Fall Creek, the intersection that borders the Indiana State Fairgrounds. Turning into the main entrance and then right towards the stables, they found the Morgan County winner's stall with fifteen minutes to spare before the show. The farmer woke up with a jolt as Mike hit a rut in the grass where they were to park. He thanked Mike and walked briskly toward the Coliseum to watch his daughter compete.

Mike decided that he would stay long enough to finish the story. He watched from the stands as the Morgan County girl was awarded the blue ribbon. She was beaming from ear to ear when she won the award, and she broke into uncontrollable tears when she spotted her dad in the stands. The farmer hurried down to give her a hug, and from their body language Mike could tell that he was giving her the news of her new baby sister. It was one of those moments when a young unmarried man looks into the joys of a family from the outside. It's the kind of thing that makes a bachelor give serious thought to marriage and children of his own—a sort of longing in the heart that he had begun to feel when Marjorie lost her husband in Paris, Texas.

Mike left the grounds of the Indiana State Fair and stopped on the corner of 38th Street and Fall Creek to eat lunch at the Tee Pee restaurant. The hamburger was great, but desert didn't work out so well. He wanted a piece of coconut cream pie, but they were out. He settled for a dried-out piece of peach pie that had obviously survived the previous night.

After lunch Mike made his way east on 38th Street. He had a real sense of the homestretch when he angled onto Pendleton Pike, which is Highway 67, the main drag between Indianapolis and Anderson.

First there was the small town of Lawrence. While still in the hospital in Hawaii Mike had met an Army Air Corps pilot from Lawrence by the name of Ricketts. Paul was visiting a friend on Mike's ward, who in turn pointed out that Mike was from Indiana. Paul came over to visit for a few minutes. It was one of those pleasant chance experiences where you meet a guy once and remember him long. Captain Ricketts had enlisted in late '43, and wouldn't have accumulated as many points as Mike. He wondered if Paul had made it home

The next town was McCordsville, where Mike decided to pay a call on Bob Frazier's parents. He gave them the cross that he had purchased from the Guadalcanal native. Mrs. Frazier said that it could have been the one that she had given Bob. She couldn't identify it for sure as the same cross, but she pressed it to her heart and blessed it with a mother's love anyway. Then the Fraziers showed Mike some of Bob's personal effects that had been returned from Guadalcanal. Among the articles was a crumpled letter that Bob had started and stopped several times. It was to the girl in Fortville. He never had the courage to finish the letter or to mail it, but he truly loved her to the day he died.

Mr. Frazier offered to drive Mike to Anderson, but Mike told them that he wanted to savor the remaining miles by walking home. He did accept their offer to stay the night to get a fresh start on the final eighteen miles.

The next town toward Anderson was Fortville, where a fellow returning from the war had opened a new liquor store. What drew Mike's attention was a giant pink elephant holding a martini glass and standing in front of the store. Mike laughed and walked on to the north end of town, where a train approached on the parallel tracks. The engineer and Mike waved to each other. It was beginning to feel more like home with every step. In Pendleton Mike saw a sign pointing to the school where Tony had hit the grand slam against the Irish. Some joker had painted "Lionel" on the railroad viaduct that served as a gateway to the downtown of Pendleton.

The little speed trap of Huntsville never looked so good. Five more miles and Mike would be to the point where Pendleton Avenue marched into the heart of Anderson and Highway 67 turned east to parallel the southern boundary of Anderson, 38th Street.

Good old Teddy Roosevelt grade school stood at the corner of State Road 67 and Brown Street Road. Mike stopped at the playground to swing in the swings and to run the bases one more time. Now it was only one mile north to 38th Street, and then it was less than a mile to his home on Ringwood Way.

He began to run. Near the small Pleasant Walk Cemetery, the horses in Doc Armington's field on the east side of the road took up the chase and ran beside him. Mike took the shortcut through Crescent Drive and headed east on 38th. He turned left at Haverhill, which angles onto Andover, which in turn leads to Ringwood Way.

Keku was in the kitchen making a salad when she sensed Mike's presence. She dropped the salad bowl and ran out of the house towards Andover Road, tearing at her apron strings to pull it off. Finally she worked herself free and threw the apron to the ground as Mike turned the corner. Joe came out of the house after Keku's mad display just in time to see her jump into Mike's arms. Joe laughed and cried, and laughed and cried, and laughed and cried. Doc and Mary Eubank came outside and gave Mike a cheer. Old Mr. Keller, who had served in the First World War, stood up on the porch and gave Mike a smile and a salute. The kids who were playing in the circle jumped up and down and made all kinds of racket when one of the older children told them who had come home. Mr. Gleeson's old mutt growled and barked and pulled at his chain.

Ringwood Way is a cul-de-sac that is shaped like a long-nosed mandolin. It has a playground in the center island, and the houses are on a hill that rings the circle. The properties are fairly close. It was nearing time for the postman's rounds, so when the neighbors heard Mr. Gleeson's dog they thought it was the mailman. Then they began to notice the commotion that Keku and Joe and Doc and Mary and Mr. Keller and the kids were making and they began to filter out of their houses. They stood on their porches and clapped and cheered Mike's homecoming. Mike waved back, a little choked up at the sight. He had not expected such a welcome home. The sight of his old friends and neighbors alone was so overwhelming that he began to weep and then just plain sob. It was all something wonderful that he had clearly not taken into account as he envisioned coming home.

Once inside, Keku hugged her son again. Joe was still laughing and crying. Then Keku unbuttoned Mike's shirt and touched the wound that Peggy Lilac had given him. As she examined the scar Mike asked, "How did you know?"

"Your sister has a big mouth and a bad temper."

"Mom, I'm so . . ."

Keku put her finger on Mike's mouth. "It doesn't matter. I'm your mother." Then she kissed the injury as if she were kissing a little boy's hurt finger.

There was a long pause and Mike asked if they had heard anything from Tony. After another somber pause Joe said, "Sit down, son. We have something to tell you."

Years later, on that same date, the people on Meridian Street gave the Pencil Man a wider berth. For some reason he was crying uncontrollably and muttering something about "coming home, coming home."

CHAPTER 30

Veronica

It took Mike another day to work up the courage to see Veronica. When he did, it was an awkward moment for both of them. They didn't jump into each other's arms as one would expect. They had both changed a lot in the past five years apart, and it was somewhat of a shock for each to realize that the other was real and not just a childhood memory.

The conversation was stilted at first. Then Mike reached for her face to see if it was flesh or just a dream. When he did, Veronica reciprocated. As they touched they accelerated their need to be touched, and they kissed and hugged with greater and greater passion. Then Veronica started saying over and over, "You're home! You're Home!" Mike for his part couldn't get a sound to seep from his throat. He just held her tighter and tighter.

After a few minutes they settled in and began to talk. Neither had expected the conversation that would develop. The truth was that Mike had not yet fully "come home." Anderson was different. He was different. Veronica was different. Mike told her as much, and for some reason she seemed to understand. She could see that Mike was different—unsettled would be the better word. They both agreed to give it some time.

Veronica had a knockout cousin Susie. The two of them had talked about taking some of the money they had earned in the factory during the war and going to Myrtle Beach for a month to relax and "drive the boys crazy."

Mike agreed. "But not too crazy," he insisted.

They both relaxed and enjoyed the feel of each other for a while. Two intense shopping days later Veronica and Susie were off on their grand adventure and Mike began work on his homecoming.

Mike's natural point of reference was still the Marine Corps, so he spent a lot of time keeping in shape. He ran a few miles every morning. Like his dad, Mike liked the early morning, before Anderson woke up and the world was his alone. For those first several weeks he spent a lot of time walking all over town. There wasn't a single street in Anderson with which he did not reacquaint himself. There were new sights and old memories.

So much of what he had known had faded or had been replaced by progress. Old Anderson High School was now populated by strangers who had been in the elementary schools when Mike and Tony were popular in high school.

Many downtown stores were getting facelifts and changing hands. Gransengetters hadn't changed a bit—Mike's dad didn't like change very much. The half of the store that had housed Mrs. Dempsey's flower shop was closed. Mrs. Dempsey had died in 1944, about the time Mike was at Peleliu.

Mr. Tuttle's old haberdashery, where Mike had worked as a boy, closed in July of 1942 and was now an optometrist's office. Mr. Tuttle himself died on August 7, 1942, the same day Mike landed on Guadalcanal.

No one seemed to know where Oscar had drifted. Some said that he had joined the Navy, others that he had been drafted into the Army and had died in France. Mike didn't think so. Oscar was still pretty young in 1941. Some speculated that Oscar was in the Pendleton Reformatory, where Dillinger had first served time. Still others thought he was in the Indiana State Prison in Michigan City, or Leavenworth, or even Alcatraz. Mike wondered if Oscar was still in town and had somehow buried himself deeper into the bricks and shadows of the city, as men who want to hide themselves can.

One day Mike walked to East Maplewood to find the grave of Mr. Tuttle. When he found Mr. Tuttle's marker, Mike spent the afternoon telling his old boss and friend all that had happened since he had left. As he spoke Mike thought he saw Oscar hiding behind one of the stones. The marker next to Mr. Tuttle's was the fairly fresh grave of Mrs. Mader.

The next day Mike walked into St. Mary's and knelt in one of the pews to pray. He didn't know why he had come or what he needed, but he knew he needed something. Mostly he just listened for God.

Fr. Williams walked into the sanctuary around 10 a.m. When he saw Mike he hesitated. He walked to the pew where Mike was kneeling and genuflected. Then he knelt next to Mike and said nothing. Neither man spoke. Neither man was really praying. Both men wanted to talk, but neither knew how to begin. Mike looked at the floor. Father Williams kept his eyes toward the altar. After an awkward pause, Father Williams began the conversation. It had the atmosphere of a confession.

"Your mother was sitting right here on the day you were wounded. I've led the consecration thousands of times, but never before or since was it like it was on that day. You boys were both dying. I don't know how I knew that, or how your mother knew it, but we did. I had this sense that I was the rope in a tug of war between Christ and death for the lives of you boys."

Neither man looked at the other as he spoke.

"I found myself in some kind of spiritual struggle, as though what I was doing meant the difference between you boys defeating death or dying. I can't explain it, but it was real. I can't help but think that if I had fought a little harder Tony would be alive."

Fr. Williams' voice was very sad as he said Tony's name.

"I'm so sorry, Mike. I should have found the strength somehow."

Fr. Williams hung his head and Mike put his arm on his shoulder.

"It was Tony's time, Father. Wasn't it enough that you saved my life? I have no right to ask for anything more. Now here I am, wasting the life that God gave back to me. That has to be a sin—at the very least a waste." There was a pause as Mike thought over what he had just said. Then, like a man saying goodbye and going to work he said, "Thank you, Father. It's time I started to live my life again."

Things were at least a little better in Mike's mind. It would be three more days before Veronica would return home, and Mike was anxious to see her. He did a lot of running and walking in those three long days. He mowed his parents' lawn, and the neighbor's lawn, and every lawn on Ringwood Way, except Mr. Gleeson's. His dog had torn out almost every blade of grass, so he could have used a pair of scissors to "mow" what was left of that yard.

On the day Veronica returned, Mike must have taken three showers and changed his clothes any number of times to get the right combination. Then he walked to her house and knocked on the door. It took her a while to let him in. She was just as nervous as Mike and kept going back to the mirror to make sure she was her best.

When Veronica opened the door Mike's knees began to buckle—just as they had when he first saw her at the state track meet. She was a little sunburned from the southern rays of Myrtle Beach, but she was wearing a summer dress that made your heart skip. Boy, did she look good!

They sat on the sofa together and began a nervous conversation. They stumbled for a bit. Mike said, "Veronica, we need to talk." Then he unbuttoned his shirt, showed her the scar, and confessed his mistake with Peggy Lilac, and his near miss with Violet, who had picked him up at the roadside park in Texas. Veronica pressed him for the details until it was all said. She wanted to clear the air so that the whole matter would become dead history with no lingering bones to threaten any future they might have together.

It was a weight off of Mike's shoulders, and the way she accepted it was amazing, and a sign of real love. Then she dropped a bomb on Mike.

"Mikey, I'm pregnant." She didn't wait for his response but confessed her whole story as Mike had done for her. She had been so angry with Mike for leaving her. During the war she took a job at Delco Remy, where she had all sorts of opportunities to meet guys who were eager to take her out.

At first there were fellows her age, but as the war wore on more and more of them were drafted. There were always men who were still plenty of fun but too old to go to war. They would take her to dinner and then to a movie or dancing. Some fellows would take her skating at the Green Lantern. The lucky fellows could work up to holding her hand. The luckier ones would score with a really passionate kiss and a heart-pounding hug. She did feel good in a man's arms.

Even the luckiest dates would make it only as far as the front door, where she would cut them off at the knees. For as much as she cursed "that mean Marine," she loved him too much to give herself to anyone else. She was such a terrible tease that it was a wonder some fellow hadn't killed her.

There was a long heartbreaking pause in the conversation before Mike said, "Are you going to marry the father?"

"Heck no, but I'd kill him if I could!"

She went on to tell Mike the whole sorry story. "It was my supervisor, Tom Kerry. He couldn't keep his dirty eyes off me. He always seemed to be angry with me—as if I couldn't do anything right. Then, about two months before you came home he called me into his office and told me that I had really messed up, but that he didn't want to chew me out where the other workers could see us. I didn't want to be embarrassed in front of my co-workers, so I followed him out to his car. We got in and he drove me to his house. By then I knew something was wrong and I tried to get away, but he was too strong. His wife was gone. He dragged me into his bedroom and raped me."

"Didn't any of the neighbors see you?"

"It was third shift—everyone was asleep."

"Did you go to the police?"

"Are you kidding? Tom Kerry is a big man in this town, and they all think I'm a little tease. I wouldn't have a chance against that guy."

Anger and adrenaline took possession of Mike.

"Is your car out back?"

"Yes."

"Show me where he lives!" Veronica had never seen such a manly rage in Mike's eyes. She was afraid of what he might do, but she wasn't about to stand in his path.

First they drove to Mike's house, where he went in to get something out of his gear. He stuck it in his shirt and told her to drive on.

When they reached the Kerry home they parked out front and Mike followed the smell of barbeque smoke to the back yard. There he saw a man standing over the grill, working the charcoal.

"Are you Kerry?"

"Yeah, what do you want?"

"I want you to quit your job and leave town forever."

"Are you crazy?"

Mike opened his shirt to reveal the scar and pulled out his Marine KA-BAR knife. He showed its handle, which was stained from the war. "Yeah, I'm crazy—real crazy, and if you want to keep your manhood you'd better do as I say."

Kerry picked up a meat fork and told Mike to "Get out of my yard before I have my wife call the cops!"

About that time Mrs. Kerry came out of the house with a platter of porterhouse steaks, and Veronica came around the corner of the house.

Not seeing his wife, Kerry first went pale at the sight of Veronica. Then he stiffened and said, "So this is what it's about. Tell you what, boy—this little whore has slept with every man in town. You can't believe her. She's just mad because I had to fire her."

"I had to quit! You raped me! I'm pregnant with your child!"

Mrs. Kerry dropped the tray and the dog eagerly went after the steaks.

"What?"

Veronica said it again. "He raped me!" Then she looked Mrs. Kerry in the eye and poured out all of the intimate details of her bedroom décor. These were details that only Mrs. Kerry would recognize.

With her veins about to burst, Mrs. Kerry told Mike, "Give me that knife!"

Fortunately, Mike had enough sense to put the knife away. He was now beginning to realize what a stupid act he had almost committed and was a little ashamed that he had lost so much control. His angry actions gave Mrs. Kerry enough backbone to take a stand that was long overdue. A few days later Tom Kerry quit his job and left town for good—and alone.

Veronica and Mike got back in the car, and Veronica drove away with Mrs. Kerry screaming so loudly that several neighbors called the cops.

Near 14th and Sycamore she pulled the car to the curb and fell on Mike crying. "I'm so sorry Mikey," she sobbed. "I wouldn't blame you if you hate me forever."

She was stunned when Mike got out of the car, thinking that he was leaving her. Instead he came around and told her to scoot over. Mike drove to City Hall, where he got out of the car and pulled Veronica to the top of the river bluffs where the original Lenape village had been. He grabbed her by the shoulders and said with great force, "Veronica, I love you. I want you to marry me!"

It was the most unromantic proposal of all time, spoken more in rage than the sappy plea of a lovesick bachelor, but Veronica understood the real intention of Mike's forceful request.

Veronica stopped crying and started crying. She jumped on Mike, and the couple fell to the ground. Her sunburned skin hurt, but she didn't care, shouting "YES! YES!" as they lost their balance on the uneven ground and rolled around like two high school wrestlers.

Mrs. Hawley was walking past on her way to the women's society at the First Presbyterian Church just in time to see the couple grappling in the grass. She quickly turned her head and picked up her pace.

Kikthawenund smiled.

Back on Ringwood Way, Keku smiled at Joe. Joe just shook his head thinking, "Now what?"

Mamalis had never thought that Veronica was good enough for her brother, but she ran the words "Aunt Toni" through her head and grinned from ear to ear.

Mike felt a hand on his head, and a warm breeze messed up his hair—just like his big brother used to do when they were boys.

CHAPTER 31

Life Begins

War is a strange thing. It takes a young man away from his life plans and puts him on a course that may lead to his early end. Therefore, a soldier lays aside his designs for the future. If he gets back from the war, there becomes a point when he realizes that he is ready to begin living again. More often than not, his maturity level has been advanced by unnatural experience, and he begins to take steps that are much less sure than his pre-war plans.

Mike went to the Plant 1 offices of Delco Remy on Columbus Avenue and applied for a job. It just so happened that there was an opening. A supervisor had suddenly quit and a longtime line worker had moved into his position, freeing up a production job. With an extra plug from Mr. Vinson, Joe's old boss, Mike was hired and began work the next Monday.

Mike wasn't fond of the factory. He was an outdoor kind of guy, but the other workers were friendly and the pay was very good. He began work on the shaft line. This was very near the winding operation where John Prieshoff worked.

This was the same John Prieshoff from "Alexander" that Fred Utt had told Mike about in Death Valley. John was all that Fred had said and more. He was a very tall man—a handsome, outgoing fellow with an easy smile. Everybody liked John, and with him being a devout cradle Catholic, they all came to him for that extra prayer for some special need. One fellow was going to ask his girl to marry him, so he asked John to pray that she would say yes. Another asked John to pray for his crabgrass, and he was serious. Then there were the really dire ones, like a child with cancer, and a man who had been terribly burned and had lost his wife and kids in a house fire.

Mike liked John for a host of reasons. John was just a little older than Mike, so he could relate to John's age and also learn from his slightly extra life experience. John had married a fine-looking W.A.V.E., Arlene, whom he had met while in service. They had a little girl named Ann Marie.

This came in handy as the weeks grew near for Mike to marry Veronica. Once he had learned the circumstances, John didn't seem judgmental that Veronica was pregnant. In fact he admired Mike for taking on the situation and showing such love and compassion for her. It seemed like a level of devotion that would make for a great marriage, and John said as much. Mike appreciated that a lot, as he was pretty much at a loss for knowing how to start being a good father. Mike had a much better example in his own loving parents than his father had had in his brutal childhood. Still one's mind is always in doubt when you are the one who has to get it right.

John assured Mike that no one instinctively knows how to be a good parent and that it was an on-going learning experience. He invited Mike and Veronica to their home in Alexandria, where they sat and talked about what to expect. Arlene was a straightforward woman who told it like it is and was very helpful. She had beautiful, expressive eyes and a sweet voice that made even the difficult parts of parenthood sound easier.

Veronica was really taken with Ann Marie. She was such a cute little girl. On the drive home she said, "Let's have a girl." Mike didn't know how she was going to control that outcome, but he wanted a boy.

Mike worked a month on first shift during his training period, but he was soon sent to second shift. It really cut into his time with Veronica. It didn't matter that much to Veronica. She had a lot to do to get ready for the wedding. Keku was a great help, and Veronica's own mother was able to take the train up from Evansville once a month to lend a hand. She had moved there when Veronica's dad got a job at Whirlpool.

Veronica's biggest concern was the dress. She wasn't sure she should wear white, being that she was pregnant out of wedlock. Keku, Veronica's mother, and Veronica were at a dress shop when it really hit her and she began to cry. Keku looked her straight in the eye and said in no uncertain terms, "First love is something a woman gives to her man. That jerk who raped you stole your virginity, not your love. You wear the whitest dress you can find! I don't care if you are sticking out to here!" She held her hands far in front of her stomach. Veronica's mom gave a strong "Amen!" The dress shop owner clapped her hands loudly, and the other customers who had heard the conversation gave a cheer.

The subject came up again in counseling with Father Williams. He put the kibosh to it in a hurry, and Mike forcefully added, "You are my bride! That is my child! Wear white!" Mike's manly stand removed all doubt, and left Veronica a little flushed.

The wedding itself was a happy affair. Her cousin Susie and her friend Betty from the factory stood up with Veronica. Luis and Rosa came up from Albuquerque. Luis stood with Mike. They left two spaces, one for Tony, and one to represent Mike's fallen Marine buddies Leroy, Bob, and Jim.

John and Arlene sat on Mike's side along with Bruce Duncan and several more of his factory friends. A few fellows who had played sports in school with Mike and Tony were there, and, of course, Rosa.

Veronica's cousins Mary Jo and Mavis were there with their husbands Sam and Ralph. They had each married just after the war. Mary Jo and Sam had just celebrated their first anniversary and Mavis and Ralph were twelve days away from their first.

Several girls from the factory came. The fair-haired Debbie came still feeling pretty blue from losing Leroy. She hadn't found another love yet and seemed to be far from it.

Mrs. Kerry sent a nice letter to Veronica with a check for $500. She said in the letter that she had hesitated to contact Veronica as she didn't want to bring up any bad memories on her wedding day. She told Veronica how much she had appreciated her brave stand and for how she had opened her eyes to Tom. The divorce was a messy one, but she got almost all of the money and possessions and was doing quite well financially.

"Tom did raise a stink over his prize MG sports car. He had a lawyer draw up a paper to demand that I give it back, or sell it and send Tom the money. It must have cost Tom $50 for that letter. I didn't want the court hassle so I sold the car for a dime and sent him a check with a copy of the sales receipt. When Tom took it back to court, Judge Smith held in my favor and made Tom pay my court costs. I wish you and Mike well, sweetheart."

On Mike's side of the church, Mamalis sat near Keku with Kikthawenund beside Mamalis. No one but Keku and Mike could see them. Mamalis had a weepy look and blew Mike a kiss. He had a hard time holding back his own tears when he saw that. Keku just let 'em flow as she watched her only living child leave home again. Joe didn't cry, but he blinked his eyes a lot. A puff of wind blew in from somewhere and caused the candles to flicker. Mike wondered if that was Tony.

Veronica's dad was pretty solemn as he walked Veronica down the aisle—so much so that Mike really felt for him. Veronica herself wore a dazzling white dress and was so pretty that he got that buckling feeling in his knees again. Her mom fought tears all through the ceremony, and her lips never stopped quivering till the reception.

Neither one socialized much. They had been talking divorce and were trying to put up a front for Veronica on her day. Sadly, they did separate a few months later. They got back together again for a while after their grandbaby was born, but their renewal would too soon take a dreadful turn.

When Veronica turned to Mike, he took her hands and said, "I am so proud of you." Veronica just smiled. Mike thought of the first time he saw Veronica smile at him after the ballgame on the Roosevelt playground. He thought of how no boy wanted Veronica to smile at him then, and of the number of men who would kill to have her smile at them as she was now—looking into the eyes of her handsome groom.

The reception was a lot of fun. For a guy like Mike it's always a relief to let down a bit after standing in front of all of those people in a suit. When things settled in, Mike introduced Veronica to Luis and Rosa. It was only then that he found out that Rosa had become pregnant a week or two after Veronica. They had a grand time comparing all of the things that made them sick.

Keku was happier than at any time Mike could remember. Joe was uncomfortable in crowds, but he hit it off with Sam and spent most of his time talking to him. He also danced with Keku and Veronica. He was actually a pretty good dancer, which surprised Mike. He had never seen his parents dance.

Mike had a good conversation with Ralph, who had also been on Okinawa. It was harder talking to Mary Jo and Mavis, but that was just a guy thing. Veronica went on and on with them, as she hadn't seen either one since before the war and was so thrilled that they had come.

Mike danced with Debbie. It was so strange that after all of these years and his young infatuation he was holding her for the first time. It's funny how you hug one person and it fits, and with others it seems a mismatch. Mike noticed right off that Debbie just didn't feel right in his arms. Once her charms had lorded over him, and now he felt sorry for her.

He lied to her and told her how much Leroy talked about her during the war. The truth was that she never seemed more than a fling to him. He would get letters from Debbie every now and then. Sometimes they would include a racy photo, which Leroy used as bragging rights among the fellows. He might have loved her—it was hard to tell. Sometimes when Leroy got really scared—and anyone who tells you he wasn't at times is a liar—Leroy would say some pretty serious things about Debbie. Maybe he really did love her. Either way it didn't matter now. Debbie had made a lot of wrong decisions, and it looked like it would be a long time, if ever, before she would meet "Mr. Right." Veronica kept an eye on them the whole time they danced.

Veronica and Mike settled into her home on Haverhill, a short walk from his parent's home. The house was fairly new. It only had two bedrooms, but it was in good repair and was a perfect starter home. Joe was near enough to lend a hand when any work was needed. Mike loved working with his dad. They had always been close, and now that he was entering a new phase of his life it was good to call on his dad for help and expertise.

Veronica was a surprisingly good cook, but she wasn't a morning person, so Mike packed his own lunch and fixed his own breakfast.

It was Veronica's job to spend as much of Mike's paycheck as she could to fix up the nursery. Mike didn't mind. Veronica had been dreading the birth of "Tom's crime," but now it was a thing of joy.

They were both uneasy about consummating the marriage. Her pediatrician, Dr. Beckoon, took them aside and had a frank discussion on what they could and shouldn't do. Still, it was after Veronica's recovery from the birth before they felt easy with the process. There was still some morning sickness and some insane cravings that dominated their first few months. A lesser man would have shot her and then divorced her, but Mike was a great and patient husband.

It was a dark and stormy night when Veronica went into labor. Actually the night was dark and Veronica was stormy. She cried, she screamed, she cursed worse than a Marine. She even punched Mike when he tried to tell her to relax. He was glad when the doctor sent him off to the waiting room for the delivery.

In the delivery waiting room there was one fellow who was lighting one cigarette after another. One fellow was praying like he was on death row. Another guy was pacing left as Mike paced right. An old guy—he must have been at least sixty—walked nonchalantly into the room and sat on the sofa. He was so calm that all of the other guys stared at him. The old geezer held up six fingers to let them know that this was old hat. Then he laid down on the sofa and slept, well, like a baby.

The nurse came in half an hour later and told the old man, "Congratulations, Harvey. This time it's triplets." Harvey leisurely sat up and stretched. As he walked out he shook his head and mumbled to the other fellows, "It's a good thing this wife is only thirty."

The next father was the chain smoker. "Congratulations, Mr. Winston. You have a little girl." Then he left to see his baby as they wheeled her to the nursery in a warming cabinet. She looked up at him as if to say, "Hello, Father. You may admire me now."

The third father was the praying man. The doctor came in to see him and led him out into the hall. A few minutes later Mike heard a loud agonizing cry. The man had lost both his baby and his wife.

Mike was scared to death when he heard the door open again. His heart and breathing almost stopped till he heard, "Mother's fine, you have a healthy baby boy."

When he walked into Veronica's room she was holding the baby on her chest and smiling from ear to ear. Mike had to put on a gown and mask, and, of course, he wasn't allowed to hold the baby. The look in Mike's eyes was all that Veronica needed to see. When they took the baby, this woman who had punched and cursed Mike pulled him into bed and held him very close.

Their first decision as new parents was what to name their son. The fact that Mike had unequivocally declared her illegitimate child as his meant the world to Veronica. It said not only that the child was legitimate, but that she was respectable as well. She had imagined what it would have been like if she had borne her son alone. She would have been forced to give him up for adoption or to rear him under the scornful eyes of society's adults and the merciless tormenting of her son's classmates. Instead she would now walk in grace with a ring on her finger and a proud father by her side.

To honor Mike, Veronica suggested that they call their son Tony. Mike smiled at her suggestion, and a part of him wanted to agree, but he also didn't want his son to be associated with a sad memory. Instead Mike wanted to call him Eddie, after the curious Marine Eddie Spencer. He wanted his son to think great thoughts like Eddie and to seek the answers to all of the mysteries of the seen and unseen world. Veronica liked Mike's thinking on the matter, so Eddie it was.

They went through the normal bottle, diaper, spit-up, and crying in the middle of the night things that all parents do. There, of course, were also the joyful times of discovery and play. Sometimes Mike would get up and see Mamalis hovering over Eddie—wanting so much to be able to hold him.

"Grandfather calls him pèthakhòn (pe tock hon—which means "it thunders"). He's proud of you, Mike. I am too. You're a great father."

Mike wanted to hug his sister more than ever, but that would never be in this life.

As to be expected, Keku was a doting grandmother. It was funny to watch his normally serious dad get down on the floor to play with his grandson. The neighbors had a shower of sorts. Mrs. Steele, Mrs. Bays, and Mrs. Vest each brought over an outfit. Mr. Jackey made a crib that he had built in his garage workshop. It was a fine piece of work. Grandma Vrouvas, the old Greek neighbor who was well into her eighties, and who didn't speak a word of English, made a beautiful hand-sewn blanket for the baby. When she gently held the baby for the first time, there was no need for a translator. With her sweet old voice she sang to him a Greek lullaby. Eddie smiled at her like she was an angel. Mike was sure she was.

When they took the baby to Evansville for the first time, Veronica's parents loaded them up with so many toys and outfits that there was hardly room in the car for the baby. Mike wondered if that was their plan—to keep their grandson there longer.

At his baptism Eddie howled like a banshee. Father just laughed and made some comment about him being a Protestant.

The first year and a half after the birth of Eddie was the most wonderful of Mike's life. Veronica met all of the demands of motherhood, but she never forgot that Mike was first in her life. She worked really hard to keep things in balance—so much so that Mamalis came to Mike and apologized for all of the bad thoughts she had had about Veronica in the past.

It seemed like everything had fallen into place.

Then it all came crashing down.

There was a thick woods at the end of Brown Street with several good trails for running. Mike loved the solitude and would run there often. One morning as he ran along the path he tripped and fell into a thorn bush. He got up from the painful encounter, and then he was pushed back into the thorns. This time he was angry and ready to clobber whoever had pushed him. To his shock, it was Kikthawenund, who pushed him down yet a third time.

"What are you doing?"

The old Indian replied, "It is time."

"What do you mean Grandfather? What's going on?"

"All men are called to go through a time of testing. Even the Great Spirit's son went through this time. Your time is now."

"But Grandfather, I've been to war. I've seen friends torn apart. What could be worse than that?"

"You have seen nothing!" Kikthawenund's voice was uncharacteristically cold.

"This time I will not be able to save you, as I did in the war. Mamalis will not be allowed to help you through this trial. Your mother will not help you. She will be with us soon."

Mike was in shock. Mamalis was crying her heart out. She reached out to her brother as her spirit and Kikthawenund's faded from his sight—never to be seen again.

Mike let out a blood curdling cry that scattered the birds and the squirrels.

Veronica's dad died the next day.

CHAPTER 32

The Wilderness

Veronica was shattered. She had been daddy's girl all the way. It was her daddy who stood by her and called her his beautiful princess when the boys and girls at school tormented her and treated her like an ugly duck. It was her daddy who tucked her in, and read her stories, and sang songs to her. It was her daddy who made her laugh when she wanted to cry. Her mother loved her, but she was more reserved. She wasn't cruel, but she was capable of only so much emotion. This may have been the source of their marriage troubles. Veronica's dad was outgoing and blue collar. Her mom was sorority and community causes.

The flash of honeymoon love grew cold between Mike and Veronica. Mike would have been lying if he said it didn't bother him, but he also knew that Veronica needed more of a husband now than a lover. He did what he could to help her through her malaise. She did what she could to snap out of it. Eddie was too young to notice the difference.

The biggest weight on Mike's shoulders was his mom. "She will be with us soon." He knew exactly what Kikthawenund had said and what he meant. Mike was working second shift in those days. Despite the late hour he would always stop by to see his mother on the way home. Joe would be in bed asleep, as he had to get up early to open the shop. Keku would be in the kitchen fixing a light snack for her son. Neither one spoke of her impending death. After a few weeks of this ruse Keku spoke up.

"We both know why you are here. Did Grandfather tell you?"

"Yes."

"Please don't tell your father. I still have some time. It will break his heart when he finds out I am dying." Keku could no longer hold her little boy. Mike was now a man who towered over her. Still she did her best to hold him as Mike cried his heart out. Likewise he could feel her tears soaking through his shirt.

"I love you, Mom."

"I love you too, son. Of all of my children you are the most like me. Go home now. Veronica needs you."

Nothing made sense. It was as though God had died and the universe was spinning out of control, or that the author of life had suddenly gone mad. The spirits that had guided Mike and Keku seemed to have abandoned them, leaving them with no idea of where to turn

Even Keku, with her great gift of clairvoyance, would be blinded to the sudden disaster to come.

There was a man in town everyone called Swede. Swede was a powerful giant of a man, but he had little more than the understanding of a three-year-old to control his massive adult body. He seemed to have no guardianship except the goodwill of the people of Anderson. At night he slept at the Christian Center Mission with a teddy bear that Reverend Lambert had given him. During the day he would roam Anderson doing anything he pleased.

Swede might point to a bald man and loudly proclaim, "He has shiny head—he's shiny head!" He might see a woman and say "funny hat" or "she pretty!" He would walk into Woolworths, take a candy bar off the shelf, tear it open, and eat it on the spot without any concept of having to pay for the candy.

Swede loved Joe's jewelry store. He called Joe "Mr. Shiny." He would enter the store and try to put his hand through the glass to pick up a sparkling piece of jewelry. Swede had no concept of barriers like glass. If he could see something, it made sense to him that he should be able to touch the attraction.

Joe would usually be able to stop Swede from hurting himself. He would open the case and let Swede hold the "shiny" up to the light and twist it around to see it sparkle and flash. When Swede had entertained himself enough he would always hand it back to

"Mr. Shiny" and would walk out of the store to find something more interesting.

Joe had a genuine love for Swede. He was the essence of innocence in a cynical world. Swede was a man who had never had to leave his childhood. Joe was a man who had never had a childhood. By rights Swede should have been locked up in an institution for his safety, but there was something in him that the citizens of Anderson needed. No one had the heart to put him away.

It was a Tuesday afternoon when Swede wondered into Gransengetters. Joe was waiting on Mrs. St. Clair and couldn't get to Swede in time to stop him. Swede had spotted a "shiny" that fancied him and he began to pound on the glass case. He had shattered the top before Joe could stop him and was bleeding profusely. This in turn made Swede afraid and then angry. He pushed the offending case backwards—propelling Joe against the brick wall of his shop. Joe hit his head and fell to the floor unconscious and bleeding. This frightened Swede. He went to Joe and started pounding on his head to wake him up—not knowing that he was inflicting even greater damage.

Mrs. St. Clair ran from the shop screaming. Her cry for help attracted the attention of Officer Graham, who was in his squad car a block away.

Officer Graham was half the size of Swede, but he knew how to handle the man-child.

"Shh—Calm down Swede. Mr. Shiny is sleeping. We must be quiet."

"He sleeping?"

"Yes, Swede. Mr. Shiny is sleeping."

Swede calmed down and sat in the broken glass on the floor. Officer Graham quickly found something to bind Swede's bleeding hand, and as he did so Swede realized that he was hurt. He began to cry and tried to crawl into Officer Graham's arms like a hurt child. Just as quickly he forgot his pain and held up the "shiny" for Officer Graham to see.

"Yes, it's beautiful, Swede."

"It beautiful—it beautiful—it shiny," Swede replied.

"Would you like to go for a ride in my police car?"

"Yes!"

"And make siren go wheeeee?"

"Yes—siren go wheeeee!"

Officer Graham coaxed Swede into the car and drove to the hospital with full lights and siren. There Swede was treated for his wounds and sedated to make him sleep.

As Officer Graham pulled away, an ambulance crew rushed in to save Joe. It was too late. Joe was bleeding in the brain and had lapsed into a coma. The hospital called Keku, but Joe died long before she could arrive. Keku had in turn called Veronica, who frantically called Mike's supervisor. The supervisor asked John Prieshoff to drive Mike to St. John's Hospital. Veronica quickly handed off Eddie to Mrs. Bays and picked up Keku on her way to the hospital. They all arrived about the same time.

The scene was horrible. Veronica dearly loved her father-in-law and was still mourning her own father. She was brokenhearted for Mike and Keku. They in turn had both prepared themselves for Keku's death, but not for this. Normally calm and in control, Keku completely lost her composure.

At the funeral she stood up to follow her husband's casket out of the church. She genuflected—she thanked Jesus for his sacrifice—she thanked God for his universal creation and love—she thanked her brother and sister trees for giving her a comfortable place to sit and kneel. Between each part she sobbed uncontrollably. In the vestibule she fell on Joe's coffin and had to be pried from it when time came to load it into the hearse. Father Williams had given thousands of funeral Masses, but he had never been so overcome. He had to stop several times during the homily to regain his composure.

Joe was buried in the Catholic cemetery just west of St. John's.

Poor Swede—everyone in town felt bad for him. Even Joe would have been saddened to see the man-child's fate. Swede was put in an institution. He was treated as well as could be expected, but, from his perspective, it was like placing a small child in a house of horrors. Everything was strange to him. He cried and would often curl up in a ball on the floor. In time he adjusted to his new surroundings, and his world went on as if nothing had happened and Mr. Shiny had never existed.

Eighty-three days after Joe's funeral, Keku died.

It was a sad Christmas for Mike and Veronica. The losses of that year were too great to bear. They continued to hold each other's broken heart and let time and love do its work. They had the extra help of a curious, happy, and adventurous baby boy, and as the months passed, they began to come around.

Mike started to believe that he had survived the trial that Kikthawenund had foretold. Little could he know that the worst was yet to come.

CHAPTER 33

The Mark of Cain

The years passed. Eddie began to talk, and stumble, and walk. He was a happy little guy who gave big wet kisses to his mom and who clung to Mike and studied his actions. He sure could get into things—especially after he learned to walk. Eddie had an uncanny aptitude for getting into the cookie jar. Several times his parents would walk in on him with a wad of cookies in his hands and crumbs smeared around his mouth. He had a killer way of getting out of that one. Eddie would calmly hold up a cookie with a look of "Here, you guys want one?" He had to take a spanking on occasion, but for the most part he just made Veronica and Mike laugh.

Love once again flourished in the home on Haverhill Drive. By the time he was four, Eddie was helping his dad with everything. He would try to push the lawnmower—the human-powered rotary sickle bar type. It was funny to watch Eddie stretch himself to reach the handle—after which he had no leverage to move the thing. Mike would stand behind and help his boy in a way that made him feel like he was really mowing on his own. He liked to crawl under the car to "help" Mike do the oil changes. It was one of the few occasions that made Veronica get angry at Mike. Boy, did she have a temper!

Eddie also liked to help Veronica push the sweeper and dust. He would hand the clothespins to his mom on sunny days. Afterwards she would pull out an empty glass milk bottle and let him drop the pins into the bottle—one of his favorite games. Eddie could actually hold the clothespins over his head and hit the opening six out of ten times. While Mike was at work they would make cookies. Well, mostly they just ate the cookie dough. When it came to cookie dough it was hard to tell who was the bigger kid.

Mike would read the bedtime stories, but Veronica would read to Eddie before his afternoon nap. He was beginning to make out words even at age three. Veronica would sing to her son the songs that her dad had sung to her. Those memories would often bring tears to her eyes. Eddie would hug his mom extra tight when she was sad.

As a family they enjoyed the simple pleasures of Halloween costumes and Easter egg hunts. They would drive to the Ace Airport to watch the small airplanes and the little skydiving club that would meet every so often.

There was Shadyside Park with its summer slides and swings and the Japanese garden that was built in the C.C.C. days. It also had the best sled hill in town. They spent summer evenings watching the water-skiers on White River near Edgewater Park, and winter Saturdays taking in the Christmas displays on the Indianapolis Circle and at the L.S. Ayres and William H. Block department stores.

It seemed as if God had again begun to smile on Mike's family. Then in August of his fourth year Eddie began to tire often—even after a good night's rest. Veronica noticed that he would bruise and bleed easily. He was getting pale and had frequent fevers and infections. Her mother tried to soothe her fears by telling Veronica that it was probably a normal childhood phase. Then Eddie began to complain of pain in his bones and joints. That's when Veronica really got scared.

Being on second shift, Mike took off work to make sure he would be home and alert the day the doctor came to the house. Dr. Luksus seemed particularly concerned about Eddie's lymph nodes. He ordered some blood tests, and a few days later he came back to give them the news. Veronica gave Eddie a milk bottle and some clothespins and sent him to play in his room. Alone with the doctor, they heard the grim news.

Dr. Luksus paused. It seemed hard for him to let go of the words, "Eddie has leukemia."

Mike and Veronica, of course, were devastated.

"What can we do?"

"There are a few experimental things we can try, but we know so little about leukemia. I can give you a prescription that will make him feel a little better, but I can't promise you a cure. I'm so sorry." Dr. Luksus had the most helpless look in his eyes as he said this.

Mike walked Dr. Luksus out to his car and asked him point blank the question that they were afraid to ask, "How long?"

"Christmas at the most—probably much sooner." The good doctor started his car and drove away.

The next evening Mike couldn't concentrate at work. People could see that something was wrong, but Mike wouldn't talk about it. The following morning John Prieshoff heard the rumor that something was eating Mike. That afternoon, at shift change, John took him aside and asked his friend to open up. Mike completely broke down as he choked out the verdict on his son. Those who saw it became unnaturally quiet. It was as if the machinery were suddenly abandoned and left running and banging in an odd cacophonous symphony sans the audience. Mike's foreman caught a glimpse of the two and took John aside to get the story on his troubled employee.

On hearing the news, Mike's supervisor called him into his office and told him to go home for the rest of the week. He didn't want Mike to make a mistake in his frame of mind that might hurt himself or someone else. Mike didn't argue. He clocked out and drove downtown to sort things out.

Mike parked at St. Mary's and prayed for an hour. He lit a candle for Eddie and one for Veronica, and then he walked downtown.

The building that had housed his dad's store had been sold for some time. There was paper across the windows, so he couldn't see in. A sign said "Opening soon," but it didn't say what was opening. He walked to the hill overlooking the river, the place where the original Indian village had stood—the place where he had proposed to Veronica and where his dad had proposed to his mom. The spirits who had sustained him throughout his life were nowhere to be found. Mike was truly alone.

It was dark now. Veronica wasn't concerned yet about Mike's absence. For all she knew, Mike was still at work. Mike walked to Anderson High School and found his way to the track. That old cinder track was the scene of a lot of glory for both Mike and Tony. Those were the good days. Those were the days when life made sense. All you had to do was run.

Mike began to run round and round that quarter-mile oval. All he could hear was the crunch-crunch of the cinders. All he felt was the pounding of his heart and the cool wind as he ran. The first lap or two were just for warm-ups. Then he let it all out for a mile run. He was nowhere near his state championship speed, and he certainly wasn't dressed for it, but he could see in his mind Gene, and John, and what's-his-name from Liberty Center.

As he crossed the line for the fourth time Mike stopped and bent over to catch his breath. He was startled to hear a lone spectator stomping on the wooden bleachers.

"That's quite a run, kid. You still have it. I would have applauded, but as you can see I can't."

The man had no hands.

"Do I know you?"

"No, but I know you. Your dad was the best friend I ever had. My name's Leon. I'm sorry about your boy."

"How do you know?"

"I know, kid, I just know. What are you gonna do?"

"What can I do? I have no choice."

"Oh, there's always a choice. Yes, sir, there is a choice. You can sell your soul to the devil—in which case you lose everything. Your son may live a while longer. Eventually he will die—maybe losing his own soul in the process."

"You can choose God. God is pure love. He will heal the boy, but his healing may be that he will take your boy to paradise. The boy wins. You and Veronica lose a child. You play your cards right, you get to see him again in another fifty years."

"We're back to the starting line. You're telling me I don't have any sure choices."

"No, son, you don't. That's where I come in. I can give you the power to save your boy's life."

"I'm listening. Go on."

"Satan is all evil. God is all good, but like I say, you may not like the kind of healing he gives your son. There is a third choice. It goes back to the day Cain killed his brother Abel. He was exiled, but his life was spared. He had life, but nothing much to live for. It was good and it was bad.

"Cain passed this 'gift' to someone else before he died. That person passed it on to another in need and so forth till it came to me.

"We were in the Ardennes—surrounded by the Germans. They were picking us off a little at a time. We were starving and dying of thirst. We had this chaplain who risked it all to crawl down to the stream to fill a few canteens. I saw a mortar round come in on him and I yelled. That's when time sort of stopped, and this strange German guy appeared. He saw what Father Courtney was doing and his heart went out to him. He told me that I could save Father Courtney, but that somebody I knew would have to lose something dear to them. Then he went on to explain the Mark of Cain. He said that it was my choice of who gets punished and that the Mark would decide what the punishment would be. The old German said he was sick of the war and that he wouldn't care if I chose to punish him to save Father Courtney.

"Well, how do you put a curse on someone else and still live with yourself? So I told him to punish me. The German asked if I was sure and I shouted for him to 'Do it!'"

Leon held up his stumps and said, "I was going to be a tailor."

"You can give this option to me?"

"He who receives the Mark can pass it on one time."

"Are you sure it will work?"

"I saw it with my own eyes. I've lived it every day since. Yes, I'm sure."

There was a long pause. Mike walked one more time around the track. He stopped in front of Leon and said, "Put the Mark on me. Save my son. Punish me."

Nothing more was said. Mike dropped his head, and when he lifted his eyes Leon was gone. In that instant he somehow knew that his son was healed. Perhaps it was an inherited gift from his mother, but Mike knew with dead moral certainty that Eddie was once again whole.

Forgetting the cost part of the deal, and in his excitement his car, Mike ran straight home. At the railroad crossing near 14th Street and Main the lights were flashing and the gates were down.

Some punks in a stolen car lost control as they raced around the corner from 14th Street and turned south to outrun the train before it crossed at Main Street. There they suddenly found themselves blocked by the crossing gates with the engine horn and light so close that it negated even a foolish notion to run the crossing.

They slammed on the brakes, struck Mike, and sent him flying into the path of the locomotive. They also hit the car stopped nearest the crossing and spun it into the side of the engine, right below where the engineer was sitting. The engineer threw on the brakes as the train drug the car down the tracks. By some miracle nobody in the car was hurt.

Mike stood up, dazed, trying to figure out what had just happened. As he shook it off he was stunned to find his own mangled body next to the tracks. It was then that he realized that he was dead and that his spirit was somehow outside of his body. Mike's thoughts began to function again and he realized that the "mark" had spared his son's life, but it had taken his. His son would live, but Veronica would be without her husband, and Eddie would be without his dad. Good and bad—life and death—win and lose.

After those thoughts had had a chance to sink in, Mike began to analyze the situation. He reasoned that his beautiful young widow would surely attract a good husband and that she would certainly choose one that would be a good father for Eddie. Perhaps it was more win than lose. He began to feel better about the deal, but the "mark" wasn't finished.

Mike looked toward the train and into an open boxcar. There he saw the lifeless body of a tramp with no legs. Some strange force suddenly grabbed Mike's spirit and rushed him into the body of the tramp.

Mike's old life was gone. He was now the Pencil Man.

CHAPTER 34

It Stinks in Here

Gathering his wits, Mike realized that the first thing he had to do was to get out of that boxcar while the train was stopped. First he had to learn to scoot this body instead of standing up and walking about. Then he had to figure a way to get down from the door. He couldn't just jump.

He quickly discovered that the tramp's hands were tough and his arms were very strong. Obviously he had learned to use his arms in place of his legs. Mike dragged himself to the open door and eased himself over the edge and down—climbing somewhat like an ape. He wormed his way under the train and crawled north toward town.

His common sense told him that he needed to find some sort of shelter, and he was more likely to find it in the downtown structures. What Mike chose was the narrow space between two buildings on an alley between Main and Meridian. It was good shelter with plenty of trash for sleeping and warmth. What Mike didn't know was that it was the same place that his father's friend Kelly had used as his home.

Once settled in, Mike began to assess his situation. Inside he was the same old Mike. His thoughts and his memories were the same as before. However, his exterior was now foreign to everyone in Anderson. When Mike tested his voice it didn't sound like him at all. No matter how hard he tried to sound like Mike, it came out like a stranger's voice.

How in the world would he would ever be able to convince anyone that he was Mike? Besides, there was that body alongside the tracks that was clearly his, right down to the dental records.

Even if Mike could have convinced Veronica that this tramp's broken body housed her husband's soul, would it be fair to make her love this? Mike decided to let it be. He had made his deal. He had saved his son. Veronica would inherit his life insurance and the money from the sale of his parent's home and the jewelry store. The thought of never again holding Veronica in his arms washed over Mike like acid.

With no other options, Mike had to begin the process of making peace with this broken bum's body. The first thing he noticed was the smell. "Man, it stinks in here," he said out loud in that strange voice. "When was the last time this guy took a bath?" His mouth felt gross. The tramp obviously hadn't brushed his teeth in some time—if ever.

The tramp's feet were cold and he could feel pain in them. He had no feet, of course, but Mike had never heard of the phantom pain that amputees experience. Finally there were the clothes. They were so filthy that they were unbearable, but if he dared to wash them they looked like they would fall apart. For a moment Mike thought that he could jump into White River and wash himself clothes and all. However, he wasn't sure but what the threadbare clothes would disintegrate in the current. He didn't relish the thought of the citizens of Anderson pointing to him—a naked and legless bum bobbing past Athletic Park.

Then he thought about money. The tramp barely had pockets —let alone money. Mike hatched a plan. He would crawl back to his old body and take the wallet and clothes that were rightfully his. After all, how could you steal from yourself?

With great effort Mike pushed the tramp's body back to the railroad. By the time he arrived, it was too late. The coroner was now on the scene, and the whole place was covered by emergency personnel. Mike went into his combat mode and tried to figure a way to outflank the operation, but he was only fooling himself. Giving it some second thought, he realized that if he had taken his former clothes it would have added a note of scandalous mystery that Veronica would have had to endure.

Mike hid beneath one of the baggage wagons that were scattered about the station ramp. About 4 a.m. Veronica arrived in a police car. She sobbed and screamed and hugged the mangled corpse of her husband. Mike wanted to shout, "I'm here, Veronica—it's me, Mike—I'm alive!"

One can only imagine the frustration and heartache. Tears streamed down his dirty cheeks, and for the first time he realized the tramp had a heart. "I'm here, I'm here," he said over and over in a low, strange, frustrated voice. He was being torn apart from the woman he loved, and was utterly helpless to do anything about it.

Over the next few days, as he made his way to St. Mary's, Mike ate from spilled garbage and drank from puddles like a dog. One night he managed to get down to the 10th Street Bridge where he slipped off his clothes and slid into the cold river for that long needed bath. He tried to wash his shirt, but as he suspected it began to tear, so he quickly ended that venture.

On the day of the funeral Mike crawled into the balcony of St. Mary's. It was so strange to hear his own funeral, but he was appreciative of the turnout and the kind words. John and Arlene Prieshoff were sitting just about where they had sat for Mike and Veronica's wedding. That's when it hit him—it hit him hard. The sight of his beautiful bride coming down the aisle with his son forming in her womb was now replaced by a devastated wife and a four-year-old boy who couldn't understand where his daddy had gone.

Mike's body was buried next to Keku and Joe. Father Williams moved on to another parish a few months later. Veronica eventually sold the house on Haverhill and moved in with her mom in Evansville. At their next doctor's appointment Eddie's cancer was completely gone. Mike would not be able to see his wife and child again except in his mad visions.

Mike went around downtown Anderson in search of some purpose and place he could call his own. No longer intimidated by his situation, he let the public see him. All-in-all the tramp wasn't a bad looking fellow. With some cleanup and better clothes he could have been seen as a gentleman. That said, he looked nothing like Mike, and no one would have suspected that he was the handsome, fit runner they had seen about town.

His progress was so slow. People either stared at the freak show of a man walking with his arms, or took a quick look and turned sharply away. Mike took pity on the tramp who had previously owned this body. He began to realize the hurt and humiliation he must have suffered.

Mike was still eating fallen garbage and was growing progressively weaker from the effort and the poor diet. Then one day he sat propped up against a storefront to rest and a man walked by and tossed him a quarter. It was the first act of human kindness shown to him since taking over the tramp's body. Mike tried to thank the man in his rough voice, but he was long gone before Mike could respond.

A few days later Mr. Kelly, the man who owned Kelly's Furniture Store, walked up to Mike and handed him a furniture mover.

"Here, I think this will work. You can keep it."

It was a square board with four small casters—one on each corner.

"You can sit on it and scoot around. I think it will be easier for you."

When Mike tried to get on the board it slipped and flipped him off. After a few tries he mastered the beast and began to roll about. At first it took off with him, and he nearly hit a wall. Soon Mike was rolling about and laughing for the first time since before Eddie was diagnosed with leukemia. Mr. Kelly recoiled a bit from the sight of the tramp's stained teeth, and when Mike saw this he closed his mouth.

At lunchtime Mr. Kelly came by again and handed Mike half of a sandwich and a full fresh cup of iced tea. He said that he was late and didn't have time to finish his lunch, but Mike knew better. It was the best meal Mike had eaten since taking possession of this wretched body.

The next morning—on his way to open the shop—Mr. Kelly handed Mike a large shopping bag from Clair Call's men's shop. He said, "Here, I threw my worthless brother-in-law out of the house last night. He left these things. Do you want them?"

Mr. Kelly didn't remain for a response or a thank you. Mike opened the sack and pulled out a nice shirt, a pair of pants, a coat, and some underwear. There was also a toothbrush and toothpaste, and a bar of soap and a washcloth and small towel. If these things were used, his "brother-in-law" must have just purchased them.

One doesn't know how much something like that means until they lose everything. Mike couldn't wait to put the clean clothes on, but he wanted to take a bath first. He started the long trek towards the river (he would still have to wait till dark to sneak in his bath). With that sack on his lap, he looked like a rolling billboard for Clair Call's.

He hadn't traveled far when he crossed paths with Mr. Cody—the old man who ran the YMCA. Mr. Cody stopped Mike and said, "I've been watching you, son. Follow me." Mike wasn't sure what to think about his statement, but it wasn't said in any threatening tone, so he did as the old man said. Mike was pretty slow on that board, but old Mr. Cody was just as slow, so they were pretty much even in their "gait."

They walked to a metal door that was located on the alley side of the Y. Mr. Cody unlocked it with a key, and they entered into a tiled hallway. The door shut and locked behind them. A few feet down and to the right were the showers for the pool. Mr. Cody pointed out one shower that had a chain hanging close to the floor. He gave it a pull and the water came on. When the handle was released the water would shut off, so it was a troublesome design. Still it was very much appreciated. In the true spirit of military adaptation Mike would later fashion a weight to attach to the chain that made it hands free.

Mr. Cody gave Mike a key to the outside door and told him when it would be safe for him to come and go.

"Go ahead and use the pool if you wish. You have about an hour before anybody will be here. There's a clock over there."

Mike thanked Mr. Cody profusely, and the old man went about his business. The shower was warm, and the soap felt so good. It felt like a million bucks to be really clean again. Mike had never fully appreciated the word "happiness" until he put on those clean clothes. He felt ashamed that he had taken so many things in his life for granted.

Mr. Cody died about a year later. Mike continued to use the key late at night for years to come. He enjoyed the pool as well. It gave him a sense of running again. The tramp's body was a virtual cork without those heavy legs, and it was a speedboat with those strong arms.

Mike decided that it was time to stop eating garbage. To buy real food, however, he needed an income. That was easier said than done. No one would hire a man with no legs. There were some amputees who were self-employed, but they were few and generally had access to some start-up capital—usually from their parents.

He tried everywhere to get a job, but most people wouldn't even look his way. It was physically hard to get into the buildings to even apply. Then one day he noticed an accountant, Mr. Michaels, who was always running back and forth to Decker's to buy pencils. He was one of those fellows who was perpetually overloaded with work and had little time for errands. He hardly went out for lunch. The wheels began to turn and Mike devised a way he could capitalize on his observations to their mutual benefit.

Mike had a dollar in loose change that he had found along the sidewalks of Anderson. He went into Decker's and asked how many pencils he could buy for a dollar. There were several mothers in the store with a list in one hand and a child in the other. The new school year would start soon, and they were looking for school supplies as if they were engaged in a winner take all scavenger hunt. Some mothers looked at Mike in fear and pulled their children close. Several children stared and either started to laugh or started to cry. The store clerk had an expression that said that he didn't know whether to wait on Mike or ask him to leave.

Mike asked the question again. "How many pencils can I buy for a dollar?" The clerk cleared his throat and curtly responded, "They are two cents each." Mike thought about it and then he asked about the cost of one of those small hand-held sharpeners. "Those are five cents," the clerk replied, still very stiff in his answer.

"I'll take one sharpener and forty-seven pencils."

Mike put his inventory into his Clair Call bag and rolled out of Decker's with forty-seven pencils, one pencil sharpener, and a penny to spare. He scoured the alleys for a suitable can for his "display." He also found a partial sheet of green construction paper to decorate the can and used someone's discarded chewing gum to attach the paper to the can. Next he set up shop between the accountant's office and the candy shop next door. Mike made sure he was on the path between Mr. Michaels' office and Decker's.

Eventually Mr. Michaels wore down his last pencil and raced out the door to buy a new supply. Mike held up and rattled his can of freshly sharpened pencils to catch Mr. Michaels' attention, and he stopped dead in his tracks.

Mr. Michaels asked, "How much?"

Mike replied, "Five cents each."

Doing a quick calculation for the labor lost in going to Decker's and sharpening a new pencil, Mr. Michaels said, "Deal" and bought three pencils. With his profit of nine cents and the spare penny from the original purchase, Mike had enough to buy a hamburger.

The next Tuesday Mike was the talk of the Rotary meeting. Soon businessmen all over town would stop by Mike's enterprise on their path to or from work to take advantage of the convenient pencil purchase. School children walking to school would buy a pencil as needed. Others would chip in a donation or buy a pencil just to be nice. They seemed to appreciate that this bum was at least trying to do something to earn his way. Mike was also passive in his sales approach. He was available, but not a panhandler.

Still, there remained a wall of separation between the normal people and this sideshow freak on his rolling board. The nights were still uneasy. He had no real shelter, and a cripple that nobody cared about was easy prey for the predators that roam society's shadows.

In all of the years that the Pencil Man worked the streets, there would be only four people who knew Mike on a personal level, or treated him like a human being. There was Mr. Cody, who died a few months after he introduced himself; Mr. Kelly; Father Metzger, who replaced Father Williams; and Rob Williams, who managed the Anderson Federal Savings and Loan.

The care shown by each of these men took only a little extra effort on their part, but each act of kindness was heroic to the lonely Pencil Man.

CHAPTER 35

Salvation, Finance, and Security

Father Metzger had a real heart for service and reaching out to people in all situations. Black or white, rich or poor, Protestant or Catholic—it didn't matter to him. Father Metzger firmly believed that since God made everybody he should consider every person his fellow and friend. That being the case, Father Metzger observed a discipline of trying to meet someone new every day.

He was the first person to ask the Pencil Man, "What is your name?" Mr. Kelly and Mr. Cody were both decent and kind to Mike, but they never really got around to asking him his name. Father Metzger made a point of trying to make Mike feel like just one of the guys in his inner circle.

On his third visit, Father Metzger sat down next to Mike and leaned against the ticket booth of the Paramount Theater. The stores had closed for the day, and the movie wouldn't start for a few more hours. It was raining. The large extended marquee provided a perfect shelter from the storm.

Father Metzger had brought with him two sandwiches from the Toast and a thermos of coffee. He made a point to have only one cup that he shared with Mike to show that he wasn't afraid to drink after this common street bum. So many people had treated the Pencil Man like he was full of fleas.

Father Metzger went straight to the point, "Mike, do you believe in God?"

"Yes, sir—I used to be a regular at Mass."

"Oh really? Why don't you come to St. Mary's? I'll pick you up anytime."

Salvation, Finance, and Security

"No thanks, Father. I don't think anyone would want to sit next to me in church."

"I won't force you, but I think you're wrong. Would you want me to bring you communion?"

"I'd like that very much, but I hate to put you out."

"It would be my pleasure Mike. When was the last time you did a confession?"

"About a year ago."

"Would you like to do one now?"

"Now? Here?"

"Sure, why not?"

"I've never done one outside of the confessional booth. It would feel funny without a curtain."

Mike wasn't thinking that moment of the one face-to-face confession he had done with Father Pelemon. Even then it had been indoors and in a private situation. It was hard to imagine God sitting on the street ministering to a wretched bum.

Father Metzger was both adventurous and resourceful. He said to Mike, "Tell you what—I'll scoot around to this side of the ticket booth and you slide over to that side and we'll do one right here. Do you remember how it starts?"

"Yes," Mike chuckled, "It hasn't been that long. Forgive me, Father, for I have sinned."

Mike started slowly, and then one thing led to another. He told Father Metzger who he was and all that had transpired to lead him to this point. Father Metzger was shocked by Mike's fantastic story. He had never heard of Cain handing down his mark. He hadn't really known Mike or his family, but Father Williams had told him some of the story before the parish changed hands. It sounded so absurd, but uncanny in its detail.

By the time Mike finished the priest was sure that Mike was not only a helpless cripple, but also very mad—and yet he sounded so sane in his speech. Keeping in mind that all people are equal in God's eyes, Father Metzger made an extra effort to see Mike as just another person.

208

Mike waited for Father Metzger to respond, and when he didn't, he asked about his penance.

"Oh, uh, your penance is . . . uh . . . to attend Wednesday night Mass at 6:00."

Anticipating what Mike might do, Father Metzger moved some boxes into one corner of the balcony. He said he needed the extra storage, adding, "There are plenty of extra seats in front if they need a place to sit. Especially the teenagers and the holiday Catholics who like to hide up there." Priests in general had a running joke about how people who sat in the balcony thought they were invisible, and about all of the funny things they had seen up there from the altar.

The real reason was to provide Mike a shelter from public view if someone should choose to sit in the balcony. Mike did exactly as Father Metzger had anticipated. He alone could see Mike watching between the openings in the rail. Father also noticed that Mike was struggling with trying to find a way to kneel. Father Metzger wondered about that for some time, "Just how does a man kneel with both legs amputated above the knee?"

The only other man in Anderson who knew Mike by name was Rob Williams. Rob was an interesting guy. He was known as the friendliest man in town, hands down. Even Father Metzger couldn't hold a candle to the way that Rob would smile at folks. He had a smile that spread across his face and encompassed his eyes as well as his mouth—and, somehow, even his nose.

Rob was very involved with his wife and kids and could be seen running to the Savings and Loan every morning—always late for work. Sometimes he would be helping with some last-minute schoolwork with his sons Doug and Mark. Sometimes he spent too much time with his wife Cindy. They loved each other even more than Mike and Veronica had. Their home was the apartment on Central where Mr. Tuttle had lived.

Each weekday morning the banker and the pencil seller would pass on the street and Rob would shout as he ran, "Morning, Mike—see you later!" Then he might trail off with some comment about selling lots of pencils, or having a nice day, or staying warm, as he ran on to the Anderson Federal Savings and Loan. That was Rob's pattern of life. He was always trying to do one thing more than his schedule allowed and therefore always running just a little bit late.

Rob and Mike met a few years into Mike's pencil business. One day after closing, Rob just walked up to Mike and asked him point blank, "What do you do with your take each day?"

Most people thought he drank it at night, and even more didn't care. Mike told Rob that he spent what he needed on food "and that was about it."

"Yes, but what about the extra? Do you have a safe place to store it? Would you like to open a savings account?"

Mike thought that was a good idea. By this stage in his enterprise he did have some extra cash on his person, and he often worried about being robbed. Besides, Joe had always instilled in his sons the need to save every penny they could, and to always put ten percent of every check into the savings. At one time Mike did have a substantial savings account in the Savings and Loan, but Veronica had withdrawn all of it when Mike's estate was settled.

Mike took Rob up on his advice and started an account. Rob took the extra step of keeping the building open to Mike after the other customers and employees had left for the night. He would make the deposit himself. Soon Mike had several hundred dollars in the account—all from small change. On some occasions, to make things easier, Rob would take Mike's money into the restaurant and buy Mike's evening meal. Then he would run home to be with his family.

The best "interest" Rob gave Mike was his sincere interest in this half-man beggar. Rob made it a point to spend at least one hour a week talking to Mike as one best friend would to another. It was during these times that Mike told Rob the intimate details of his life and travels, and of his time both before and after he had lost his legs.

Rob was a native of Anderson, but he had attended different schools and was just a little younger than Mike, so he had never known Mike as a boy. He had a health problem that kept him out of service, and had met his wife at Indiana University about a year after Mike had passed through with Dr. Wells. He and his family had returned to Anderson after Veronica and Eddie had left, so he didn't know Mike's family, but he was fascinated by every detail that Mike was willing to share.

The one thing that Mike kept private was the Mark of Cain and how he had lost his legs. Rob was enough of a friend to not ask. He tried several times to invite Mike home, but Mike always refused.

On the business of staying warm and dry—that was a bigger problem, which was resolved by Mr. Kelly. One day near the close of business Mr. Kelly walked over to the Pencil Man and made him an offer.

"Some punk's been trying to break into my place at night. I can see the marks on the back door. I'll give you a key to the alley entrance. You can sleep in the back storeroom, but don't sleep past midnight. That's when the thief is likely to break in. I want you to stay up and watch the place. I'll leave a phone on the floor so you can call the cops. Deal?"

"Sure thing, Mr. Kelly. I won't let you down."

Life wasn't what he would have preferred, but it was coming together for the Pencil Man. Mike had two friends who knew him by name, business was good enough that Mike could eat and even put some aside, and now he had a place to stay at night.

For the longest time Mike thought that Mr. Kelly was just putting on a show to cover his soft heart. There wasn't the slightest sound all night, except for the three or four cuckoo clocks throughout the store. A furniture store is an interesting place for a man who is only thirty-three inches tall. There are partitions for simulated rooms and tables, sofas, chairs, plants, and lamps of every description to impede the view.

Although Mike doubted Mr. Kelly's claim that he was under siege, he decided to prepare for the worst. He was at a decided disadvantage for jumping an intruder, so Mike laid out his defenses as would a Marine taking up positions in jungle warfare. He educated himself to every nuance of the floor plan and positioned the tools he would need in case of an "invasion."

After several months of staying up most of the night, it finally happened. Mike heard a truck stop in the alley and the sound of someone using a crowbar on the back door. Mike hurried to his first line of defense to scout the enemy. There was one adult and a teenage boy—no more. They had flashlights that they used only in short bursts so as not to alert any possible patrolling policemen. Mike waited till they passed deeper into the store. If they had overheard him calling the police, the intruders could have easily killed Mike with that crowbar. Mike waited until they were well into their mischief, then he loudly slammed the door.

"What's that!" The boy waved the flashlight everywhere to see who was there.

"Shut up! Turn that thing off! It's just the wind."

They hesitated and listened for a while before going back to work.

"There's a big grandfather clock in here somewhere. We'll take that first."

In the maze of partitions and furniture they were disoriented. Finally the older man told the kid to take one path while he checked the other and to let him know if he found the clock.

Meanwhile Mike had silently scampered into position a few feet in front of the kid. He carefully placed his board in the boy's path. Wham! The kid stepped on the board, and it rolled out from under him. He hit his head hard on the floor and was knocked out cold. Mike quickly rolled to his next position.

"What's that?"

The man wheeled around and shined his flashlight on the boy. Mike shouted in his spookiest voice, "You're next!" Then he threw a baseball at the man, giving him quite a welt. He shined his flashlight all over the store and growled, "You're a dead man!" Mike set up for his next attack. As the burglar passed Mike's hiding spot, he sent the man flying with a lamp cord.

Mike jumped on the thief's back and held on with a hammerlock. The thief struggled to his feet with something on his back that felt like a wild ape. His crowbar had gone flying across the store, so he tried to knock Mike off with his flashlight. The flashlight was on and making quite a light show for Officer Bowman, who was patrolling Meridian Street. In short order they rushed into the building with Mike yelling "Yieehah!" and the burglar screaming "Get it off! Get it off!"

The man was going crazy, the cops were doubled over laughing, the teenager was crying and begging for mercy, and Mike was having the time of his life. Word spread quickly that there was some kind of spook at Kelly's and that "you'd better lay off that place."

Mr. Kelly was more than pleased with Mike's work and gave him a fifty dollar reward. Mike slept in Kelly's furniture store for another seven months, and then Mr. Kelly up and retired. He sold the store, and moved to Charleston, South Carolina, where he sold locally made baskets and cane chairs at ungodly prices to gullible tourists. The new store owners kept the name, but they didn't keep Mike. Once more he was out in the cold.

CHAPTER 36

The Final Years

There isn't much more to tell about the Pencil Man's story. Like the Mark of Cain, his remaining years were neither good nor bad. They became a hopeless spiral of frustration and sameness. They spun both up and down.

For a year or two Mike was able to use his YMCA key to find nighttime shelter and a bath, but it was not like the days when he first met Mr. Cody. He now had to sneak in at night and work around the watchman's schedule. The showers were brief, the swim time was gone. Mike alternated his sleeping places so as not to get caught, but one night he was found and they took his key.

From that time on, Mike slept where he could. The Christian Center and St. Mary's were available to him anytime, but they were too far from where he worked. He saved those nighttime shelters for the worst weather. Mike did make the effort to go to Mass on Wednesday. On those nights he would usually sleep in the church.

There were two lean and mean years when a group of teenagers led by a heartless punk kept harassing Mike. They roughed him up. They scattered his pencils. They would steal his board and leave it far down the street.

There were also a few nice kids who would come to his defense, but they were quickly run off by the bad ones. As with all teenagers they grew up and the problem moved away.

Over the years there were a few people who treated Mike very well. Mary McKee would often end her early morning shift at the Joy Lynn Bakery and bring Mike a large cup of coffee and a discount doughnut or two.

Mr. Chance, who worked at the drugstore, would take a smoke break in mid afternoon and sometimes bring Mike a small bag of pretzels and a pop. He never looked at Mike when he talked and always addressed Mike as "Bud." They'd talk about the weather, or politics. Sometimes they would talk about the war.

Mr. Chance had served in the combat engineers in Italy. He had some harrowing stories. Mike would talk about the 1st Marine Division. Mr. Chance never brought up the question of how Mike had lost his legs. He figured it was a touchy subject, so he just assumed that Mike had lost them in the war. Years later he became a pseudo expert on the Pencil Man, and when the subject came up about his legs that was his answer—"He never said for sure, but I'm pretty certain it was a mine. You could tell by the way the fellow reacted when we talked about the war."

One bitterly cold winter morning the First Methodist Church caught fire. Too tired to push himself up the hill to the Christian Center, Mike had spent the night amongst the garbage cans behind the Alibi restaurant. When he noticed the fire he rolled toward the nearest fire alarm box, but he couldn't pull himself up to reach the button. He finally spotted a Post Office worker who was just getting off third shift and yelled to get his attention. The man quickly saw the situation and pressed the fire alarm till his thumb nearly froze.

The firemen suffered terribly in the cold. When the fire was finally extinguished the remains of the church looked like a burned out ice castle.

As they fought the fire, several onlookers in the gathering crowd spotted the Pencil Man and the rumor quickly spread that he had accidentally started the fire in an effort to keep warm. The police cleared him the next day when it was determined that a mentally ill custodian had set the fire in the sanctuary after the church had to let him go. Mike was glad to be cleared of the accusations but it hurt deeply to be so easily blamed. It was a real low spot that left him feeling more isolated from the townsfolk than ever.

The Pencil Man's years droned on. He was seen by everyone and known by so very few. Everyone seemed to have an opinion on the man, but almost no one saw him as a man.

At the beginning of one school year Mike met a sad little girl named Nila. She was a Korean War orphan, very shy, and so different from her classmates that they picked on her terribly. English was hard for her to grasp, isolating her even more from the mainstream. Mike could relate to that, giving him great empathy for the little girl.

Nila walked by Mike every day on her way to and from school. She always walked alone. Nila was afraid of Mike, as she was with most people, but she could relate to his missing legs. There were so many men, women, and children in her native Korea who had lost their limbs to the war and to the land mines that were scattered all up and down the peninsula.

Mike tried to encourage Nila on her daily visits. He would compliment her on her dress or ask how she was doing with a certain subject. Sometimes he would help her with a school problem with which she was struggling.

Sad to say, Nila did not take to the mentoring. A few years later she fell in with a rough crowd. She would dress trashy and come downtown with her gang. To impress her "friends" Nila would walk over to Mike and ask for a light. He of course refused. She thought that gave her an excuse to knock the Pencil Man off his board—leading her gang in laughter at the "crippled freak." That was hard for him to take.

Mike did, however, have many good experiences. He had a greater appreciation for warm summer days than most. He studied the pigeons that lined the rooflines of the building, and gave a few of them names. He enjoyed the gift of a pretty woman in a summer dress and the fragrance of the air made sweet by her passing.

He had mixed feelings about the men of town. He enjoyed studying the professionals vs. the laborers. There were things about them that were so different and other habits that were very same. It was enjoyable to watch them coming to and from their jobs, but it hurt to realize that he had been robbed of the camaraderie and pride of work.

Mike watched the rushed and strong pace of the young men. He imagined them when they would be like the old men who shuffled as best as they could, and who sat in idle groups watching the young women pass, in a vain effort to touch the feel of their glory days.

Melancholy was the word for the way Mike watched the lovers. There were fresh eyed teenage lovers full of energy. They would hold hands as they strolled down the sidewalks on the way to the Rivera Theater. Their skin would tingle and their hearts would beat rapidly as they touched. There were husbands and wives who would casually connect their hands when those hands weren't busy corralling their children.

There was one old couple who would come to town once a month to dine at the Farris Cafeteria. They would arrive on the North Anderson bus and walk arm-in-arm down Meridian Street to 12th. Both were dressed out of current style, but to the nines. He would hold her close and she him—somewhat to keep each other from falling. There was a divine smile on each face. This was their date, and they were just as giddy in romance as the teenage lovers.

As Mike watched he would sometimes think the word, and other times say it out loud, "Veronica."

Mike especially loved to watch the children. They would pass with a tired pout or the joy of going to town. Often they would carry a teddy bear, a doll, a newly purchased toy, or a small shopping bag.

The Pencil Man could be a pleasant curiosity to the children. He was the only adult who was physically at their level, and that made some of them feel secure enough to speak with him openly. One such child was a boy with a burr haircut and large wire-rimmed glasses that made his head look small. His name was George. Mike called him Curious George because he always had a pouch full of straightforward questions.

"Hi, I'm George."

Mike stuck out his hand, "My name is Mike."

George looked at him funny as if Mike was pulling his leg.

"Nah, you're the Pencil Man, mister—everybody knows that."

"Oh, I'm sorry, George—I forgot."

"You're silly, mister. What happened to your legs?"

"Oh, no! Did I leave them at home again?"

To tell you the truth, that was a hard question to answer. Mike really didn't know how the tramp had lost his legs, or how he died, or where he came from. He had some empathy for the man—having now suffered much of the same fate. Did the tramp have a family? How old was he when he lost his legs? Did people torment him? Did they ignore him? All of these questions were a mystery to Mike.

As the years passed Mike began to notice that the tramp's body and his own tired soul were wearing thin. There was no home for Mike—worse, there was no hope. He had lost everyone he had ever loved. He was unknown except as a fixture in downtown Anderson. He was less important than the fireplug across the street, and even the fireplug had a dog that loved him. Mike's reason for living and his desire to do so was gone.

To make matters worse, after seven years at St. Mary's, Father Metzger moved on to a parish in Oklahoma. The new priest was a man who commanded respect and preached a powerful homily, but he was not the pastor that Father Metzger had been. One of the first things he did was to clean up "those boxes in the balcony." He couldn't understand why someone had stacked them there. He had no idea who Mike was, and he made no effort to speak to the strange bum who sold pencils on Meridian Street.

Mike's one remaining friend was Rob Williams, but Rob was so busy. They had added two more children to their nest. Joyce was born two years after Mark, and Susan was born four years later. By now Doug and Mark were involved in school activities. Joyce was still pretty dependent on her mom and dad, and Susan was a baby.

Rob continued to say hello each morning, but he had to ask Mike to cut his day short so he could make Mike's deposits and get home sooner. He tried his best to keep Mike in his circle, but Rob was stretched farther and farther each day by his family and community obligations. Rob was a man with a growing list of needs and a dwindling supply of money. There were medical bills, clothing bills, food bills, school bills, and always something to fix or replace. They had moved into a house on Pearl Street to accommodate their growing family.

One evening Mike implored Rob to stay over at work. Rob said that he couldn't. Mike again asked Rob to stay—adding that it was very important. Seeing the seriousness in Mike's eyes, Rob agreed. He called his wife to take the kids to the school program, saying "I'll be there as soon as I can."

There was a deep sadness and a look of finality on Mike's face. Rob was ashamed of how long it had been since he had really looked at Mike eye to eye. The Pencil Man had aged so much in just the past few months. His color was pale. His eyes were sunken. There was a noticeable rasp and weakness to his already rough voice.

Fearing the worst, Rob began the conversation.

"What's wrong, Mike?"

"I can't do this anymore, Rob. I'm so tired." There was a look of hopeless surrender in his eyes.

"Do you need a doctor? Is there anything I can do?"

"Yes, there is. Look at my account balance."

Rob hesitated a moment as if to non-verbally ask why. Then he stepped to the files and was astounded to see that Mike had saved several thousand dollars in the past several years. When I die I want to give that to your kids for college. Rob was stunned. That was enough money to educate at least two of their four children, with money left over to pay for much of the third and fourth.

"What do you mean die, Mike? You aren't much older than me."

Mike said it again—this time with a look of firm conviction in his eyes. "When I die, Rob."

Rob was cut to the quick by the tone of Mike's voice. It sounded more like a fatal diagnosis than an offer of future help. Nothing more was said between the two, not even "goodnights." They left the Savings and Loan together, and Rob locked the building. That night Rob didn't run home—he walked very slowly.

When he met Cindy at the school, Rob tried to tell her what the Pencil Man had said. For the longest time all he could do was to choke on the words. At first she feared that Rob was sick or had lost his job.

A few days later they went to an attorney by the name of Hartley to draw up the papers. Mr. Hartley was fascinated by Mike's acumen. Here before him was an articulate and well-reasoned man, where before he had seen Mike only as a bum selling pencils.

Winter was coming on, and Mike was definitely on a downhill slide. One weekend in November he endured two days of cold rain without proper clothes or shelter. Rob and his family had been in Bedford that weekend visiting Cindy's parents. When Rob saw Mike on Monday morning he was ashamed that he hadn't been there for his friend. Several times Rob had asked Mike to stay with them when he needed shelter, but Mike had always refused.

Rob put aside his work obligations—even though the state auditors were already at the Savings and Loan waiting for him to arrive for their six-month audit. He walked straight to Clair Call's and waited for the men's store to open. Rob bought Mike a raincoat with a warm lining and implored him to go to his house.

"At least stay on the porch and Cindy will give you a blanket."

Still Mike refused. "I have to work, Rob—I don't want people to think I'm a bum."

Rob didn't laugh at the self-deprecating joke.

Mike's condition turned into pneumonia. His cough was so bad that he lost a lot of customers. No one wanted to catch what the dirty bum had.

By January Mike was a shell of a shell. His lungs were shot, and the phantom pains that amputees experience were exacerbated by the cold moist air. The end was getting near and yet it was just out of his reach. Reach he did. Death was now a prize of great value and Mike was coming in second with every dawn. There were days when he would wake up and cry that he was still alive.

Still, nothing hurt him more than the expression on Rob's face when he saw him on the morning of January 13th. Rob was not running as usual. He was early for work. He walked very slowly with his head down.

Rob walked past Mike without a word. Mike followed him to the Savings and Loan and rolled into Rob's office without an invite. Rob was sitting on the floor in the corner, collapsed in on himself.

"Joyce has leukemia, Mike. There's nothing they can do."

Rob melted into a pool of tears. The news cut Mike to the quick as he thought of his own Eddie.

"What are we gonna do, Mike? What are we gonna do? She's my little girl and I can't do anything to save her."

Mike rolled over and closed Rob's office door. Then he rolled back and sat next to his embattled friend. For the next several minutes they sat together in silence, two dear friends, one a broken man and the other heart-broken. Mike thought of all those terrible losses in his own past and how bitter his life had become. He had the feeling that his whole existence had boiled down to this moment.

Finally Mike spoke.

"I can save your little girl."

At first Rob was incensed at Mike's poor joke, but when he saw Mike's deadly serious expression he said, "I'm listening."

Mike thought of the moment he had said those same words to Leon. He had never told Rob about the Mark of Cain.

"My son was dying of leukemia. I met this man with no hands. He said he knew my father in the war . . ."

Mike went on to explain the whole incident and how he became the Pencil Man.

Rob didn't know what to think. It was all too much. He was numb with confusion.

"I can save your little girl. All I ask is that you put the curse on me. Please, Rob—I can't live like this anymore. Put the curse on me—finish me off.

Rob jumped up. He was horrified at Mike's offer.

"What are you asking? How could I ever make a decision that might kill an innocent man—let alone one of my best friends? Are you crazy? I couldn't live with myself."

Rob squeezed his head with his hands as if he could somehow press all of this madness from his tormented mind.

Mike implored his friend, "Please, Rob—look at me—I'm a physical derelict—I have no hope—no family—I have no reason to live. Please Rob—save your little girl—save Joyce!"

Mike lowered his voice and paused. He grabbed Rob's arms and pulled him down to his level. Looking him squarely in the eyes, Mike begged, his only remaining friend.

"Please, Rob, save Joyce—give me peace."

CHAPTER 37

Epilogue

The life of the Pencil man was like no other, and yet it was so very same. He was a man who had laughed, and danced, and ran. He was a man who had faced temptation. Sometimes he bravely stared it down. Sometimes he fell beneath its step. Sometimes he lucked into the right decisions.

He was as brave as any man and probably braver than most. He was a good son, a good brother, a good husband, and no one could say he didn't give all to his son.

He had felt the pangs of love with a teenage girl in Goldthwaite, Texas, and the virtuous Norma June. He had found true love in Veronica, a girl he had first rejected on the Roosevelt playground.

Mike was an observer. His teachers were both major and minor influences in his life, but they each had a lesson. Keku, Joe, and certainly Kikthawenund and Father Pelemon and the Sisters in Ferdinand had had a great impact. One could not exclude the lesser "lessons" of Art and Belle, Bert T, the Quaker farmer, Landis, Professor Dewing, and Marjorie Blocker, the woman whose husband was dying in Paris, Texas. Even the tempting Violet and the sad trucker Adolph had taught him much.

Despite the cruel loss he had suffered, the Pencil Man taught him more than any normal life could have. In a strange way Mike had been grateful to the old tramp.

Anyone could have speculated, but no one could have guessed the life Mike would live or how it would end. That end would be bizarre, made more so by his fate being firmly laid in the hands of his best friend.

Rob chose not to use the Mark of Cain to save his daughter. Anyone who could have known the situation would probably have thought him cruel, or at least crazy. Anyone who knew Rob intimately, as Mike did, might possibly have seen the nobility of his choice. Even then it was hard to understand.

It was a bitter decision that would haunt Rob for the rest of his life. It changed him in the worst way, and in the process he became separated from his wife and children. In time he left Anderson.

Joyce suffered for a few more months, and then, by the grace of God, St. Jude's Hospital, and Danny Thomas, the doctors found a way to arrest the cancer. She remained in remission for another 25 years. Eventually the cancer returned and took her life, but not until she had had the chance to finish school, to marry, and to bear a daughter who would go on to become a leading scientist in cancer research.

When Cindy took Joyce to St. Jude's, the folks of Anderson pitched in to pay for her medical expenses. The money poured in from banks and businesses all over town. Factory workers, students, parishioners, and regulars at the local bars put their money and their hearts into helping the little girl.

Cindy remarried. Doug became a state senator. Mark was ordained in the Methodist church and eventually became the senior pastor at the North Methodist Church in Indianapolis, which Mike had passed on his way to boot camp. Susan became the head of the orthopedics ward at St. John's Hospital in Anderson.

Word eventually came to St. Mary's that Father Williams had passed. By then few remained who knew him well, but those who did deeply grieved his loss. He had been, for many Andersonions, the definition of a good pastor and friend.

In South Carolina, Mr. Kelly developed some form of dementia and wandered into the path of a car on a busy highway. As he lay dying he mumbled something about a "Pencil Man."

In his Christmas homilies Father Metzger would often tell a moving tale about a man named Mike.

Few if any people in Anderson remember when the Pencil Man came on the scene. Just as many can't remember when they saw him no more. He had been just a fixture—an odd memory of those downtown days, now governed by the fading recollections of those who then called Anderson home. Many remembered the Pencil Man, but hardly anyone knew who he was.

The last time I saw Mike was years ago. He was running to his recently acquired job at the Anderson Federal Savings and Loan. He was always running late. It could have been that his son Eddie needed some last-minute help with his schoolwork. More likely than not, Mike had stayed at home too long with his beautiful wife Veronica.

As he ran past, Mike shouted his usual morning greeting and wished me well. He didn't know my name yet, but at least he treated me like a man. It was the goodness of his character that led him to treat me well. It was not the memory of his Pencil Man days that drove him to be so kind, for those days were gone from his mind. Mike had no memory of who I was nor of the man who had made the painful choice to use the Mark of Cain—not to spare his own daughter, but to restore his friend.

I'm sure we could have become good friends in time, but I decided to leave town for a place with a healthier climate—far from the people and places that I had dearly loved, but that had become oppressive reminders of the life I had enjoyed.

My only friends now are the spirits who have driven me to reveal this account. Perhaps it is entirely true. Perhaps I am thoroughly mad.

And who am I?

I'm the man who wrote this journal.

My name is Rob Williams.

I'm the Pencil Man.